INFINITE RICHES

Ben Okri has published nine novels, including *Infinite Riches*, as well as collections of poetry, short stories and essays. His work has been translated into more than 20 languages. He is a Fellow of the Royal Society of Literature and has been awarded the OBE as well as numerous international prizes, including the Commonwealth Writers Prize for Africa, the Aga Khan Prize for Fiction and the Chianti Rufino-Antico Fattore. He is a Vice-President of the English Centre of International PEN and was presented with a Crystal Award by the World Economic Forum. He was born in Nigeria and lives in London.

ALSO BY BEN OKRI

Fiction

Flowers and Shadows
The Landscapes Within
Incidents at the Shrine
Stars of the New Curfew
The Famished Road
Songs of Enchantment
Astonishing the Gods
Dangerous Love
In Arcadia
Starbook

Non-fiction

Birds of Heaven
A Way of Being Free

Poetry

An African Elegy
Mental Flight

BEN OKRI

Infinite Riches

VINTAGE BOOKS
London

Published by Vintage 2009

10 9

Copyright © Ben Okri 1998

Ben Okri has asserted his right under the Copyright, Designs and
Patents Act 1988 to be identified as the author of this work

First published in Great Britain in 1998 by Phoenix House

First published in paperback in 1999 by Phoenix

Vintage
Random House, 20 Vauxhall Bridge Road,
London, SW1V 2SA

www.vintage-books.co.uk

Addresses for companies within The Random House Group Limited
can be found at: www.randomhouse.co.uk/offices.htm

The Random House Group Limited Reg. No. 954009

A CIP catalogue record for this book
is available from the British Library

ISBN 9780099540335

Penguin Random House is committed to a sustainable future for
our business, our readers and our planet. This book is made from
Forest Stewardship Council® certified paper.

Printed and bound in Great Britain by Clays Ltd, St Ives plc

Acknowledgements

I am grateful to Graham Greene who, in 1989, at the Oxford & Cambridge Club, told us the anecdote on which I based the Rain Queen story;

And to Harould Courlander's collection of oral African tales, *The Crest and the Hide*, for reminding me of a story from my childhood;

And to Rosemary Clunie.

To my beloved Mother
Grace Okri
1936–1996

Now that serenely
You rest on high
Forgive your son
Who couldn't say goodbye

But Death was a tyrant
On the rich land
And you had written
Enigmas in my hand

The more they try
To press you down
The more beautiful
Grows your crown

And now that you
Are as a spiritual dove
Dwell forever
In our eternal love

'Infinite riches in a little room'

Christopher Marlowe

I

BOOK ONE

ONE

The little room

'Who can be certain where the end begins?' said Dad, shortly before he was arrested for the murder of the carpenter.

'Time is growing,' he added. 'And our suffering is growing too. When will our suffering bear fruit? One great thought can alter the future of the world. One revelation. One dream. But who will dream that dream? And who will make it real?'

TWO

The leopard

While the whole community dreamt of the dead carpenter, Dad sat in our darkened room, talking deep into the night.

I listened to him, with dread in my heart, as he spoke words which heated up the air of the room. With blazing eyes, almost without purpose, he said: 'Some people who are born don't want to live. Others who are dead don't want to die. Azaro, are you awake?'

I was surprised by the question.

'Yes,' I replied.

He carried on, as if I hadn't said anything.

'My son, sometimes we find ourselves living in the dreams of the dead. Who knows the destination of a dream? How many worlds do we live in at the same time? When we sleep do we wake up in another world, in another time? When we sleep in that other world do we wake up here, in this world? Is history the converging dreams of many millions of people, living and dead? Have I just died and am I now living in another zone? Are we asleep all the time? When we wake, is it to one level above the deep sleep of our days? Do we wake when we die? My son, I feel as if I have just died and yet I have never felt more awake.'

He stopped again. His speech frightened me. Something incredible must have happened to him in the forest when he was burying the dead carpenter. It was as if he had burst out of a tight space which had been confining his raging spirit.

Then, in a sleepwalking voice, he suddenly cried out:

'I have never felt more awake, but I see a leopard coming towards me. Am I a leopard? Is the leopard my dream? Look!' he said, with an illuminated anguish in his voice, 'The room is becoming brighter!'

THREE

Disappearance

I looked with widened eyes. My heart was still. The room was flooded with a subdued green intensity. The smell of herbaceous earth overwhelmed my senses. The forest darkness compacted into corners of the room. And, condensing beside Dad, as if the green were alive, its own light, contracting into an unmistakable form – was the leopard.

It was old. Its eyes were like blue jewels. And it sat peacefully at Dad's feet. The leopard was phosphorescent, spreading no shadows, as if it had come to the end of its dreaming.

Then something odd occurred to me.

'Are you awake, Dad?' I asked.

The light of the great animal flickered. Dad was silent. I asked the question again, louder. Mum turned on the bed. For an instant the room darkened again. Then the green radiance glowed, filling out the place. I got up from my mat. As I neared Dad, the leopard's illumination dimmed. I stopped, and whispered hard into his ear.

'ARE YOU AWAKE, DAD?'

'WHAT?' he cried, jumping up suddenly, plunging the room into night.

8

The leopard was gone. I stayed silent for a moment.

Then, as if he had woken into sleep, Dad brushed past me, muttering something about seeing things for the first time. He went out of the room. For a moment I was confused. Then I went out after him, ran to the housefront, and looked both ways. Dad wasn't anywhere. I went to the backyard, but he wasn't there either. I hurried to the street again, ran one way, then another. It was very strange, and the thought scared me, but it seemed as if Dad simply stepped out of our door, and out of reality. I went back to the room and waited for him. While I waited it occurred to me that Dad had been talking from his sleep. I had entered another of his dreams.

FOUR

Circling

I was restless. I waited a long time in the dark. I lay on the bed. Then I rose out of myself, and began circling. I circled in and out of the dreams of the community. Circled in the dreams of spirit-children who keep coming back to the same place, trying to break the chains of history. Circled in the dreams of the dead carpenter, who grew bigger in his coffin, till his swelling body split his wooden encasement.

As I circled, I saw that the dead carpenter had left his grave without moving the mighty rock that was above him. He had white flowers all over his body. He went from place to place, stirring the spirits of the dead. He wandered from one sleeper's house to another. Rattling their roofs. Trying to get into their lives. Trying to manifest himself to them in some way.

The dead carpenter knocked on people's doors. Banged on their windows. Grimaced into the blind faces of dreamers. Held long conversations with sensitive children. Roamed around the kitchens clattering the cooking utensils. Out in the open air, he glowed in the dark. Soon he drifted up into the sky, and hung in mid-space, threatening pestilence until his murderers had confessed their crime. Until he had been properly buried. He stirred revolt in the universal air of dreams.

I went on circling. Mum turned again on the bed. She was dreaming about the time, many years on, when she would be serenaded by a man who sold cement. Her dream changed. She found herself with her mother, who had been dead for twenty years and was now living on another continent, near the silver mountains. In the dream she stood with her mother beneath an Elysian sky. Together they stared at the faces of great women sculpted on the rocks by nature.

Then, I saw someone staggering down our street, with a bucket on his head. The man's face was completely wrapped in cloth, except for the eyes. When the wind blew against our window, our room was invaded by a bad smell. A reminder of our wretched condition, in which we live instantaneously with all the consequences of our actions.

After some time, I lay down again, and resumed circling. Twenty miles away, the future rulers of the nation slept in peace. They dreamt of power. They dreamt of bottomless coffers to steal from. Houses in every famous city. Concubines in every major town. Power removing them from the consequences of their own actions, which we suffered in advance. And suffered for long afterwards.

Meanwhile, the man with the bucket was shouting incoherent abuse as he staggered past the houses. The smell of his bucket altered our dreams. After he went past, we heard a loud cry, and then silence.

Twenty miles away, in a richer part of the city, on mattresses that would be transformed into palatial beds, the future rulers of the nation breathed easily. They were reliving their ascension, their victories. Numbering their enemies. They were dreaming their nation-destroying policies in advance. Tribal dreams of domination that would ignite civil war.

Thirty miles away, the English Governor-General, who hated being photographed, was dreaming about his colonial rule. In his dream he was destroying all the documents. Burning all the evidence. Shredding history. As I lingered in the Governor-General's dream a wave of darkness washed me to an island, across the ocean, where many of our troubles began, and on whose roads, in a future life, I would wander and suffer and find a new kind of light.

I wasn't long in that world when someone appeared at our door, stinking of a crude perfume made from the bitter aloes of the desert. I stopped circling. I descended into my body, woke up, and saw Dad. He was freshly bathed and looked thoroughly scrubbed. He also stank of carbolic. Wrinkles were deep on his forehead. His eyes bulged. A candle was alight on the centre table.

Dad was in his chair, silent, as if he hadn't moved. He smoked serenely. He didn't look at me. His thoughts were very intense. When he finished smoking, he put out the candle. Then, without a word, he got into bed with Mum, and fell into a profound slumber.

FIVE

Prelude to trouble

Dad was still asleep when we woke up in the morning. His perfume chastened us, and hung densely in the room. The perfume was so appalling that it drove Mum out hawking much earlier than usual.

Mum was dressed like a prophetess that morning, as if she were cleansing the day in advance. She wore a white smock, white beads, white kerchief and a fish-patterned wrapper. She made food for us, and left Dad's breakfast covered on the table. She ate with me, but did not speak. Her face was shadowed as if her spirit were conserving its energies for the trials ahead.

After we had eaten, she got her basins of oranges, mosquito coils and soap. She prayed at the door, and then begged me not to wander far from home. She went out into the early sunlight. I listened as she advertised her wares in a new singing voice. Advertised them to a people who were too poor to buy oil for their lamps.

She went down the street, in the direction opposite Madame Koto's bar. Breaking the settled crust of the sleeping earth with her antiquated sandals.

Walking innocently through all the rumours gathering. She was beginning her day as she would end it. Seeking elusive things. Calling out to people who weren't listening. Soaking in the dust and murmurs of the road.

Meanwhile, Dad was deep in the last decent sleep he would have for a long time. He slept soundly, gathering his secret strengths. While he grew heavier on the bed, our door was wide open for trouble to come and pay us a lengthy visit.

SIX

Dialogue with my dead friend

Mum left and I waited patiently for Dad to wake up. But Dad snored noisily. I got tired of waiting. I went out into the street and encountered the new cycle. It had begun at night and was now real.

There were loud cries from Madame Koto's bar. It was as if many women had fallen into trances and were possessed. The street was crowded with neighbours and new people with odd faces. Soon I pieced together what was happening. People were talking about the old leopard they had glimpsed in the forest. Its breathing was poor and its growling was hoarse. People had gone hunting for the leopard with dane guns and machetes, but hadn't found it. On their way back they had come upon the enormous figure of Madame Koto, rolling on the ground, raving.

That was when the community discovered that someone had dumped a bucket of something disgusting in front of her bar. I hurried over to see for myself. The crowd there was solid. Madame Koto seemed quite insane. She lunged at us, uttering the most terrifying threats. Her women stood around, with handkerchiefs to their noses. And right next to Madame Koto's new car, in the middle of her frontyard, was the appalling bucket. We looked on with fear, knowing that retaliation would come at us in unpleasant ways.

She kept jumping up and down. Cursing. Crying out with the pain of her bad foot and her abnormal pregnancy. She was like a mad witch. In a harsh voice, she ordered her men to fetch people to clear the mess from her barfront. She seemed like her own nemesis. Everyone looked on, thinking about the dead carpenter. Thinking about his son, whom Madame Koto's driver had killed.

While I watched Madame Koto shrieking, a cool wind blew around me. A flash of dazzling light shot through my brain. Then something nearby electrified my skin. I turned and saw that it was the spirit of Ade. The dead son of the dead carpenter. My friend. In his blue suit, he seemed very healthy. With a mischievous smile, he said:

'How is my father?'

'He has been buried,' I replied.

'But who killed him?'

'I don't know. I saw a thug . . .'

'Who gave the thug the order?'

'I'm not sure.'

'How is your father?' he asked.

'He's asleep.'

'How do you know?'

'Because he was fast asleep when I left him.'

'Your mother was singing when she left you, but she is not singing now.'

'Why not?'

'Because she knows something bad is happening.'

'Where?'

'I'll tell you when my father has been buried.'

'He has.'

'How do you know?'

'I was there.'

'Where?'

'In the forest.'

'What forest?'

'That one.' I pointed, turning.

But when I looked, I was amazed to find that the forest had vanished. I turned back to my friend, but he too had disappeared. Instead, I saw Madame Koto descending on me. She began hitting me on the head, howling. I ran, fell, and got up. A man in the crowd held me and said:

'Why do you talk to yourself when your father is in trouble?'

'What?' I asked, confused.

'Wake up!' he shouted.

I was stunned into a new alertness. Everything was turning too fast. I ran home. The world was spinning. The road kept opening and shutting. Voices were whispering. The forest had reappeared. When I got to our room, five policemen, acting on rumours spread by the Party of the Poor, had come to arrest Dad for the murder of the carpenter.

SEVEN

The arrest

Dad was serene. He didn't even smile at the absurdity of their accusation. He put on his boots with a dignity that got on their nerves. The policemen began to hurry and hassle him, but Dad put on his boots more slowly, so they lost their tempers, punching and kicking him. Dad regarded them coolly, with pity almost. I jumped on one of the policemen, who threw me on the bed.

'Sit still and watch, you cricket!' Dad said to me, his voice raised.

I sat still. I watched as they dragged him out with only one boot on. Dad didn't resist, but didn't comply. They had to carry him out into the street, where our neighbours were gathered, demanding in angry voices why the policemen were arresting a good man. But when the policemen threatened them with imprisonment, everyone fell silent.

We all followed the policemen as they carried Dad to their van. But before they managed to throw him into the back, Dad managed a defiant cry and a cryptic statement:

'JUSTICE IS A BLACK GOD!' He shouted.

They slammed the door on his mad voice and drove away before we could find out where they were taking him.

EIGHT

The gathering wrath of women

Mum came back that evening, having sold very little, her face swollen with the bitterness of the road, her feet blistered, her eyes red with dust.

When she heard that Dad had been arrested for the murder of the carpenter whom he had been brave enough to bury, she immediately set out on the road again. She sang a song which appeared joyful, but which was actually seamed with anger. I followed her down the street but she turned and shouted at me. She said to keep our door open as Dad had commanded, and to remain in the room. She said I had to be their eyes and ears. Reluctantly, I went back home.

With their ears I heard the insistence of Mum's song to the road that carries people to their unsuspected destinies. I heard her song to the spirits of the dead, who know all the truths obscured to us in pain and ignorance. And I heard her song to the great angels of all women, sisters of justice, handmaidens of fate.

And with their eyes I followed Mum down the roads which keep growing the more human beings dream of places to go. The roads which led to bridges. The bridges which led to highways. The highways built on reclaimed rivers, whose goddesses sue constantly at the higher courts of justice for the annexing of their ancient territories.

Mum walked without knowing where she was going. She walked on rage, her mind dimming and brightening. Incendiary visions flamed in her eyes. She was crossing a road, talking furiously to herself, when she walked into a red space. When she recovered she found lorries all around her, blaring their horns. A crowd of women bore her across the road, fanning her, asking her a thousand questions; and all she said, fighting the waves of her mind's blackout, was:

'Police station!'

When one of the women said she knew where the police station was, Mum instantly overcame her dizziness and jumped up and began wildly in the direction indicated. The women followed her, urging her to rest, to recover properly, but Mum pushed on. Her unaccountable single-mindedness magnetized the women. Without knowing why, they accompanied her, as if they were all on the same angry pilgrimage.

The woman who knew the police station led the way. Mum did not speak to the women who accompanied her. She spoke to the road and the air and the wind, complaining about the relentless injustice of the world, singing snatches of defiant village songs. In stirring her spirit, she stirred the women. And the women, chanting and singing, caught the interest of other women who sold beans and roasted corn and fruits along the bustling roadsides. Eternally curious, endlessly harassed by history, the women of the roadside joined the surging mass of women. Their numbers swelled, their flow directed by Mum's anger.

They poured down the roads, halting the traffic, overwhelming the traffic wardens. They flowed past the law courts whose buildings were changing to the colour of dust. They swarmed past the banks, and past the inquisitive schoolchildren, who joined the women for short distances, and fell away to other distractions.

And when the women got to the police station which used to be a madhouse they were surprised to see the lone figure of a sergeant-major at the desk, filling out his overtime coupon. The poor sergeant-major looked up and found himself overrun by a scary-looking mob of women, all in their different cracked voices demanding the release of husbands, sons, in-laws, brothers, fathers, uncles, and the missing sons of their friends. The sergeant-major panicked and blew his whistle, thinking that colonial order was being overthrown, or that a new war of liberation had been launched. Two policemen in khaki shorts came running out with batons, but the women overpowered them and stormed into the labyrinths of the police station.

The cells were bursting with faces that were like forest carvings and raw-eyed sculptings. The faces of those who battled tirelessly against the colonial order. Faces of the hungry who had turned to crime. The knotted faces of murderers who no longer dreamt at night, no longer slept, but who with paranoid eyes kept awake and ready for the return of the spirits of those they had murdered. The pinched faces of pickpockets from creeks deep in the country, money-doublers from towns not mentioned on any maps, armed robbers from tribes whose numbers were very small, and whose languages were dying out. The remorseless faces of thugs, who had taken punishment on behalf of their masters, whose lives blazed with a hunger soul-deep, a rage without a language, their faces raw like wounds which have no intention of ever healing. Faces burning with the fierce intensity of the last of a dying breed of men, who would not let the world forget the unique stamp of their soul's identity. Faces of the half-insane and the downright insane. Faces of university professors who had woken up from their idealistic dreams to find the promises of Independence betrayed in advance, and who had spoken out with all the brashness of those unused to the brackish waters of politics.

The women saw these faces and recognized townspeople, relatives, friends of old enemies, familiar customers. And the police station, with its overcrowded cells, its stench of unwashed bodies and crypts without light, yielded its hoard of vanished names, forgotten heroes, prominent figures in anonymous holes. Among them was a professor insisting that he was a baker, and a money-doubler swearing that he was of royal birth. The prisoners were all weaving in and out of their dissolving identities.

The women, inflamed by their goddess, blurrer of the boundaries of justice, found the keys to the cells and flung open the creaking gates. They unleashed on the roads hordes of criminals who did not dream any more, forgers who believed they were aristocrats, thieves who never said thank you, thugs who had no respect for gratitude. Faces poured out of cells which were big enough for seven standing coffins, and held thirty-six men. But none of the faces was recognized by Mum, and none of the faces belonged to Dad.

Her simple search had undammed so much chaos. All around her the women were revelling in the new dimensions of their power. They sang and spoke boldly. But Mum left the precinct and went on walking, seeking the next police station. Again the women followed her.

The story of their rampage, their cry for an unstated justice, found the ears of the city, the judges, the newspapers, and the night.

They didn't get very far. The darkness brought Mum exhaustion, but brought the other women exhilaration. Mum sank on the roadside, her feet bleeding, her eyes raw, her mind going on and off, hot lights in her brain.

The women around her, some of them quite mad, others spoiling for a confrontation, planned their next invasion, their next assault on the political structure. While they made their plans, Mum slept with her back to a concrete wall, with the road babbling all around her. She dreamt of all the faces in all the prisons. She dreamt that the freed prisoners were running mad over the city, burning down vehicles and government houses, starting fantastic riots.

NINE

The imprisoned tyger

And with my parents' eyes, in my lonely place, I saw Dad in a dark unidentifiable room. It was a room in which they kept murderers, where they created them. Initially, in isolation, they softened their skulls. They softened them for the beating with clubs that was to come at the first excuse, the first question that was not respectfully answered.

Dad saw the leopard again that night. The leopard grew brighter as it neared its death. Dad heard the uncadenced growl of an old beast that knew the ferocity and freedom of prowling the boundaries of dreams, that knew the rage of blood, the salt caves where elephants polish their tusks, and the awesome solitude of the forests.

Dad saw the beast, his being swelling with visions he couldn't understand. And when, at midnight, they came to question him about the murder of the carpenter, Dad did the most characteristic thing. He raged, interminably, about injustice.

He was surrounded by twelve underpaid police-men, all of them illiterate, all of them irritated by Dad's crude eloquence. And so they fell on him and beat the phosphorescent leopard out of his brain. They softened the edges of his bones, hoping to dissolve his energies, little realizing that they were doing in thirty minutes what he couldn't do in thirty years. In beating him as they did they opened the gates of his body, broke down its walls, and shifted the massive rock of his self-limiting ego. In beating him as they did they opened all the doors of his body for his bad blood and dream spirit to come flowing out, through pain and unconsciousness. Then darkness invaded the precincts of his mind.

In the deep night of his body, his brain overwhelmed with visions of blood revenge, Dad saw his father, priest of roads. He saw his father wandering in the village square of his mind, pouring out advice that wasn't understood, singing proverbs and parables in the deep idiom of a vanishing language. Then his father disappeared. Light shone in his eyes. He heard voices. He felt rusted bars. And found himself among the compact mess of bodies jammed tight in a hot cell. He saw faces marked with gashes. Faces of erratic criminals. Some of them were evangelists. One of them spoke all night long about the agonies of black people. Another insisted justice was an idea invented by the big crooks who run the world, an idea designed to keep small people in their corners.

Dad listened to their farting, their excreting and their cursing. He listened to the insurgent ideas of his fellow inmates, and soaked in the rough secrets of their spirits. Each element he absorbed pushed him outwards into an unknown space between heaven and earth. And that night, because of the visions in his brain, because of the secrets he was soaking in, because the agony of his broken body was too much for his comprehension – expanding and cracking the bowl of his knowledge – he released a frightening cry which sent me running to the door, to the housefront and the street: and I kept looking both ways, because I could smell the fury of his presence. But he was nowhere about. After a while I returned to the room and stayed on the mat, with my back to the wall. A mosquito coil was alight on the table.

I watched our open door. I listened to the footsteps of invisible beings padding up and down our corridor, looking for ways into the lives of unfortified sleepers. And as I listened with all my senses, small amongst the fluid shadows of the room, I heard a new voice singing in the forest.

At last the silence of the forest had been broken. The voice sang in the sweetness of a dirge meant not for the passing away of silence, but for a death announced in advance.

It could have been a spirit or a woman or a bird singing with the voice of humans. Or it could have been a birth uncelebrated. But the night, concentrated in the voice, tightened over our community, and yielded a morning that began with fresh disasters.

TEN

The fantastic ravings of Madame Koto

When I woke up, Mum had not returned. My neck was stiff. I cleaned the room, as she would have done. I made food for myself, and ate, and went out to investigate the world. Everywhere I went I asked if anyone had seen Mum. Some said they had seen her that morning, seen her setting out to hawk her wares. A woman even said she had seen Dad prowling about in the forest, shouting.

Neighbours were concerned about Dad's imprisonment. They wanted to do something. Some talked of going to protest to the Governor-General. Others threatened journeys to police stations and newspaper offices. But no one did anything. The men went to work. The women fed their children, fetched water from the well, and washed clothes. Then we heard that Madame Koto was raving again.

Her cries of a mad bird with broken wings, cries like the sounds of certain musical instruments forbidden to human ears, came over to us in the hot air. We rushed to her barfront, and saw something quite horrible. We saw that someone had placed a coffin on top of her new car. We knew at once that the coffin contained the body of the dead carpenter.

It seemed to have been burst open on all sides by the corpse which had been growing during the nights.

We could see the dead carpenter's head with its snarling mouth full of earth, as if he had died of overeating. His ears were large and black. He had stones in his eye sockets. His hands stuck out from both sides of the coffin, his fingers swollen. His feet were big and frightening; they had grown larger than their shoes. And his gleaming body was the colour of palm oil.

When we saw the coffin and the grotesque corpse, we let out a collective cry of astonishment and horror, a cry that was silenced by Madame Koto storming at us from the backyard. Her white beads were in her hands and her hands inscribed the air with the crude shapes of nightmares. Her face was swollen and ugly. A wound in her shoulder seeped blood through her expensive lace blouse. She had an aluminium libation on her lips. Her stomach heaved. And her wrapper fell from round her waist, revealing luminous rashes and cicatrices. She began to rage at us. She raged the most startling torrent of confessions, an eruptive flashing thrust of words crowded with burning dreams that held us fast to the shifting earth. Our mouths hung open. Our eyes twitched in the mercury of the sun's lash. While we listened to many portents within the incoherent rage of Madame Koto's words, white birds poured out of the cloudless sky, winging down on us in the oddest formations.

'So what if a man comes to my bar and is blinded by what he shouldn't have seen?' she shouted in a jagged voice. 'So what if I grow fat when all of you have lost your eyes? I did not plant a dead man in ashes. The rock is my mother and I did not eat your children in the wombs of your women. I did not make sores come out in your ears. But, yes, I sit on the head of my enemies. I take power where I find it and if you sleep and let your spirits float about unprotected, I will drink in their secrets. I will speak to the air, such is my nature. But I cannot plant a dead man and reap a bucket of nonsense.'

She glared at us out of insane eyes. Before we could breathe, she plunged back into the hallucinated sea of her rage.

'So what if two thousand years ago when you thought the world was the size of your village and your rumours, so what if my crocodiles cried for your flesh and I answered with the children of those who opposed our religion? So what if when I plucked a flower from the farm three men died? And what about the toad I cooked and gave you all to eat? You ate it and grew strong; you hailed my powers, you followed my politics. I do not drink blood from leaking calabashes. All over the country children call my name at night; the people I have saved outnumber my enemies by five to one; people I have sent to school, mothers to whom I have brought justice, marketwomen whom I have protected from thugs and gangs, unions that I have helped. It is not my fault if a carpenter died because he wanted someone to kill him. You all stare at me as if I am giving birth to a horse, but which one of you can give birth to a country and not die of exhaustion, eh? Which one of you can live in three continents at the same moment? Which one of you can enter the dreams of one hundred thousand people? Which one of you can talk to white people in their sleep and listen to their plans of making us smaller while they get bigger, eh? Which one of you can bear the responsibility of power, can fight off all the demons of the poor, tame the devils of the rich, ride the colonized air of the country? Which one of you, I want to know, can do battle with the six hundred and fifty-two spirits chaining up our future with a single diamond key, a key thrown into the deepest parts of the Atlantic where the bones of a sunken continent dream our history backwards as if it cannot be improved?'

Madame Koto paused a moment and we glimpsed a terrifying intelligence in the madness of her eyes, an intelligence so fascinating that we lost all consciousness of being in our bodies, under the fiery sun. And then, gently at first, as if seducing us with a forgotten tenderness, but rising again to fury and to shouting, Madame Koto continued:

'So, the secret of our failure is buried in the brain of a dead tortoise: why don't we eat the tortoise? Why come and dump a bucket of nonsense at my bar, why put the coffin of a man who wanted to die on my new car that hasn't even tasted the sweetness of our new roads? I did not cut off the fingers of my husband, and even if I did do you see him complain? I did not poison your dreams, and even if I did can you swear that you did not want it? Which one of you can ride a horse in your sleep and still hold on when the horse turns into a giant bird that takes you to the great white egg of the moon? You people believe in scattered gods; you don't even worship at your shrines. Your gods have too many names; and because you have forgotten why the gods were born there are holes in your souls through which your lives leak out. I plug the holes with rocks. The trees grow on my body, leaving all these rashes. I cut down the trees. They grow again, and I burn them, and lightning flashes while you sleep. Some flowers have roots of millipedes. When they die the air begins to boil. The sun bakes the barks of the trees, and they die – all the young trees that are not good for carving and the plants that are good for eating. They die and the great trees that were here before we knew the name of our continent, they give shade to two thousand caravans of spirits. I cannot cut down old trees. Take away your dead. Plant him in your sleep. I will carry the noise and the cries of those whose blood makes my body swell. I will carry the responsibility for those who say I killed them, poisoned them, planted bad dreams in their kidneys – but take your dead, put him on the great river and let him swell up in the sky. I have no words for the blind, nothing to show the deaf, so when you look at me it is your mothers' fevers that you mock, and when you judge me with your hungry ears it is the words of your fathers that you judge. I am the tree that you planted, a tree that you can't find a use for; don't complain if I give you strange shade.'

ELEVEN

Seeds of mutiny

Madame Koto stopped. No one moved. The birds had vanished from the sky. The only thing that fluttered in our midst was terror at Madame Koto's ravings. Like statues, we stood entranced by the flame of her words. The earth sizzled beneath our feet while she broke again into her confessions. We stood there, rooted at the crossroads of many eras which met simultaneously in our brains. And Madame Koto proceeded to confess to crimes committed in other continents, as an inquisitor who burned innocent women on oakwood fires, and made love to their cries. She confessed to murders committed hundreds of years ago in an Empire which flourished on the edge of a desert. She confessed to the deaths of children, to the destruction of villages, to driving men mad, like the husband who cut off three of his fingers under her hallucinative spells.

On and on she went, accusing us of eternal cowardice, of refusing to use our powers and envying those who do. On and on she shouted, mingling her agony with rage at the coffin. She attacked the air with her thick fingers. She flung her beads about. She jumped and fell, and tore her clothes, till she was nearly naked. She repeatedly screamed at us to get rid of the coffin, as she had already got rid of the disgusting bucket and drenched her barfront with basins of disinfectant. When none of us moved, none of us spoke, she charged at us, and we fled howling.

We didn't stop till we heard her commanding the men to remove the coffin from her car and dump it in the middle of the street for all to see. She said the corpse was our collective responsibility. But her men were silent, and they did not move. And from their silence we knew that they were more afraid of the corpse than of her. We should have known then that the seeds of mutiny had been planted in that silence. But, as always, we looked at the shapes of our ordinary reality – the chickens strutting about, the sun bleaching our walls and our clothes – and we didn't see the things perceived, but only the myths we brought to them.

Each moment offered us clarity and liberation but we settled for the comforting shapes of legends, no matter how monstrous or useless.

TWELVE

Birth of a three-day legend

That morning a three-day legend was born. I stayed at home, with Madame Koto's words growing larger in my brain. Then our neighbours brought me the day's newspapers which all carried pictures of a chaotic group of women who had taken hold of the city's imagination. The women had fearlessly raided a police station and released all its prisoners. Among the faces of the women was Mum. She looked exhausted, her eyes dull, her gesture defiant.

The newspaper said they weren't quite able to make out the grievances of the women, but listed complaints of malnutrition, poor social services, hospitals that didn't treat their children, governors who don't listen, inequality before the law, and above all the case of the man who was arrested – without being charged – for the public good of burying a dead body festering at a street corner.

There were editorials about the women. The story of the women storming the precincts of a police station went round our area, and became more elaborate as it travelled. By the time it got back to me again the story had multiplied like weeds on fertile patches of earth. I heard of Mum leading an organization of women, gathering them from the streets. The women drew other women, all of them lean with undernourishment, their children ill, their husbands listless under the pressures of the days. I heard that Mum led the women from one police station to another, with newspaper photographers following them everywhere they went. At busstops and market-places Mum called on the women of the unborn nation to stage a mighty strike, and to protest for Independence.

Mum changed in our eyes. Her absence nourished her myth. Women of our street, noticing how their comrades were seizing the national stage in acts of boldness, became quarrelsome, and staged strikes against their husbands. They had meetings in which they discussed the formation of organizations, in which they discussed how they could help Mum's group. They made sure that I was fed, and bathed, and beautifully clothed. They fussed over me as if I had suddenly become a hero. They talked about politics all day long. The word politics took on a warmer meaning.

I heard amazing stories of Mum addressing crowds of bewildered women. She spoke in six languages. She spoke of freedom, and of justice, which she said was the language of women. She spoke of Independence and of an end to tribalism. She spoke of the unity of all women who have to bring children into this world made difficult by selfish men. She spoke of all the things she had always been silent about. She talked of the special way of African women, their way of intervening, their way of balancing, of turning hatred into friendship, their talent for redemption, their long memory for histories and secrets that men too quickly forget, their gift of nourishing, of healing, of making good things grow, their secret ways of undermining, their great love of humankind.

Mum always spoke from a height, on top of battered cars, on hastily rigged platforms.

But when, alone among the shadows, I saw her, she was different. What I saw was starker than the legend. She was always overwhelmed by the noise of the women chattering and arguing in twenty-six languages. Often they did not understand one another. Mum was oppressed by the chaos of toddlers and their smells of malnutrition. And the women's rage overran her simple desire to locate her husband. Meanwhile Dad slept upside down in an empty space. His feet had been beaten with rough wood, his face softened by batons and knuckles. His eyes burned in the dark as he stared at the bright leopard crouching before him, ready to leap into his consciousness, and range around in the expanding bowl of his philosophy.

THIRTEEN

Hidden view of the Governor-General

All that time, Mum was brave and silent. The women who surrounded her wanted to sweep into Government House and storm the doors of the Governor-General.

The Governor-General had spent seventeen days burning the crucial papers relating to the governance of a country whose people he did not much like, and seldom saw except as shapes with menacing eyes and too many languages, too many gods, too many leaders. A people who took too little interest in the preservation of their culture.

He still had twenty-eight days to burn all the secret documents, all the evidence of important negotiations, the notes about dividing up the country, the new map of the nation, the redrawn boundaries, memos about meetings with religious leaders and political figures. He also burnt diary references to the three African women who consoled him while his wife badgered him about the plums of summer and the seashores of Cornwall. The women bore him seven children, whom he denied, though he was to send each of them fifty pounds a year for life, anonymously.

' And when he heard the story of the marauding women, I saw his eyes light up their green and blue of lovely deep sea fishes.

FOURTEEN

Distorting the rage

The women wanted to storm the Governor-General's door. They wanted to create a new parliament. But suddenly elite women appeared amongst them. These new women, with beautiful dresses and polished manners, had flown on aeroplanes. They had spent the same day in three countries, had seen ice fall from the sky, and had spoken into instruments that could send their words across a hundred miles without roads. The elite women were impressive; they talked in languages which none of the original women had heard.

The new women, with their bright bangles, glimmering eyelashes and wristwatches which actually made time visible, tried to lead the original women in another direction, quieting their urge to rebel, their desire to raid stations, descend on law courts and hospitals. The new women distorted the rage of the originals, confused them with orderly plans, with decent processions. The new women with their new words were largely successful.

Their success left Mum free to continue her search for Dad, taking with her the core of women who first joined in her campaign against injustice. Together, all eight of them – hard-headed women who, in another place, in a freer time, could have been eminent lawyers, doctors, engineers and wrestlers – spent the whole day tramping the labyrinthine streets of the heated city, looking for the police station where Dad might be held.

But at the first precinct they came upon, the policemen were patiently waiting for them.

FIFTEEN

The re-emergence of an old deity

The eight women had just entered the police station to ask whether Dad was imprisoned there, when the door was slammed shut behind them. When three Alsatian dogs leapt at them from behind the counter, they realized they had walked into a trap. I dread to think of those dogs slavering for a bite of human flesh, pouncing on the women, barking, while cameras flashed. The women screamed. The policemen blew their whistles. Prisoners in numerous hidden cells clanged on their bars, cursing the organs of justice. While the dogs tore off the women's wrappers, the policemen were ready with their batons for an invasion, seeing more women than were actually there.

The police station, for a moment, in that chaotic violent air, changed into an underworld crypt that flowed into all the other crypts in the years to come. The flies sizzled in the heat and the stench of the prison latrine buckets circulated in the closed spaces. When the dogs jumped on the women, spreading fear and panic, the most extraordinary thing happened. One of the women who had stayed silent the whole time, released a cultic cry which created a counter-panic. She was short and heavy-faced, had bold cicatrices on her forehead, and peculiar hand-writing on her bare arms. After her mesmeric cry, the lights flashed. And when the women looked from behind the vain protection of their cowering hands they saw that the dogs were perfectly still, sitting on their haunches, their tongues drooping from their mouths. In the moment of wonder that lasted for a few seconds, the police station was completely silent, and then a voice from one of the cells hidden below said:

'Your husband isn't here. Black Tyger is not in this station. Why trouble yourselves, eh?'

Then the woman who had stilled the dogs with her dark enchanted scream went to the door, and unbolted it. The policemen in their khaki shorts watched in utter astonishment. The women and the photographers started to leave. They were outside on the steps when the police officer, released from the spell, recovered his sense of authority, and barked out an instruction.

The Alsatian dogs, trained in two international cities, did not bite the women. But the policemen, galvanized by the instruction, leapt on them, fell on their defenceless backs, and clubbed them down the steps. The policemen pursued them into the streets, upsetting a gigantic cage of monkeys which a Brazilian revenant was bringing as presents for his relatives and in-laws. Five of the monkeys escaped, screeching along the road, causing cars to run into one another. Ignoring the extraordinary traffic chaos, the policemen went on pursuing the women, hitting passers-by who got in the way. The monkeys fled over cars, and made faces from the backs of lorries.

The Brazilian was surrounded by the shrieking of car tyres, the wailing of women and the general howl of the city. He ran across the road to the police station, began screaming his complaints about the cruel behaviour of the police, and was promptly bundled into a cell as a political agitator.

Meanwhile, the policemen went mad in the streets, stepping into a future time when public madness would be their norm. The entire road filled with the cacophony of dented fenders, exploding tyres, combusting engines and the cries of monkeys being run over by lorries. The road was jubilant at the taste of such novel blood. And the monkeys, ground into the road as sacrifice to the god who also likes the taste of dogs, probably saved the lives of the women. For the road, convulsing in its hunger, possessed the drivers, who saw forms rising from the tarmac, spirits with calabash heads and six eyes and thin legs and long fragile arms. The lorry drivers, fearful of committing an unknown sacrilege, crying out the names of all the gods they worshipped, entirely lost control of their vehicles. The lorries ran into parked cars, and crashed into buildings, their tyres spinning in the air, their engines groaning.

Having been faced with what they thought was a mutiny of women, the policemen now had a larger problem to occupy them: the re-emergence of an old deity, the great god of chaos, who would revel in decades of unprecedented rule, a new reign beginning with the birth of a nation.

The women regrouped, limping along with their

torn wrappers, battered faces, wrenched shoulders, dislocated ankles. Blood flowed down from their hair-lines, fertilizing the nightmares of the road. They gathered together, collapsing into a heap, groaning, cursing, expressing gratitude for their lives in fifteen languages. The cameras went on flashing at them. After a while, they got up, limping, ankles swelling, bones aching, welts forming on their necks. As they began to leave, as Mum pushed on with unconquerable determination to the next precinct, a man came towards her. He lowered his camera, jolting me as I watched them all in my dark circling space in the room, and said:

'Don't you remember me?'

'No,' Mum replied, wearily.

'I'm the Photographer, the International Photographer. I killed all your rats. You protected me when the Party of the Rich were trying to get me. How is Azaro?'

Mum recognized him instantly. In spite of her agony and exhaustion, she cried out in joy at seeing a familiar face.

'I've been following your campaign,' the Photographer said, with an important air. 'And I want you to meet someone who might be able to help.'

A short man, briefcase in one hand, a parting in his hair, stepped forward and shook Mum's hand.

'He is a lawyer. He has just returned from England. He believes in social justice and he wants to offer his services free of charge. This will be his first case.'

At the next police station, they got an entirely different reception.

SIXTEEN

Dad dissolves into seven selves

As the women were getting closer, Dad sat in a boiling cell, his chest constricted from all the beating. His ears were so wounded that he heard the language of his blood in the beating heart of the prison walls. His eyes hurt so much that he saw shapes hovering between the metal bars. Angel or demon, spirit or ancestor, he couldn't be sure. The form was bright one moment like a passionate annunciation, and dark the next like a death sentence. It was as if all prisons have a special god of their own, whose menacing face keeps changing, and whose features are never remembered.

Dad's broken skin made the air feel peppery. It was as if he had bruised eyes all over his body.

He sat in a small cell, the standing space of two coffins, unable to breathe. He sat there in great agony, his being dissolving into seven selves. I saw three of them while I sat at our housefront, watching the street, waiting for Mum to return. There was a moment when Dad was beside me, holding his head, but when I asked him a question he vanished. Then he was walking down the street and when I ran up to him he turned into a stranger. And then he called my name from our room and when I got there he was pacing for an instant, lighting a cigarette, but the match-flare dissolved him. My head widened. I feared that I was returning without warning to the land of spirits.

After a while I stretched out on the bed and felt myself floating in a green space, where Madame Koto lay, encircled by powerful herbalists.

SEVENTEEN

Madame Koto and the shadows

The herbalists were toughening the walls of Madame Koto's spirit. Fortifying the foundations of her power. They were drawing back the seven breaths which had escaped from her being. Pulling her back from the realms of madness.

The blind old man, sorcerer of the ghetto, was preparing for his own reign. He sent out ten spells, and reclaimed a terrain he had colonized for Madame Koto. He hurled out his ministrant incantations which altered the geography of the air, sealing out the powers of his associates.

Madame Koto shivered on the floor, making the house tremble. As the herbalists drew the breaths back into her, she began to swell. They purified her blood and her milk. They made more potent the chemical constituents of her body, and realigned her spirit. They solidified her womb in preparation for the birth of her three children.

These special herbalists struggled to restore her strength. They cast their cowries, and listened to the obscure language of divination. They saw that their seventeen interpretations led to the same dreaded crossroads, and became actors, foretelling wonders for her, while swiftly reconsidering their alliances.

I saw them retreat. Leaving only their shadows behind. Or was it that they remained but their shadows left? Madame Koto lay alone in her enormous room. She was delirious. She muttered dark confessions which ran back two centuries and forward one hundred years. Her words took form and crowded the air. I fought to get back into my body.

EIGHTEEN

A dream of hope

I found myself in another space, staring into the eyes of the policeman who had imprisoned me in his house many years ago. The policeman who tried to make me a substitute for his dead son. I was shocked that he was still alive, still in office, and that he couldn't see me. He stared past me to a group of women who tramped in like beggars, led by a young lawyer, predictably arrogant for his age. The lawyer proceeded to make a speech which the policeman forestalled by raising his hand and saying:

'I know this woman. She is a brave woman. Her husband is not locked up here, but I will do everything to help.'

After two sleepless days on the road, set upon by dogs, hassled by miracles, beaten by policemen, to find someone who actually offered to help was too much for Mum. She collapsed on the floor, and was laid out on a bench, where she slept without moving for five hours.

When she woke up she found herself in a strange house full of unfamiliar women. She was still so exhausted that she took it all for a dream. She turned over on the bench to have a nicer dream when a voice said:

'They have found the station where your husband is held. Go back to sleep. Nothing can be done till the morning.'

Mum heard it as a dream, for the night had conquered her body, and she had surrendered her spirit to the waning moon which shone like Madame Koto's egg, or like a white bowl of palm-wine which an exiled god had balanced over our house, and which intoxicated the rooftops.

NINETEEN

Dad summons his ancestors, and fails

That night, while the voices of the forest started again, vaster in number, sweeter than ever, as if a whole secret age of dreaming was coming to an end, Dad was suffering in the aftermath of his second beating. He sweated all night long, covered in heat rashes. Lice and fleas crawled all over his body. Microscopic worms festered in his wounds.

He had been incandescent that day, daring the policemen to torture him and see if they could kill him. He boasted all afternoon that his spirit was made of the inexorable stuff of justice. He poured out a torrent of calumny, listing the crimes of the government, denouncing all forms of police brutality, shouting that the prisons were erupting with innocent people who would one day destroy the administration.

The more they tortured him the louder he cried about the love of injustice that would tear the unborn country apart. He poured out visions of future coups and riots, tribal massacres and famine, plagues of beetles and explosions at oil sites, the genocide of war and the decades of hardship to come. When the policemen got tired of beating him, breaking innumerable batons on his head, dislocating their wrists and cracking their knuckles on the solid bones of his tigerine face, they incited the other prisoners to set upon him and silence him altogether. When they did set upon him Dad was so broken by the treachery of his fellow inmates that after they had finished with him he sat in a corner nearest the bucket latrine, the only free space in the cell, and began to call out the names of his ancestors.

He called out their royal titles, their chieftaincy titles, listing their achievements and legends, in order to lift the leaden weight of his betrayed spirit. On and on, he called to them, as if he expected them to appear before him, answering his harsh summons. His brain was all in a tumble, and his lips were so swollen that the names came out differently. He got stuck in the grove of his spirit. He uttered the famous name of Aziza, the road-maker, who built roads over marshes, and who charmed the silver spirits of the great forest surrounding the village. He incanted the name of Ojomo, the Image-maker, who felled a great boar with a single blow, who tamed the spirits of the valley, who discovered an ancient grove of monoliths in the forest, who initiated a religion without a name, who could discern the shapes of the ever-changing gods and built statues and masks to their ascendant attributes. He chanted the mighty name of Ozoro, warrior, blacksmith, who fought in one of the white man's wars, who survived wrestling with the fabulous spirits of two oceans, who stopped seven bullets and killed five white men and was surprised by the softness of their spirits. He returned home an uncrowned hero, forgotten by those whose war he had fought; but he brought with him the message that the white man's power was both real and an illusion, a reality that hadn't been faced, and an illusion that had been accepted. Dad chanted the great name of Ozoro more than any other, the Ozoro who claimed that spirits are essentially the same the world over, and that power resides in hard work, in scientific investigation, in intellectual curiosity, in creative greatness and freedom, in the fullest exploration of our human powers, and in the truest independence. He sang Ozoro's name with reverence, the Ozoro who returned home after the great war, opened a factory and became the first man of the village to build a radio. Before he died he announced that in the spirit-world we had already gone past the age of technology and entered the era of pure power, the power that moves the volcanic planets, the distant constellations, the wind, the moon, the heart and all destiny. Dad cried out the name of the legendary Ozoro who died an enlightened man, who saw the world being made smaller, who saw his people worshipping alien dreams, exiled from the mighty spirit world where the atom had been split thousands of years ago; and whose last cry to the world, the essence of his legacy, was: 'CATCH UP WITH YOURSELVES!'

Dad went on calling his ancestors in a heated voice, as if he had gone entirely mad. None of his ancestors appeared. None of his ancestors gave any sign that they had heard him. Dad fell to wailing, to throwing himself about. And when the darkness cleared from his mind he saw three forms over him. Thinking that they were his ancestors at last made manifest, he assumed an attitude of utmost reverence.

The three men lifted him out of the cell and took him to a small room with a fan on the ceiling, a telephone on an empty table and an imperial map on the wall. The three men left and after a while a white man came in and sat six feet away from him, and looked out of the window. Then the three men came back in and asked him questions about agitations, planned riots, protest movements, political organizations, assassination attempts on the Governor-General, and underground efforts to destabilize the regime. Dad was unable to hear anything clearly because of his swollen ears. He heard only the pulsing of blood through the arteries of the world. He answered their questions with the names and legends of his ancestors. Then the white man, who had already wasted more time than he had intended on so worthless a specimen of humanity, turned angrily to the three minions in khaki shorts, and shouted:

'You brought me a mad man, not an agitator! Take him away!'

They bundled Dad back into a tiny cell, where he sat crouched, listening to the worms eating the walls and foundations of the building. Then, with horror, he realized that they were eating away at him. He screamed and his voice bounced back at him. He had been left with worms and fleas, in a cell of lice and diseases, with only a little window through which he could see a patch of the sky. But it was dark that night because he couldn't see through his swollen eyes and the congealing blood on his eyeballs.

TWENTY

Dad summons a dreaded deity

In his crushed space, with his wounds burning, his spirit tightening, Dad fell into a hole in his mind, from which he couldn't get out. And not knowing the full range of his desire, the depth of his belief, the vibrating power of his summons, Dad began to call out the attributes of a deity. He called upon the god to manifest itself, to open the gates of his spirit, to show him wonders and images of redemption, to help him out of his abyss, to unleash revolution on the tormentors of his people. He called on the god of revolution, stern brother to the god of justice, to flatten the evil places of the world, to lash thunderstorms and hurricanes on all oppressors, to burn away the corruptions of the nation, to destroy the shacks and malarial abodes of the wretched, to drive their excessive tolerance of suffering from their backward lives, to goad them to rage and revolt, goad them into changing their conditions for ever, into something wonderful.

Dad listed the awesome attributes of the god, inventing songs to an undiscovered deity, a deity so terrible that humans have always dreaded to include him in the pantheon for fear of his monstrous destructive presence.

Then, quite suddenly, in the midst of Dad's summons, came a sound which he had never heard before. He looked around the darkened cell. He heard the sound again, like the hesitant footsteps of a giant, or a monster. Dad couldn't see clearly, but he perceived a light growing brighter in front of him, from a point in the wall. The footsteps resonated all around him in the cell. The brightness intensified and the light became so hard that he felt it was burning his brain. He covered his face, crying out. Spasms of the most delicious and agonizing intensity were tearing his being apart. Even with the shutting of his eyes he could not escape the blinding illumination that surrounded him like tongues of hard flame. And it occurred to Dad that he was in the very presence of an unbearable fire which was roasting his being and brain, turning all that he was into living ashes.

He saw the flame all over his body. Burning his flesh and hair and face. Burning him all over as if he were covered in phosphorus. Purifying his being even as it wracked and consumed him. And he crouched there in the awesome flames, enchanted and terrified, hearing clear voices in the fire, voices that were varying registers of one voice, chanting codes over him. The voices spoke to him in an unearthly accent, in an entirely incomprehensible language. The words intensified the flames. And the flames climbed high in brilliant colours, till the whole cell and the whole city seemed illuminated.

Then in the lightning flash of a moment, Dad saw a boy with a face of sublime beauty. His hair was haloed with a golden crown. In his hand a black sceptre shone like diamonds. Then the boy was gone. The flames vanished. There was no smoke in the air of the cell. And everything was plunged into primeval darkness. In that darkness Dad saw a mighty form, darker than the darkness. The form had green eyes. Then Dad heard words that were not spoken. Harsh words that were like electric shocks on his body. Words that broke him out in violent tremulations, inflaming and destabilizing his brain for many years to come. He heard words that shortened his life. Burning away his years in the consummation of enduring the presence, not of the deity he thought he had summoned, but of another one altogether, whose name is too terrible for words. All night long Dad burned in the aftermath of the manifestation. But the burning did not stop then, did not stop till the end of his cycle.

In the morning his jailers found him covered in white ash. They found that all his wounds and welts, his cuts and bruises had healed miraculously over-night. They found him with his eyes open, staring straight ahead, as if into a visage of pure golden horror.

They found his spirit serene. He didn't speak, his neck was stiff, and he could barely support himself. They found that the white ash wouldn't come off his body, that the cell smelt of the sweetest perfume, and that the walls were all charred, not with black, but with aquamarine, with streaks of yellow and gold and red, as if a goldsmith had patterned the walls in rough medieval splendour.

They found Dad's hair matted with gold dust. Diamond powder clung to his face. They led him out

58

in wonder and horror and took him to an empty room. He stood against the wall, his mind empty, his eyes staring vacantly but wondrously ahead, as if he had finally seen the constituent secret of all objects, all trees and metal, as if he could perceive once and for all the secret of the world – that all things are alive, and all things are manifest by virtue of fire. The flames were all he saw. He saw faces as flames. Saw wood as flames. Saw the air as incandescent, with everything burning at different speeds. He saw wonders in that sight, but he could not speak. The things he saw were too much for the words with which to say them.

TWENTY-ONE

A public confession

That night, while Dad burned in the visitation, the forest broke into voices of the dead. The forest was populated with voices which breathed out melodies of incomparable clarity, sweet like a choir of angels trapped in an earthly sphere. Voices that longed for a different space. A space that was pure reality.

The songs in strange languages found me and lifted me one foot above the bed. I remained like that in the intense lucidity of pure dream. Then the spell was broken. A sudden rash came out in my spirit. And I crashed down and landed awkwardly back into my body.

Startled and disorientated, I jumped out of bed. And through the vicious headache which pounded in my brain I heard coarse voices of two men raving in the night like jackals.

I was not the only one who heard them. The whole community listened as the two men began screaming that insects and slugs were eating up their brains. We listened to them shouting out incriminating words very clearly so that the earth and sky could hear them, words from which I made out public confessions and livid descriptions of their crimes. They confessed to the beating up of men who had done them no wrong, the kidnapping of children, and the brutalization of women. They confessed to partaking in schemes to rig the forthcoming elections, to acts of rape on women who flashed their sexuality at them on hot nights, to armed robberies and murders, to intimidations and fetishistic rituals for breaking the spirit of whole communities. They shouted out a horrific confession of why and when they murdered the carpenter, of how they stabbed him in the navel and throat and forehead and dumped his body on a patch of weeds.

They confessed to having performed crude abortions on a great number of women for money, to how they dug around in their wombs with metal spokes, in barbaric ignorance of the business. They confessed to the vile number of wombs they had destroyed permanently for the sake of two weeks drinking at Madame Koto's bar. But what they said next made my headache worse, made the air – innocent in its existence – take on the form of beasts without memory. In the heat of their confessions, for they sounded quite mad, screaming as if the words they uttered would somehow save them from the turbulence of their thoughts, they said that their crimes were great, they begged no forgiveness, they called on the heavens to break hurricanes on their spirits, but they warned that they had greater masters above them, a hierarchy of masters, who never committed crimes, whose hands were always clean, and who delegated the thoughts, the acts and the consequences of their crimes and wickedness to lesser beings, to their minions, their servants and their disposable friends.

Then, quite suddenly, the men turned from confession to growls without words, antiphonal gnashings, tuberculous coughs, coarse sounds of spitting, noises like the mindless grinding of teeth. They went on like that, as if their energies were jammed in the production of horrid noises. They went on all night.

And in the morning, the people of our street found the two men in the forest. Their bodies were covered with sores and gashes, pus oozed from their ears. They were still shouting their confession to the murder of the dead carpenter in hoarse voices, begging that they be punished and beaten without mercy. But the people of the street merely bound them with ropes and carted them off to the nearest police station, where they kept on raving their confessions to the bewildered policemen.

TWENTY-TWO

The vacant Tyger

Twelve miles away, in another police station, Dad answered all the questions of his interrogators with an unconquerable silence. His silence was such that they felt he had truly gone mad, or that they had overdone their torture. His silence was unnatural. It wasn't self-willed, wasn't determined and had no intensity. It was a sort of neutral emptiness, as if his head were entirely devoid of thought, his eyes empty of emotion, as if he were locked in the hermetic space of a spell or curse.

The policemen were suddenly afraid of him and sought ways to get him off their hands. His vacancy had become a weight, a nightmare responsibility. He stared at them as if he had no soul. He seemed a complete vegetable of a man, staring at them with vacuous, almost enchanted eyes, or maybe even mad eyes.

The policemen could have coped with his death, and put it down to suicide. They could have coped with massive wounds, and called them self-inflicted. But how could they cope with madness, emptiness, the absence of soul or animation in the eyes, the limbless serenity of an insane baby, the stillness of a hypnotized chicken, the immobility of a hallucinating snake? They couldn't very well say that he willed himself into becoming a zombie. They couldn't say that he tore his soul from inside him and hurled it against the prison walls. And they didn't dare goad answers out of him now, for his vacant stare suggested an awesome godlike power uncontrolled by fear or desire. And who has the courage or the equal madness to beat an insane man to death?

So the policemen left Dad standing at the Information Desk, unchained, free. But he stood there, staring at the walls, at the policemen, at the ceiling, with an equal vacancy, as if things had become pure signs, and as if he were just another sign in the universe where everything flared or blazed, was more itself or less, according to the secret will of its ascendancy.

TWENTY-THREE

Homecoming of the heroes

And when the lawyer, the Photographer and the eight ragged women burst into the police station, demanding the release of an innocent man who had not even been charged, the police were only too glad to get rid of Dad. Though not without the lengthy formality of questions to be answered, forms to sign, addresses taken, superiors consulted. Dad meanwhile was returned to the crowded cell. He had stared at his rescuers with such empty eyes that Mum cried out that the police had stolen her husband's vigorous brain.

The lawyer told Mum to hold back her anger. The Photographer flashed his camera. And the policemen, though they didn't betray it, sweating into the coarse material of their colonial uniforms, were glad to be rid of Dad, to be rid of his silence of a great river at night which couldn't be seen, his stillness of a mountain range in a deep darkness which was the weight and size of an unnamed premonition in the brain. They were glad to be rid of his queer ravings, his undaunted body with the inexplicable gold ash on his skin, the diamond powder rimming his eyes, and the phosphorus of his rock-like face. And as soon as all the formalities were completed, the policemen released him to the clamorous women, and quickly bolted the door behind them.

The women's joy at their triumph was not as complete as it could have been. Neither was the reunion between Mum and Dad. After Mum had thrown herself at Dad outside the police station, after she wept with gratitude at seeing her husband again, she slowly became acquainted with the fact that Dad didn't seem to recognize her. He stared at her with a stupid sort of longing, a vacant unfocused gratitude, as if his gratitude also included, with equal weight, the dust on the ground and the flies in the air, the birdshit on the statues and the dust-covered trees that no longer bore fruit.

'What have they done to my husband!' Mum kept shrieking, as she tried to reanimate his eyes, and get Dad to recognize her.

But Dad's eyes retained their serene vacant compassion. He wholly submitted himself, or seemed to have no choice whether he did submit, to their excited buffeting, to their leading him one way and then another, to their many voices of conflicting advice. Some said take him to the hospital. Others said return him to the police station and ask them to give you back your real husband. The lawyer offered his services to sue for police brutality. The Photographer offered to expose the scandal to all the newspapers. One woman suggested they go to a herbalist. And another recommended that he be rushed to his village. At that moment, the hint of a smile appeared on Dad's face.

Mum saw the smile, and immediately took charge of the situation. Holding on to Dad as if he were a defenceless child, ill and broken of bone, she led the way home.

As they set off, the lawyer gave Mum his business card in case she wanted to bring charges against the police. The Photographer took a picture of that moment. And the eight women caught a bus to our place, talking rowdily about all the things that could be done about Dad's condition. The Photographer frowned in a curious fashion through all their disagreements.

Dad sat in the bus silently, his face impassive except for the faint lingering smile. He was limp, and his fingers twitched occasionally. His eyes deepened in their emptiness, and the emptiness was made freakish by the gold dust inflaming the corners of his eyes.

They talked about Dad as if he wasn't there. And, in truth, he wasn't there. He was in the midst of his sufferance of a manifestation. The brightness was still burning at the root of his tongue. His thoughts were stilled. And the world was turning in a fire which fixed his gaze at an equal distance, a distance without focus.

When they all disembarked at the main road near our street, the women were still disagreeing. The Photographer marvelled at how nothing had changed since he left. Dad lagged behind. He stared at everything. He kept wandering away from the street to examine the dried fishes and black-eyed beans and shoelaces and candles sold at the stalls. He studied the mud huts and zinc abodes with their rusted rooftops. He kept looking into buckets of water as into magic mirrors. And he kept peering into people's faces, as if to determine the precise location of their secret fire. He frequently had to be restrained and led on by Mum. He seemed to have lost all sense of discrimination. He took a democratic interest in everything, as if he perceived no essential difference between wood or worm, metal or paint, between human beings and wells.

Mum found his silence and his absence of focus rather trying. She kept talking to him, asking him questions about his imprisonment. But he looked at her emptily and then looked away. He remained silent.

As they neared our house, the people of the street began to recognize Dad. A great cry of jubilation rang around the houses, and the news was passed from mouth to mouth. People stopped what they were doing and rushed at him. The cry of his homecoming preceded his advance. Children ran to him, singing out his nickname. Soon the whole weary group were besieged by the people of the street. Voices hailed Dad, calling him a hero. A hundred hands touched him, felt him, embraced him, drawing his spirit back into the community, reminding him of who he was, earthing him in his vacancy, threading his legend in songs of homecoming. But Dad stared at the many faces crushed by poverty, faces with intense or resigned eyes, faces of the thousand shapes of suffering, all of them bearing the unalterable stamp of a single condition – he stared at them all and gave no response to their enthusiastic welcome. He even seemed quite annoyed. His brow lowered in passive hostility.

As Dad neared our house the crowd around him

thickened. The children pulled his shirt, and he glared at them with wide open eyes that did not frighten them. And when quite suddenly the excitement mounted, and the men of the street hoisted him up in the air, lifting him on their shoulders, bearing him home in a conquering hero's welcome, singing songs with his communal name, something odd happened to Dad. It may have been a panic brought on by his sudden elevation. It may even have been that, in raising him up high, they upset his impassivity. He immediately began to kick and struggle, till the men bearing him had to throw him down.

When he hit the ground with his face, rolling on his wounded arms, on which no wounds showed, he jumped up and pounced on the men who had been celebrating him. He punched one of them, knocking him out. He kicked another, and sent him reeling. He caught the barber round the waist, and hurled him rather spitefully on the hard earth. Then the eight women, the Photographer and all the people of the street backed away from him, wondering what they had done wrong. They were puzzled at his violent response to their triumphant welcome. On their faces jubilation was mixed with bewilderment.

Then, with the ferocious single-mindedness of a lustful soldier, Dad strode towards Mum. He seemed so like a barbarian on a battlefield that Mum fled. Dad pursued her round the crowd which kept shifting and scattering at his insane advance. He chased after Mum relentlessly, his face unemotional, his eyes calm, and she bolted towards the main road as if a blood-crazed murderer were after her.

Terrified by Dad's zomboid vacancy, she was

69

fleeing and screaming when a powerful voice, part thunderous, part demonic, made her stop, as if paralysed. Then, to our astonishment, Dad swooped down on her and roughly bundled her on his shoulder, in an act rather crudely proclaiming her the true returning hero.

With his face sweating and impassive he came up the street, and the crowds surged round him again hailing Mum in sweet songs, embellishing her legend of a woman who brought the city to its knees and defied the might of the administration and freed innocent prisoners from the dark holes of injustice. The seven women joined the triumphal procession, and sang loudly of a new era of women's liberty. The Photographer recorded it all with his famous camera, darting amongst the singing procession and taking pictures from his unique angles. The children too sang and called out Mum's communal nicknames in their excited high-pitched voices.

And I heard them, and ran out from our room, out into the street, into the sunlight and dust, and saw Mum high up on Dad's mighty shoulder, her face bright and scared, her figure lean and broken, her eyes intense, shining with new knowledge. Dad was striding along, ahead of the procession, curiously smaller, strangely bigger, his face swollen, his eyes clear. I ran towards them, with joy surging in my lonely heart, but Dad pushed on, not acknowledging my bursting joy, mistaking me, it seemed, for one of the many children racing around him.

He saw me but his eyes didn't change. It was only when Mum demanded to be lowered, when she jumped down and knelt on the ground and embraced me tightly and lifted me up, turning and laughing and fondling my hair, weeping on my face, calling my one hundred and one names of a spirit-child who needs many names to feel real and wanted, that Dad bent his mighty frame and touched my face with his bristly cheek. Then he raised me up high into the benevolent smile of the gods. And afterwards he led the procession to our little room, where I had been crying for three days, sleeping amongst ghosts and shadows, circling the spirit of my parents through the stories of their absence.

TWENTY-FOUR

Dialogue with the Photographer

The crowds of people who came to welcome Dad back from prison brought their smells and anxieties and celebration into our little room. Mum bustled about and tried to make everyone comfortable. She organized folding chairs and bought drinks on credit. The crowd also brought with them the air of a chaotic fiesta. The seven women, in clashing voices and elliptical languages, gave us fantastical renditions of their adventures, their battles with policemen, gigantic European hounds, disorientated monkeys, spirits wearing wristwatches, and all the demons of the quivering roads. At the same time, in a hundred voices, each interrupting with an important nuance or missed detail, the inhabitants of our street related the incredible scenes of Madame Koto's ravings and the confessions of the two delirious murderers.

Voices were loud, faces were animated, misunderstandings abounded, laughter circulated, and chaos – a great lover of crowds – made itself at home among so many languages, so many hearts, drinking happily from the wine of celebration. The bustle of bodies, and the waving of hands sent shadows flying round our room like maddened birds. Dad sat in the midst of it all, smoking a cigarette on his three-legged chair, his face inturned as if he were alone in a dark space.

He was very silent and he stared through everyone. It wasn't long before the guests began to refer to him as if he were invisible. I sat watching him, frightened by his transformation, and by his silence. It was as if a river had swept through his mind, washing away all signs of identity. He did not respond to the homecoming festivities. He did not rage. He was not exultant and feverish in his desire to entertain. He was absent. He was like a man who had witnessed a terror greater than anything he had seen on earth. His deep ghostly silence made all the celebrations in his honour seem hollow and a little frivolous.

There were voices all around him. People talked about the disappearance of the dead carpenter's coffin. Children with dazed faces occasionally mentioned Dad's fighting name in their games. The seven women argued about what to do next. Some suggested the formation of an organization, a nationwide society of ordinary women to rival the one that the elite women had swiftly created. One of the women referred to the elite society as vampires who had made a national spotlight for themselves out of the energies of the suffering women of the streets.

The celebration went on for hours. Mum strove to keep it vibrant. She bustled in the kitchen and hurried to the traders and haggled with them and bought more drinks on credit. Tired as she was, she would come into the room, see the celebrations flagging a little, and would move from one group to another, infusing their discussions with fresh vigour.

She made sure everyone was happy: she went up and down the little room, initiating a cycle of songs and mediating between quarrelling factions. She did all this with an unusual charge of energy.

But Mum's initial enthusiasm gave way to exhaustion. Forcing herself to be the living spirit of the party, her gestures became slightly manic and her face strained, her smile enervated. A dark light burned around her, the light that exhaustion gives when one still has to give out energy. The fact is that the three days away, her adventures, her resilience, and the successful outcome of her campaign had quickened the growth of Mum's spirit, and deepened her powers.

And while Dad sat sunken in the silence of a new childhood, as if he were in a world of shadows without objects, his eyes registering nothing, a thin smile fixed on his mouth, as if he were indulging in a hidden pleasure, Mum glowed with a dark exhausted animistic light. Her voice was high, her neck taut, her body tense, her shadow sharp, her eyes raw, and her presence lacerating. Her voice took on a brittle authority. When the crowd had eaten and drunk us into a long list of credits, when they had thoroughly imprinted their anxieties and quirky passions on the walls, and drained our vitality, till we hung about in our own room listless and half-asleep, Mum could bear it no longer and began roughly ordering people to leave. Her transformation amazed us. She thanked everyone for coming, but proceeded, without sentimentality, to hustle the drunken guests out of the room. Her forthrightness was extremely effective.

People started to leave. They left unwillingly, thanking Mum for her wonderful hospitality. Receiving these tributes with a brusque graciousness, she ushered them out nonetheless. One by one, in ragged drunken groups, still continuing their interminable songs and disagreements, they reluctantly staggered out of the house.

While there were still some people who hadn't been dislodged, inventing legends in their happy drunkenness, the Photographer, who was not yet ready to leave, and who had been sitting on the floor silently next to Dad's chair, looked over at me and flashed me a mischievous smile. Then he got up and came over.

'You do remember me, don't you?' he said.

'How can I forget you?' I replied.

He smiled happily.

'Your parents have become famous. Did the rats come back?'

'What rats?'

'The rats that used to eat your food before you did, remember?'

I found myself staring at him with Dad's impassivity. The Photographer was as crickety as ever, with his quick jerky movements, his sad humorous face and vaguely paranoid eyes. There was also something about him that wasn't there before. A slight oiliness had crept over his manners, as if a good deal of his time had been spent in obliging people he didn't like.

From across the room I heard Mum apologizing to the seven women for her roughness, thanking them for their great support, and asking them to stay the night if they wanted. They didn't. They were anxious to return to their homes, to their husbands and children. I heard them swear oaths of eternal friendship and allegiance, vowing to create their society for the liberation of ordinary women. Mum saw them to the street and she was out for a long time while the Photographer kept pestering me with questions about whether the thugs and political spies who were after him had returned during the time he had been away. He asked about women whom he had been passively interested in; some had moved away from the area, and some had vanished into the forest to join the nocturnal choir of Elysian voices, but I didn't tell him so. He asked me questions about neighbours, about his landlord, and if any rival photographers had appeared in the area to fill the vacancy his absence had created. I didn't answer many of his questions at all and I didn't reply to his queries for a while because I was watching Dad, who sat rocking his three-legged chair, with the vacant smile still on his mouth, and a dissolved expression in his dead eyes. Dad's transformation was curiously magnetic. He seemed to spread a bizarre contemplative somnolence over the room, making my eyes droopy.

'So what on earth has been happening here since I left?' the Photographer asked, with some exasperation.

'Many, many things,' I said.

'Like what?'

'Madame Koto is pregnant with spirit-children.'

'How do you know?'

'I know. I saw them.'

76

He stared at me dubiously.

'What else?'

'The blind old man is going to take over the world.'

'What blind old man?'

I stared at him, bewildered. I went on.

'The forest has been singing.'

'How can a forest sing?'

'Many people have disappeared into the forest. I saw white antelopes with jewels round their necks. Thugs killed the carpenter and Madame Koto's driver ran over Ade, my friend, the carpenter's son. The carpenter's body has been walking about the street and he held me one night . . .'

'A dead man?'

'Yes.'

He stared at me again, as if I were in a fever, or as if I had appeared without explanation in a dream he was having.

'Tell me something else. Tell me something I can believe,' he said, eventually.

'I am,' I said.

'Tell me something else anyway.'

'There is an old leopard in the forest which only Dad can see.'

'Is that so?'

'Yes.'

The Photographer turned to look at Dad. I tugged at his shirt.

'Madame Koto has been going mad. There was a mighty evil wind with rain and earthquakes which destroyed people's houses. Dad went blind because of the dead carpenter. Madame Koto's masquerade rode a white horse killing spirits. The political thugs came and stoned our windows. Soon there is going to be a great rally where . . .'

'I know about the rally,' he interrupted.

'Will you come?'

'Of course.'

He was silent for a moment. Then he spoke again.

'You are the strangest child I have ever met,' he said. 'No one mentioned anything about a masquerade on a white horse killing spirits, or a dead man walking. Are you well?'

I nodded.

'Tell me about the old leopard.'

'Only Dad can see it.'

'Why?'

'I don't know. Maybe it's because Madame Koto has been sitting on his head. Maybe it's because he went blind.'

'Blind?'

'Yes.'

'How could he see a leopard if he was blind?'

'I don't know.'

'What a crazy family,' he said. 'Everything seems to have changed. What happened to the rats?'

'They didn't come back.'

'Didn't I tell you?'

'You did.'

'I killed all the rats in the house of a millionaire. One hundred and six rats died in his house. That's how I got my job.'

'What job?'

'Working for a newspaper. I take their photographs.'

78

'So you are a big man now?'

'No,' he said, laughing. Then, lowering his voice, he asked:

'Can I photograph the leopard?'

Dad mysteriously stirred on his chair. The smile had widened imperceptibly on his face.

'I have taken photographs of all kinds of things, of white men flogging their black servants, of riots and strikes, political rallies, boxers being knocked out, wrestlers lifting cars with their teeth, houses collapsing because of the storms, goats being slaughtered for religious feasts, people of new churches, in white dresses, praying at the beach, prisoners rioting, politicians making speeches about Independence, birds flying out of a huge magic saxophone, but I want to take the sort of picture I've never taken before. I want to photograph an old leopard, a free leopard, in the forest of the city. I can see it in my mind already.'

'But only Dad can see the leopard.'

'Nonsense,' the Photographer said, unwisely.

Suddenly, like an apparition rising from the earth, Dad got up from his chair. He towered over us. His presence was menacingly serene. The Photographer stood up hurriedly, and said:

'Well, I suppose I must be going. Yes, I will go and develop the photographs. Thank you for all the drinks. I will be back before the rally.'

He made for the door. Dad caught him on the shoulder. They shook hands.

'You are a strange family, but you are my favourite family in the whole world,' the Photographer said, with a grand gesture, leaving.

Outside I heard Mum thanking him for his tenacious support. I heard them talking about newspapers and fame. Their voices went towards the street. Dad sat back down in his chair. He looked at me with wide-open eyes. Then he smiled, and said:

'My son, I have seen wonders.'

Then he became silent again, his eyes vacuous, his face almost foolish with his smile of a hidden pleasure. Not long afterwards Mum came back into the room. She sat beside me on the bed. She put her arm round me and held me close. We sat alone in the room full of shadows. We stared at one another in silence. It felt like we were at the bottom of a sacred river.

TWENTY-FIVE

Destroying the veil

On the day after Dad was released from prison, Madame Koto stopped raving. Her bar was shut and none of her women were seen around. No one went there to drink palm-wine and peppersoup. There were no political meetings. There were no rehearsals for the great rally. It had been postponed so many times because the voices of the oracles were not yet favourable and the alignment of the planets had not been propitious.

The continual postponement of the rally left us in a state of frustrated expectancy. The people of the area, the shopkeepers, petty traders, sellers of fried food and soft drinks had made great preparations for what would be a fiesta of sales. The rally had come to assume mythic proportions in our minds. We looked forward to big bands, magicians swallowing gold coins, somersaulters, fire-eaters, dancers, acrobats, contortionists, jugglers and bombastic speech-makers. There were no circuses in those days and the rally focused our minds on the spectacle of politics.

With Madame Koto's bar empty and silent, a fabulous lightness filled our beings. But we waited that morning for her appearance. We waited for her daily public confessions, her forty-five minutes of delirium, her curses, her sinister utterances; and when she failed to appear we were disappointed. We became somewhat irritable. With her disappearance also went her tragic drama. We felt cheated through the day, and in the afternoon it rained.

The dead carpenter also temporarily disappeared from our lives. When the government pressed on with the destruction of the forest the dead carpenter's grave was discovered. The grave was freshly carpeted with wild flowers and it had the most expensive gravestone we ever saw, bearing the legend: 'HERE LIES A CARPENTER WHO REFUSES TO DIE.' We had no idea who had erected this wonderful memorial.

After the discovery of the grave, and one week after Dad had been released, the two murderers were rumoured to have gone insane in prison. One of them had managed to scratch out his eye, apparently thinking it was a weird kind of slug that was burrowing its way into his head. They were both carted off to a maximum security prison and we didn't hear anything about them any more.

But on the night that the dead carpenter's grave was found sinister new voices sounded in our street. The forest was silent. There were no empty spaces in public spectacle in those days but it came as a shock to us to hear gruff voices, red-hot with drink and vengeance, accusing Madame Koto of being a traitor. 'THOSE WHO BREAK SACRED OATHS MUST DIE!' the voices cried, obscurely.

We didn't know what it all meant. For three days the voices continued. Madame Koto retreated to her

secret palace to recuperate, and her absence intensified the myths about her which the voices made
more ominous.

The rains fell, and turned our roads into muddy
streams. Eventually the voices, hoarse from their
chanting and their threats, were silent. Fresh winds,
unsifted by wild leaves and aromatic climbers, blew
through the gaps in the forest. The gaps widened
daily.

The forest once represented the beginnings of
dreams, the boundary of our visible community, the
dreaming place of spirits, the dwelling place of
mysteries and innumerable old stories that reincar-
nate in the diverse minds of human beings. The
forest was once a place where we saw the dreams of
our ancestors take form. It was once a place where
antelopes roamed with crowns on their heads. It was
a rich homeland of the spirit. Its nocturnal darkness
was the crucible of all our experiments in imagination. The darkness there had always been a spell, a
hallucination, a benign god. In its silences old herbs
kept their secrets of future cures. The trees stored the
stories of our lives on their gnarled and intelligent
faces. In the dark forest snakes swam on dead leaves,
spiders laid eggs that shone at night, and the eyes of
strange animals turned yellow and flared intermittently.

The forest was once a place where the spirits and
elves came awake at night and played and wove their
spells of mischief and delight. This forest of dreams
and nightmares, dense like all the suffering of our
unrecorded days, was being altered for ever. This
forest of our living souls was beginning to show

gaps. We saw the sky beyond. We also began to see other communities. But they were as a dream, fading and reappearing in a yellow mist.

The destruction of the forest, the unfamiliar gaping holes, the great wound of it, seemed to our horror like a veil rent asunder, cut through with flashing knives, to reveal not mysteries, but nothingness. It was as if the veil itself were the mystery.

At first the gaps in the forest were not noticeable. The rent in the trees had not yet begun to eat away at our psyches. But the forest dwellers compacted their living spaces. The spirits and tangential beings fled from the exposure, from the shallow reality of daylight.

At first, the spirits thought only of the continuation of their mysterious lives. The destruction of their crepuscular abodes had not yet begun to drain our souls. Vengeance had not yet entered a new war. The war humans were waging on the spirits' realm. The war they would rage on ours.

At first we humans didn't notice the great trees dying, crying out as they fell in the agonized voices of slain benign giants. At first the falling trees, crashing down on their mortally wounded colleagues, didn't alter the stories of our lives. We still had our spectacles, and our daily dramas to divert us.

TWENTY-SIX

The silence of the Tyger

When the Photographer's pictures were published in the newspapers we became famous for three days. The seven women who had made the search with Mum turned up at our house, bearing the newspapers. They talked all day long about their future plans. Mum took to fame very badly. She became loud-voiced. She talked of becoming a wrestler. She spoke of becoming a politician. She dressed in very bright clothes and even stopped hawking for a while. She invited her new friends round and made frenzied plans and bought drinks on credit.

All that time Dad slept, woke, went off to work, came back, and stayed silent, with an unconquerable smile on his lips and a depthless emptiness in his glassy eyes. He resented the new interest in him. He didn't speak to anybody. He stayed indoors, in the dark, with the door always open, and with a complete absence of expectancy on his face, always staring through people and things as if he were in a realm where perspectives were radically different from ours.

For three days Mum was famous and when we began to starve again she went out hawking, and took the newspapers with her, telling strangers about her prominence when they wanted to buy her wares. She took her fame badly and no one wanted to buy anything from her and she came back in the evenings dehydrated and depressed, having alienated all her customers with her self-obsession. One evening when she returned from a bad day's hawking, she said:

'We are in the newspapers and still we are hungry.'

We said nothing to her. It was just as well, for the next day we read in the papers that the elite women and the lawyer were claiming all the glory for freeing Dad from prison. Mum was furious and she set out immediately to the newspaper to correct the lies. She returned in the evening thoroughly disillusioned and hungry because she had spent the whole day searching for the newspaper offices and had been unable to find them.

'Newspapers are printed by devils,' she said.

For days afterwards we heard more stories about other people the lawyer had freed, and the cases he had won. We learned that the leader of the elite women had become a politician and an official candidate for one of the political parties. Mum became bitter because the elite women had somehow entered a higher zone of public life on the basis of three days of her agony. She was bitter, but she didn't know what to be bitter about.

'My husband is free,' she said. 'He doesn't talk, and sits around like a fool, but at least he is safe. And my son is well. What more do I want?'

But Mum wanted more. She had tasted more. She had learnt more. Somehow she felt that a new life, a greater opportunity, a new freedom had been snatched from her. She felt that a door had been shut on her new possibilities. The seven women came often to discuss, to plan; but with the birth of the famous Society of Women headed by the elite group, with all the interest they had generated in the newspapers, their fund-raising events, their highly publicized speeches and well-organized demonstrations, their meetings with members of the government, what chance did eight women from eight different ghettoes stand? Their meetings in our little room turned into squabbles and power struggles. The group splintered. They quarrelled endlessly. Their friendships turned sour and then the whole idea died and then they stopped coming to our place.

I was very sad when the seven women stopped coming. They brought activity, twelve languages, strange philosophies, and many interesting dishes of food with tastes like the memory of a rich dream in our mouths. They brought hope and activity and argument and lovely voices. They had dreams of improving the lives of women, dreams of getting the government to change our society's perception of women, of creating better hospitals, and setting up schools and universities to educate women for the best jobs that the land had to offer. Their dreams were chaotic and related to their experiences and they always argued. But they argued with lots of food in the house. They talked a great deal about politics and they made the word take on a better taste, like the taste of succulent mangoes, or sun-ripened oranges.

When they stopped coming our room became small and sad again, devoid of different lovely voices and languages and faces, devoid of the laughter of those who dream intensely from intense suffering. And Mum became more shrill, more irritable. Her brief fame had cheated her and she took out her annoyance on us. That was when it occurred to me that fame is often a devourer of the best things in our spirit. I suffered Mum's annoyance the most. I was made to run long errands, was sent to the market, and made to wash clothes under the merciless sunlight. Mum became a stern disciplinarian, shouting at me, putting me through my paces, and bellowing stories to me of what happens to lazy people, how they become criminals, how they go mad in jail.

Through all the comings and goings of the seven women, through all the dying of their dreams, through Madame Koto's absence, and the destruction of the forest, Dad remained silent. He was silent for several weeks. Not even the groans of the devastated trees stirred him.

During the long weeks of his vacancy, we became aware that we were being spied upon. Policemen in mufti would hang around outside our compound, watching our movements. The secret policemen spied on us, thinking we were agitators. But after observing the comings and goings of the seven women, their public arguments about who should be chairwoman, their quarrels which flared in the street, after observing Dad's wandering off to work, his staggering back, his complete silence, his idiotic stare, his fixed smile, they lost interest in us. They saw us as buffoons who had somehow stumbled into national prominence.

When the spies stopped watching us, our sense of significance diminished. When the seven women vanished from our lives, we were fairly dazed. We were left only with Dad's silence and his holographic smile. His dead-eyed stare continued. His wounds and bruises had gone, but the pain of them remained. He groaned in agony every night. He ached all over. As the weeks passed the pain increased, as if he were paying an additional price for having all evidence of his wounds disappear from the surface of his flesh in the first place. The gold dust rimming his eyes gave him an increasingly demented, sleepless expression. The ash in his hair, the diamond-powder streaks, which had been a continuous source of mystery, made him look older and at the same time more striking, curiously distinguished, almost demonic.

Dad's silence was deep and on many nights he took us with him deep down into a hole or abyss which left us frustrated by the beginnings of sentences that he would launch into once every ten days. He would say something, an oblique word. We would become tense. We would listen, waiting. Then we would find ourselves following his silence into coral reefs and dark caves, into places deep under the earth, and deep into the sea, where fishes of the diamond seabeds utter strange melodies. And it would be another ten days before Dad would speak again, saying one word, a word like 'wood' or 'tree' or 'sun', and then again his silence would suffocate us. He made our lives so airless.

While we watched the invading phenomena of a new time full of sinister omens, Dad lay on the seabed, the moonbed, of a long agonizing dream, an unfathomable meditation on the nature of the gods and on the fifth stage of history. While Independence approached with all its signs and cross-currents, while the trees died, and Madame Koto regained her strength, while the rainy season unleashed an avalanche of dead leaves and dead birds, of streams and primeval mud on our destinies, Dad did nothing but make us suffer the silence of a man who has survived the manifestation of a dreaded deity, a new god.

BOOK TWO

ONE

Circling spirit (1)

There is a famous story of a chief who ordered all the frogs to be killed because they disturbed his sleep. The frogs were killed and he slept well till the mosquitoes came and destroyed his kingdom. His people fled the realm because of the diseases the mosquito brought and what was once a proud land became an empty waste.

Mum told this story several times through Dad's long silence. I never understood the story till one day after it rained. A horde of frogs appeared in our street, croaking all night. The frogs got into our buckets, into our wells, and into our water from the aluminium tanks. The people of the street fell into an orgy of murdering frogs and the more we killed the more appeared, and the more they croaked at night, till none of us could sleep.

'Where are the frogs coming from?' I asked Mum one day.

'From the forest,' she replied.

I didn't believe her. It seemed as if yet another plague had descended upon us. Not long afterwards toads and snakes appeared in our street. Mighty spiders turned up in our rooms. Wolves and hyenas roamed the area at night. A white antelope was found dead in an unfinished house. Through the days we listened to the woodcutters chopping down the trees. Our area filled up with strangers who came to the city from their villages deep in the country. There were no houses for them and sometimes ten of them lived in one room and when the diseases began to visit us from the forest many people died while the trees fell one by one. Things changed rapidly and at night all kinds of animal cries kept us awake.

One afternoon, as I played outside our compound, I heard a giant cry from the forest. Without knowing why, I ran towards it. I ran past Madame Koto's bar, which was still shut, her signboard taken down. I made my way into the forest. I saw blobs of snakespit everywhere on the matted grass. Animals gasped for breath in the undergrowth. I heard the roar of the distant river. The forest had the dense odour of crushed leaves, fervent tree sap, broken bark, dead animals, the cruel fragrance of uprooted herbs and the intoxicating aroma of overfertile earth. I went deep into the forest, following the great cry that sounded from the treetops.

Soon I came to the place where Dad had originally buried the dead carpenter. The great black rock Dad had hefted over to mark the grave was still there. It bristled with furry growths, green mushrooms, snails, and things that looked like eyes but which were actually tiny plants with a bitter smell. The black rock had grown curiously bigger. All manner of noises crackled inside it. Beneath the rock, where the grave had been, the earth was gashed and torn open. I fled from the ugly sight of the gutted earth and went on following the cry till I came to a place where machinery and electric saws filled the air with grating cacophony. All around were the hulks of great trees, their trunks bleeding. All around were bulbous men, with heaving muscled chests, cloth-covered faces, saws and huge axes in their hands.

'What are you doing here?' one of the men shouted at me. 'Or do you want a tree to fall on your small head, eh?'

Behind the men was a majestic iroko tree. It was beautiful. Its trunk span was so vast that ten men couldn't link their arms around it. The iroko stood a third sawn through. The men had thick ropes attached to its higher parts.

Men were shouting everywhere and the noise of weeping sounded all around like a giant in agony.

'Someone is crying,' I said.

The man who had shouted at me came closer. His sweat was pungent.

'Who?' he asked.

'I don't know. I heard it from the street, so I came.'

'No one is crying. Go away!'

'Can't you hear it?'

'Get away from here, you mad child, before I crack your head with this axe!'

I stood still, rooted by the spectral weeping. The men went on sawing away at the tree. Their chainsaws produced buzzing noises which started a headache in me. The men started hacking at the tree again, their axes bouncing off as if the tree trunk were made of metallic rubber. Their chainsaws coughed and clogged with wood fibre, eventually stuttering to a halt. The men, meanwhile, hacked and sawed and cursed. One of the burly men said something about the tree being full of devils. The man who had shouted at me turned and saw me still standing there.

'I said GET AWAY FROM HERE!' he bellowed, taking a few menacing steps towards me, lifting the axe above his head as he did so.

I turned and started back home. The weird weeping intensified all around me. I wandered for a long time in the forest. Banks of leaves, dense canopy of branches, crowded jungle foliage, all shut out the sunlight. I walked in a green darkness. Thunder sounded above the green ceiling of the forest. I began to run. The trails multiplied. Many paths intersected. Red cloths were tied to tree branches. Snails everywhere. A leopard coughed far behind me. Rubber pods exploded and fell through the leaves. The paths confused me. I followed one of them and it led me deeper into the foliage. Led me to parts of the forest I had never seen before. I beheld a settlement, a cluster of white huts, with a fence round them, with white dresses out drying on the lines, with odd-looking animals wandering around in the premises. I took the path back, and came to another intersection. Another path led me to a stream. Another one just went on and on, as if the forest had been inwardly growing, as if the trees had been walking.

Everything confused me. White faces appeared amongst the climbers. Tortoises watched me from the vegetation. A boar rooted around a tree. Antelopes fled into green wastes. Dogs barked at me and vanished. Trees crashed down a short distance away, and rays of the sun slashed at me from chinks in the leaves and branches. The forest had again become a labyrinth, a fiendish maze, and I couldn't find my way out. As I stood there in the deep shadows, listening to the lisp of forest voices, something fell on my head, filling my eyes with whiteness. When I turned around I saw a girl sitting with her back against a tree. She had one good leg and a wooden one. She had greenish eyes.

'I can't stand up,' she said, staring at me.

A praying mantis leapt past my face. I heard footsteps coming towards me.

'Help me up,' the girl said. 'They are coming for me.'

'Who?'

'Them,' she said, pointing in the direction opposite where the footsteps sounded from.

I looked and saw only trees, lianas, undergrowth.

I went towards her. The forest became silent. The noises of trees being chopped down had stilled. I could no longer hear footsteps. When I got near her she gave out a cry and leapt on my back, clinging to my hair, shouting into my ears:

'Go! Run!'

Galvanized by a feeling of panic, for she was so heavy, I started to run.

'That way!' she cried.

I ran in the direction she pointed, giant footsteps all around us, shadows weaving. A strong wind blowing the treetops, sending pods crashing through the leaves.

'No, that way!'

She indicated another direction. There there were

no paths, only soft earth, covered with decomposing leaves. I ran on, changing direction with her cries, till I burst into a yellow realm, where I saw butterflies vibrating in the wind. Everywhere I looked a settlement was vanishing out of sight. Figures with the faces of antelopes were disappearing into the trees. An old woman sitting outside a green hut was weaving a cloth of many colours. She looked up at us, and smiled. A horse with the feet of men was galloping into the forest roads. Giants with gold teeth sitting on stools the height of baobab trees were telling stories in their yellow time. Their beards were green, and their laughter disturbed the wind.

'Stop!' the girl cried.

I couldn't. My feet ran on, independent of my will. With my burning feet I ran past ochre huts whose walls were made of matted flowers. I ran past a blue and green mushroom on which a thoughtful cricket sat. I fled past an anthill seething with red ants, past honeycombs with bees frantic in the hot air. Went on running till I heard the omnipresent cry again and saw the sky falling down in the shape of a mighty treetop falling slowly over us. Voices seared the wind from the earth and flowers. And it was only then, with the old woman pausing in her design, the figures with antelope faces pausing to stare in our direction, only then could I stop, and it was too late – for the tree had crashed down, bringing three others along with it. And its branches, rich with fruit and bird nests with silver eggs, fell on me and knocked me out on the soft earth.

When I recovered, the girl had gone. Deep in the forest the old woman was singing a haunting dirge.

The earth was soaked with blood. I tried to move. I breathed in deeply the air of wounded plants. Tears stung my eyes. I looked about me and found myself buried in a bank of leaves and branches. I screamed. Suddenly the wind changed and I disentangled my ethereal self from the wreckage of dead trees and saw a silver egg near my head. I floated above the great elephant of a tree and wandered like a bird through the bewildering expanse of forest, circling the air, weaving in and out of visions. I saw the world through a blue fire. My being fractured into several selves. There was agony in my brain, and butterflies in my ears, stirring my blood. Footsteps sounded about me like the pounding of an enormous heart. I circled in the forest, round and round, like a bird trapped in a labyrinth of trees, unable to reach the sky. My vision swirled. Then suddenly everything settled, and I found that I could control my flight when I stopped being afraid.

I dared the wind, rode its seven humps, and found myself at another site. Eleven men, two of them white, were surrounded by complex machinery for the destruction of trees. I saw them through a blue haze. They stood amongst great indifferent shadows. And one of the labourers, in a despairing voice, said:

'But, sir, we have been trying to cut down this tree for five weeks!'

One of the white men, wearing crash helmet, glasses, khaki outfit and boots, with a gun under his arm, said:

'Superstitious Africans!'

And the shadows changed around him and I saw all the footsteps of his life marked by the vibrations of his utterance. Wood sprites in the form of chameleons stared at him from the undergrowth. A spirit with liverish eyes, riding the wind, went into the second white man who said:

'Ghastly people!'

And the spirit stayed in him for a while. The earth turned slowly. The wind heaved above the trees. The smell of trouble forefelt wafted over their heads in the fragrance of secret nameless herbs which understood the diseases, ailments and afflictions of the future. The herbs whispered their potencies on the wind, naming diseases incurable that they could cure. And the white man with the liver-eyed spirit in him took off his dark glasses, and polished them. He looked around. Then, holding on to his colleague, he said, in a controlled voice:

'There are devils in this forest.'

'Steady on,' his colleague said. 'You don't believe in the so-called spirits of Africa, do you? Surely science has conquered all that nonsense.'

'Absolutely,' the man with the spirit in him said. 'But I feel ill. Something's come over me, Harry.'

The butterflies stirred in my ears and the winds of the new space blew me on, carrying me off like a cotton waft, and I saw the beautiful girl with the wooden leg sitting beside the old woman, helping her with the weaving of the long cloth of stories. They were both singing dirges under the spell of the sun. The wind blew me on and on. The footsteps about me diminished. The agony in my head increased. Then I came to another place where two woodcutters had gone mad from destroying a sacred grove and releasing a host of angry spirits. The plants there were bleeding a purple ink which left a bizarre epic on the red soil.

The two woodcutters were jumping about, screaming that they could see the future. One said that five devils were dancing in his head. The other yelled all the names of his lineage, a line which would end with insanity. The anthill which they had also destroyed poured out its army of poisonous ants which brought out ugly welts on the faces of the two deranged tree-cutters, who went tramping around the forest, and spreading terror before them. They disturbed the silent spaces where secrets dwelled in peace with the dreams of the dead, where forgotten diseases lived in calm quarantined content-ment. And when the diseases were dislodged they too began to roam about looking for beings that would give their agitation a new home.

Everywhere the two deranged men went things dwelling in solitude roused themselves. The dead stirred, and spirits fled out from their crepuscular abodes. Leopards with the feet of white men, antelopes with jewels round their necks, fled their lairs, moved deeper into the forest, closer to their extinction.

The new wind blew openings through the forest roof, and exposed the dark rich places of solitude to the merciless glare of distant planets.

TWO

Circling spirit (2)

I was blown on and on, and like a spider's web I caught the surrounding stories as they drifted in the wind. In the distance I heard women calling my name. Their voices resounded through the forest, each syllable changing as the trees altered the sound of my name, changing it into theirs. The trees named themselves through the distorted voices of the women who were searching for me.

Beyond them, in a spell-sealed place, the old woman began to laugh at all the vicious ironies of time and history that she had witnessed in her life of a recluse. The old woman had been exiled from society because she looked frightening. A strange disease had deformed her, humped her back, twisted her eyes, made her voice ghostly, made her legs swell, and made her complexion more radiant. She was driven from society, isolated, avoided. Nobody would do business with her. Landlords refused to rent her rooms. And so she came to the forest and built her hut and watched the changes in society. She lived the life of a hermit, of a herbalist and benign witch. She cured her disease, but she retained her ugliness so that she would never again have to live with the wickedness and hypocrisy of human beings.

She began to care for lost animals, wounded beasts, children left in the forest to die because their mothers couldn't abort them – strange children with powers of transformation. During all her years in the forest the old woman grew to know the secrets of plants and the earth, the disruptive and benign influences of unseen planets, the unsuspected winds, the undeciphered voices, the vast realm of spirits, and all the permutations of omens and signs.

The old woman laughed now, standing up because she had unfurled the full length of tapestry she had been weaving. And the wind in contemplation rushed across the full length of cloth with all its stories of trees and animals and plants. The wind smoothed out the annals of the origin of human beings, from their beginnings in the silver egg which the great god put in space and which hatched into millennia of stories. There were tales of exile and war, the birth and descent of the gods, the hubris of mankind, the flood, and the cycle of vanities. And there was the end which all true stories threaten: the second deluge of fire. It illuminates the choice that has to be made between blindness and vision. Blindness leading to the apocalyptic. But vision postponing it so long as we can keep to the bright side of all creation, and to the shining original dream.

The wind seemed in love with the tapestry of stories and fates which the old woman had been weaving all her days isolated in the forest. And when the beautiful girl with the wooden leg saw the tapestry, she wept. The weaving was not yet complete, but the end was in sight. The tapestry was admired not only by the wind but also by the sun, by the birds who were her servants, the animals she had tamed, and the spirits she had befriended. The splendour of the old woman's labours made the girl weep, for she too had been woven into the cloth of fates. And as the old woman laughed, the white man whom the liverish spirit had entered said:

'Listen, Harry, I'm feeling sick. It's as if I've got live eels inside me.'

'Quite so,' his colleague said absent-mindedly as he commanded his nine woodcutters to resume their assault on the great sacred iroko.

'Look, Harry, you believe in *Zeitgeist*, and the residing spirit of a place. You used to like the great German Romantics.'

'So, what of it?'

'I tell you, Harry, this place has a weird spirit to it. And I feel bloody awful. And I feel drunk as a kite and I haven't had a drop to drink. It's the damn heat, Harry, the heat's gone mad, Harry.'

'Quite so, quite so. Have some whisky or something, old chap.'

The man with the spirit in him staggered to the jeep. His African servant rushed forward to help him.

'Don't touch me, you ugly creature,' he screamed.

The servant ignored the remark and helped him into the jeep. He spread himself out on the back seat, his feet on the door. Then he opened a flask of whisky, and drank, and the liverish spirit expanded in him, sitting sideways, a mischievous expression on its woebegone face.

Drunk on the heat, he was suddenly invaded by hallucinations. He saw bats with the faces of pale white women, owls with binoculars round their necks, and he shouted:

'Damn you, Harry! Damn your imperial dreams, Harry! We've been trying to cut down this tree for a whole month. It's destroyed our saws, blunted our axes, exhausted our workers, taxed our patience, and we haven't even dented its African face, Harry!'

'Shut up, old chap, and mind your language with the natives,' snapped his friend.

And the possessed man, drunk on hallucinations, fell into hysterical laughter. His laughter tickled the air. The forest began to laugh as well, distorting the original laughter. The hyenas took it up and played their variations on it. As did the wolves, the trees, the frogs, the spiders, the lost dogs, the hidden leopard, and even the two deranged men, with the sacred grove spinning in their eyes.

As they fled past the trees, the two men saw beings they last glimpsed in their childhood. Women who walked upside down in a serene realm of sepia. Old men with yellow eyes flying through a silvery air. Old women with one eye each in the middle of their heads. A horse with the face of a village chief. Spirits with many heads all talking and singing at once. A stomach without a body, rolling along an ancient path, followed by the most beautiful girl in the world. The two men saw these forgotten sights of childhood and laughed even harder. The forest distorted their laughter, sifted it, sanitized it, and the white man with the spirit in him sat up in the jeep, his eyes clearing for an instant, and said:

'Africa is laughing at us, Harry.'

And the old woman said:

'Stop weeping, girl. Go and prepare food, but first help me to fold this cloth.'

The girl with the wooden leg didn't move. The two mad men, still fleeing, stopped laughing. The old woman, folding the cloth slowly, looked up, and said:

'Feed the animals. I'm going to the moon tonight. Make sure my special candle stays alight. I want you to sit up and protect it from the wind till I return.'

Then she went into her hut and began to study her fate-sealed carvings of the men and women who had banished her to a forest solitude. She didn't handle the figures. Her heart was suddenly, unexpectedly, touched with a profound nostalgia for the life from which she had been exiled. The feeling was like a bitter herb giving off a divine fragrance in her spirit. Moved by the depth of the feeling, she started to alter her spells. She rearranged the end she had foreseen, and redesigned the spell she had shaped over the lives of the community. But when she cast her divinatory beads she was horrified at the answers. She cried out, and the birds flew from her rooftop. The bat with green eyes stirred on her wall. She had begun her alterations too late: the figures had set, their future was fixed forever. She staggered out of her hut, looked out over the forest, and wept. When she stopped weeping she uttered a cry which brought the yellow owl circling above her head. And with another cry of command she sent the owl winging beneath the roof of the forest, circling and calling out, while the white man said:

'Harry, I'm going back to the hotel. There's

another owl with binoculars on that tree. I feel ill, Harry. Can you hear me, Harry?'

'The whole world can hear you,' said his exasperated friend.

At that moment the two mad men burst into their midst, jabbering, pulling faces, laughing, screaming, imitating the noises of owls and hyenas, sending confusion through the camp. The woodcutters cried out in terror. Harry backed away, his exasperation changing into incomprehension as he said:

'Are these devils or men?'

The two mad men rushed towards Harry. He stood his ground, clutching his gun, upper lip quivering. The two men made ugly faces at him. Screeching and scratching their bleeding ears. Dancing round him. Imitating his expression of horror. As if they recognized him neither as beast nor man. Then Harry's companion in the jeep, drunk on whisky, suffocating from the heat and from the spirit which had now completely occupied his being, jumped to the front of the vehicle, started it, and shouted:

'Are you coming or not? These creatures have smelt your blood, Harry!'

And Harry, confronted by the mad men, backed away slowly, his finger on the trigger of the gun. The two mad men made faces, crowding him, while his friend said, in a tone of hysterical mockery:

'Get Africans to deal with Africa, Harry. That's always been our policy. They know their jungle better than we do.'

When the two mad men pounced at Harry, the owl circling the scene cried out three times. The mad men imitated the cry, and Harry fired twice, startling them. He leapt into the jeep, and fired three more times, grazing two trees and hitting the innocent shell of tortoise in the undergrowth. The vehicle's wheels spun on the red earth, gained solid ground, and shot off along the dirt track towards the distant road. They fled the site, never to return.

Much later, African supervisors took their places. They recruited powerful sorcerers, neutralized the spirit-dwellers, and drove away the witches from their meeting ground within the trees. Then the levelling of the forest began.

But that day, after Harry and his mate had sped off, the owl circled the trees, and sent its messages back to the old woman. The woodcutters of the camp scattered into the forest. Trapped in its labyrinth, they were prey to the vengeance of spirits. They roamed from path to path, ran round in confusing circles, and saw trees dissolve before them as they hallucinated in a forest fever.

THREE

An incomplete ascension

The owl completed its circling, returned to its flowering tree near the old woman's hut, and was fed a white mash by the girl with the wooden leg. The old woman, saddened by the day's discoveries, and late for her meeting, retired into her hut to sleep. Beneath her bedspread of stories the old woman changed into a nightbird and then into a spirit with six eyes. Then she soared past me, up through the treetops, a luminous shroud, ascending to the crescent moon.

But the air was dense, and a green mist hovered above the forest. The old woman found her spirit heavy that night. She who had borne exile in her own land. Suffered half a century of solitude. Mastered spirits of air and tree and earth. Listened to the whisperings of gods in her dreams. She was heavy that night. All the cries and sufferings of the earth tugged at her heart for the first time in many years. The agony of innocent human beings. The genocide of the trees. The insomnia of the beasts of the forest. The homeless spirits and the dislodged diseases. The rising seas and shrinking forests. The unstable earth and the misery to come. All tugged at her and made her heart a mass affected by their force of gravity. Her sorrows made her heavy. The unalterable destiny of her people which she had willed and changed too late filled her with nostalgia. And her longing for an earlier time, a golden time of childhood among mysteries, started a powerful wind, which blew round her hut. The wind knocked the door open, startled the birds which slept on branches, and swept a somnolence on the air which made the girl protecting the flame fall asleep. When the wind blew out the candle I heard a great cry from above and saw a bird with a hooked, aged beak fall down. When the bird hit the ground, it turned into an antelope, and then into the old woman. Then to my horror she looked up at me, and said:

'I can't stand up. Help me.'

'How?' I asked.

'Just help me.'

'Why?'

'I know your father and mother. They are good people. If you help me I will do something for you.'

'What?'

'I will help you too.'

'How?'

'I will free you from under that tree, I will help you out of this forest, and I will tell you a secret.'

'Is it the same secret my father has?'

'No.'

It was very dark and all around me I could hear birds stirring. A strange wind was turning my body to wood. I could hear noises from the silver egg. As I hovered in two places, I began to hear words all around me on the silver wind. The wind spoke with the voice of the old woman. A voice light like the feathers of birds that fly without ever perching. All night the voice spoke to me of the nitrogen shadows and the air of moss and bark which protects the dreams of forest dwellers from being blasted away by the heat. The voice spoke of the special mysteries invaded by the new chemical secretions in the soil, of marshes and rivers reclaimed by limestone and sand. The voice told of the many beings left homeless and unprotected with the death of trees. It hinted at the rage of the spirits at the disturbance of their centuries of dreaming. It whispered about the trees which had grown magnificent in particular places in the forest. Places where the earth's lines of vital forces met. Acupuncture points of the land. The voice talked of trees that were like the essence of a civilization, masterpieces of sculpture and survival, with future destinies coded on their trunks. The voice spoke of the tree of mysteries which grew up into the three realms – the earth, the ancestral plane, and the sphere of higher spirits.

The voice dwelt on the indecipherable powers resident on earth in ordinary or invisible forms, seen only by antelopes and cats, dogs and the dying, the inspired and the enlightened, strange children who are half human, one quarter spirit, and one quarter dream. The voice said the function of labyrinths was to confront the trapped one with the light of an inescapable truth. Once the confrontation is effected the spell of the labyrinth is broken, and the fata Morgana, the lure, disappears. Then the bird unique to the entrapped one leads him out to the new realm that was the old familiar place where the labyrinth began.

The voice spoke all night, soothingly. A voice without language in which many things were heard simultaneously. The voice became more urgent as night neared dawn.

'You must help me or I will die!' the old woman cried.

So I lowered my floating form over her and she clung to the back of my spirit. Uttering a wail that was almost a laugh she turned swiftly round, knocking the nightspace from my mind. I felt feathers beating rapidly on my face and heard a steady noise of axes on wood, moving towards my head. The smell of wood smoke was rich on the air. Voices in the distance were calling my name. I opened my eyes and saw a tiny bird of blue and yellow plumage standing on my forehead. Its feathers quivered above my eyes. I awoke beneath a cascade of leafy branches.

I stayed like that for a while, bewildered. I stared up at the chaotic canopy of leaves. My head hurt. My brain was spinning from a hundred livid dreams. When I moved the bird flew from my face, twittering and circling the branches. Slugs were crawling up my legs, ants were busy on my arms, worms wriggled on my chest, and lianas were tangled about my head. Weaving in and out of different spaces of clarity and pain, I listened to the sound of wood-chopping coming closer and closer, and to the rough voices of men marvelling at the fallen tree. Then I saw several faces above me. The bark faces of hungry men. I panicked. Screaming and wailing, I wrenched myself from beneath the weight of branches. And when I rose frantically the men saw me and shouted, fleeing. They shouted that the tree was turning into a human being, that the place was possessed.

Clumsy and confused, I managed to get myself out from under the branches completely. I stood swaying before the most beautiful ancient god of a dead tree that I had ever seen. Blood was streaming down my head. The blue and yellow bird was circling the air above me. And I gazed in awe at the magnificent tree. It was the length of ten elephants and its flowers were in full bloom. Bird nests were scattered around and silver eggs broken on the red earth.

Following the erratic flight of the blue and yellow bird through the labyrinth of the forest, I came to a place where a group of women in white smocks were performing a ceremony. The women were deep in their ritual. A white goat was tethered to a root and white chickens flapped, terrified in anticipation of their sacrifice. I ignored the women and wandered on. My stomach was empty. My head reeled with forest fevers. I came to the fabulous rhinoceros tree that had grown from Madame Koto's fetish. It seemed so long ago now that I first rode it in complete innocence. Further on, the voices calling my name were louder. Soon I could see them. Our neighbours and street people. With cutlasses and sticks. Mum wasn't with them, and neither was Dad. They stopped when they saw me. I felt like a ghost returning to a forgotten home.

Our neighbours were so amazed at my appearance that none of them spoke. I must have seemed to them like a sleepwalker or an apparition. I gazed through them with Dad's impassivity. They let me wander amongst them. Muttering strange words about our family, they followed me home. At the door to our room, certain now that I had got home safely, they left me alone, and gathered at the backyard, to whisper weird legends about our little family.

Dad sat in his chair, nodding his head. He was staring through everything with a smile on his face, as if he hadn't moved for seven years. Mum lay on the floor, weeping in her sleep, exhausted from spending all night looking for me along the silent roads of the world.

FOUR

The unaccountable passion of mothers

Dad didn't move or express any emotion at my return. As soon as I went and sat on his lap, Mum woke up and saw me. Yelling for joy, she snatched me under the arms and swung me round. She embraced me. Then, still joyful, Mum threw me up and swung me right into a yellow terrain where the old woman woke up on her bed and, complaining of backaches and a throbbing head, scolded the girl for not protecting the candlelight while she ascended.

When I opened my eyes woodsmoke was thick in the air and Mum was dressing the wounds on my head, saying:

'What happened to you, my son? We have been looking for you for two days.'

I stared at her. She had changed. Her eyes were fiercer, her face longer.

'They were cutting down a tree and it fell on me,' I said.

'A tree fell on you?'

'Yes.'

'Where?'

'In the forest.'

'Who cut down the tree?'

'I don't know.'

She turned abruptly to Dad, raising her voice, and said:

'So, while you were sitting in your chair, nodding like a lizard, a tree fell on our only child, eh?'

Dad turned his head towards me. Nodding. Smiling. With the gold ash ghoulish round his eyes, he stared without seeing me.

For a while Mum stayed silent.

When she had finished bandaging my head she prepared food and watched me eat. My head kept swelling, my eyes hurt and the room swayed.

Mum cleared the plates. Then, in an outburst of rage, she hurled the table over, and left the room. She soon came back, straightened the table, and sat next to me. For a long while she stared at me. She stared at Dad. She kissed her teeth, cursing. Then she proceeded to gather what little money she had from her various tin cans. She tied the money at the end of her wrapper, laid me on the bed, and went out.

An hour later, she returned with a herbalist. They had both hardly stepped into the room when Dad, setting eyes on the wizened sorcerer, gave out a disdainful cry. The herbalist had come with his charms: crow's feet, beads, vulture's liver, and a bag of potions. Dad grabbed the sorcerer by the scruff of the neck, and threw him out into the startled compound. Mum was horrified. The herbalist was reputed to be so powerful that he could drive out demons with a single inscrutable syllable. But he picked himself up, dusted his trousers, and said to Mum:

'Your husband is a strange character. He's too strong for my powers. Don't ever consult me again!'

And, without malice, he stamped off.

Dad went back to his chair. His eyes were red from the effort of rage without words. He had a demonic smile on his face. He turned his fierce eyes on me. Then I told him about what had happened to me in the forest. He smiled all through my narration, rocking in his chair. Why did my father smile at my terrible experiences? I had no idea. And while Dad smiled, Mum got angrier. She turned on him again, and accused him of being a monstrous coward since he'd come out of jail. She taunted him, saying she wished she had never taken the trouble to free him, saying that it was all right for him to be brave when there was no suffering involved but as soon as he feels the true suffering that comes with real courage he turns into a speechless chicken. Dad went on rocking his three-legged chair, staring without focus. Mum couldn't stand his colossal impassivity. She began crying out that people had nearly killed her son with a tree and he was doing absolutely nothing about it.

'What did they do to you in prison, eh?' Mum screamed at him. 'You are a great fighter. What has happened to you? Did they poison you? Did they cut off your prick? Did they eat your heart, eh? What did they do that has made you so timid – you who used to be afraid of nothing under God's sun, eh? Now you're just a big dunce, eating up all the food in the house, and doing nothing!'

But Dad smiled on. The shadows on his cheeks

made him look leaner. Mum got exasperated, and stormed out of the room again.

Later we heard stories about what Mum did when she left. She became quite strange. She took to stopping people in the street and telling them that the sacred forest was being destroyed, that her child was nearly killed by a falling tree. She talked to neighbours at great length and with unaccountable passion about roaming spirits and about forgotten diseases stirring from their resting places in the forest. She bewildered everyone, especially when she began to talk of the woman that the community had driven into the forest because they were afraid of her pustules.

Mum didn't go hawking that day and she didn't prepare any food for us. She went from house to house, her hair dishevelled, her clothes dirty. Trying to gain the support of the women in our area. Trying to organize them into expressing revolt at what the woodcutters were doing to the sacred forest. No one paid much attention, and people began to speak of her as mad.

While Mum was going up and down the street shouting, Dad rose from his chair and polished his boots till they shone like new steel. He washed his safari and French suits. He had a shave. Then he came and sat down again in his fabulous chair. The smile had dissolved from his face.

We starved till late in the evening when Mum returned, exhausted from too much talking. We had a small meal. After eating Dad spread out the mat and lay down. Mum went on and on about the tree that nearly killed me. I remained bed-ridden, unable to move, watching the room expand and contract. Dad blew out the candle. By slow degrees Mum fell quiet. Not long afterwards they struggled gently on the floor.

FIVE

The old woman's circular narrative

That night the old woman went to the moon as a flying spark of light. She circled the moon three times before attending the meeting of other lights from all over the world. In the morning, when she returned full of the energies and enlightenment her journey had given her – the life extension and the weight of future sight – she resumed the weaving of our narrative.

Simultaneous narratives of past, present, and future were also being woven in other places around the world by other people.

The old woman wove our secret narratives into her bloody and eventful cloth. Our narratives in pictures, in angled images and mysterious signs, were like a labyrinth from which there was no escape.

Our stories were patterned and circular, trapped in history. Unable to rise above a problem older than millennia our circular stories continued, trapped by the things we wouldn't face.

The old woman seemed older than ever that morning as she wove the terrible and wonderful narratives of our lives. Divining the future had accelerated her ageing. It weighed heavily upon her that she was unable to alter the future in any

significant way: the signs must be properly interpreted and acted upon. All she could do was divine
and weave. And when she finished her morning's
weavings the past also weighed on her in that deep
forest space.

She was so disturbed that morning by the new
gaps opening up in the trees, by the great irokos
crashing down from their ancient heights, that she
went in circles round her hut, holding back the rage
that swelled in her heart. And while she went round
in circles, fuming at the sacred groves exposed to the
sky, hobbling and limping with a walking stick,
shouting instructions at the one-legged girl, Mum
left our room and set out for the forest to find out
who had cut down the tree that had fallen on me.

Dad didn't go to work that morning. He stayed in
and his smile became sinister, and his eyes took on a
dangerous aspect.

That same morning, the old woman, hobbling round
her hut, felt an unnatural explosion shaking the earth
on the margin of the nation. The tremor made her
kick a stone with her good foot, and she let out a
great cry. At that same moment the explosion,
quaking the earth and the seas, disturbed the forest
and woke a giant spirit from its long slumber. The
spirit woke up, and found that it had been made
homeless. Confused, it began to wander through the
forest looking for its familiar abode, its great baobab
tree with its moss and serene lianas. And the
agitation of the wandering spirit started a wind
which blasted Mum back as she entered the forest,
following the noise of the tree-cutters. But Mum

fought her way through the wind and rested in the shadow of the black rock.

She followed the trail of broken silver eggs. Ambiguous birds hovered above her unseen. Thin wisps of smoke and wood-sprites floated beside her, listening to her being. As she went deeper into the forest, pursuing the disembodied noise of trees being felled, the noise kept moving, kept eluding her. The forest itself was echoing the sound, carrying it from place to place. It was as if the noises of trees being destroyed had themselves become forest dwellers.

In the room, my head splitting with agony, I saw the mischievous spirits imitating the tree-cutting noises. Deceiving my mother. Luring her in. Drawing her deeper into the labyrinth. And then a yellow smoke obscured her, and I didn't see her again for a long time.

SIX

A curious interchange

That morning Dad cleaned out the room, swept the floor, scrubbed the walls, and went to prepare food for the family. It was amazing to witness Dad's sudden domestication. The compound people stared at him in astonishment as he fetched water from the well and washed our clothes. They were particularly astounded at the concentration with which he washed Mum's undergarments. They stared with disbelief as he split firewood, and ground the pepper and tomatoes and melon seeds on our rough grinding stone. And they watched open-mouthed as he pounded the yams, his mighty chest heaving, and as he fried the meats, his eyes watering in the smoke-filled kitchen.

When he finished with the cooking he came into the room with the steaming pots of fragrant stews, deposited them in the cupboard, and then set out with Mum's basket for the market-place. Two hours later, his face caked with dust, veins throbbing on his forehead, he returned weighed down with excess shopping. He unloaded the yam tubers, the vegetables, the snails, the bundles of dried fish, chuckling to himself as he arranged them in pots and basins.

He sat down, had a cigarette, and then took Mum's tray of goods and went out to hawk her provisions.

I was confused that day. There was yellow smoke in my eyes. There were silver eggs in my dreams. Mum was in the labyrinth, raging with a passion that belonged to Dad. And Dad was sweating in the homestead, performing the tasks that Mum did every day. It was strange how Dad's brief domestication spread outrageous rumours through our streets. But it was wonderful to note how his serenity finally conquered them.

SEVEN

The battle of rewritten histories

I didn't move from bed the rest of that day, but the whole world was in the room. All the events of our history were alive in the little space. Like ghost dramas. Is history the livid hallucinations of time? I slept through the seepages of many events wracking and tossing me on the bed. The ghosts of historical consequences wandered through our room, looking for their destinations. The rumours of violence and the faintest echoes of gunshots reverberated through the floor. Continental liberation wars were being fought in nine places on the ceiling. And the Governor-General, an Englishman with a polyp on the end of his nose, had just completed the destruction of all the incriminating documents relating to the soon-to-be-created nation. When he had finished he proceeded, in his sloping calligraphic hand, to rewrite our history.

He rewrote the space in which I slept. He rewrote the long silences of the country which were really passionate dreams. He rewrote the seas and the wind, the atmospheric conditions and the humidity. He rewrote the seasons, and made them limited and unlyrical. He reinvented the geography of the nation and the whole continent. He redrew the continent's size on the world map, made it smaller, made it odder. He changed the names of places which were older than the places themselves. He redesigned the phonality of African names, softened the consonants, flattened the vowels. In altering the sound of the names he altered their meaning and affected the destiny of the named. He rewrote the names of fishes and bees, of trees and flowers, of mountains and herbs, of rocks and plants. He rewrote the names of our food, our clothes, our abodes, our rivers. The renamed things lost their ancient weight in our memory. The renamed things lost their old reality. They became lighter, and stranger. They became divorced from their old selves. They lost their significance and sometimes their shape. And they suddenly seemed new to us – new to us who had given them the names by which they responded to our touch.

Caught in his passionate objectivity, the Governor-General made our history begin with the arrival of his people on our shores. Sweating into his loose cotton shirt, he turned himself into a fairy-tale figure awakening stone-age man from an immemorial slumber, a slumber that began shortly after the creation of the human race. The Governor-General, in his rewriting of our history, deprived us of language, of poetry, of stories, of architecture, of civic laws, of social organization, of art, science, mathematics, sculpture, abstract conception, and philosophy. He deprived us of history, of civilization and, unintentionally, deprived us of humanity too. Unwittingly, he effaced us from creation. And then, somewhat startled at where his rigorous logic had led him, he performed the dexterous feat of investing us with life the moment his ancestors set eyes on us as we slept through the great roll of historical time. With a stroke of his splendid calligraphic style, he invested us with life. History came to us with his Promethean touch, as his pen touched our Adamic souls. And we awoke into history, stunned and ungrateful, as he renamed our meadows and valleys, and forgot the slave trade.

He rewrote our nightspaces, made them weirder, peopled them with monsters and stupid fetishes; he rewrote our daylight, made it cruder, made things manifest in the light of dawn seem unfinished and even unbegun. In the process he laid before our eyes the written evidence of our recent awakening into civilization – we who bear within us ancient dreams and future revelations. We who began the naming of the world and all its gods. We who fertilized the banks of the Nile with the sacred word which sprouted the earliest and most mysterious civilization, the forgotten foundation of civilizations. We whose secret ways have entered into the bloodstream of world-wonders silently.

And as the Governor-General rewrote time (made his longer, made ours shorter), as he rendered invisible our accomplishments, wiped out traces of our ancient civilizations, rewrote the meaning and beauty of our customs, as he abolished the world of spirits, diminished our feats of memory, turned our philosophies into crude superstitions, our rituals into childish dances, our religions into animal worship and animistic trances, our art into crude relics and primitive forms, our drums into instruments of jest, our music into simplistic babbling – as he rewrote our past, he altered our present. And the alteration created new spirits which fed the bottomless appetite of the great god of chaos.

As he sat there, in his large office, with the picture of the Queen just above his head, as he rewrote destiny (made his brighter, made ours dimmer), the old woman in the forest pressed on with the weaving of our true secret history, a history that was frightening and wondrous, bloody and comic, labyrinthine, circular, always turning, always surprising, with events becoming signs, and signs becoming reality. The old woman in the forest coded the secrets of plants and their infinite curative properties; she coded the language of spirits, the epic speech of trees, the convergent lines of vital earth-forces, the healing uses of thunder, the magic properties of lightning, the interpenetrations of the human and spirit world, the delicate balances of unseen powers, and the ancient formula for glimpsing the unalterable movement of fate. She even coded fragments of the great jigsaw that the creator spread all over the diverse peoples of the earth, hinting that no one race or people can have the complete picture or monopoly of the ultimate possibilities of the human genius alone. With her magic she suggested that it's only when all peoples meet and know and love one another that we begin to get an inkling of this awesome picture, or jigsaw, or majestic power. These fragments of the grand picture of humanity were the most haunting and beautiful parts of her weaving that day.

The old woman kept the deciphering of the code

to herself; for she had entirely forgotten that during fifty years in the forest she had invented a private language. And with this language of signs and symbols, of angles and colours and forms, she recorded legends and moments of history lost to her people. She recorded bawdy ancient jokes, drinking songs, riddles that had never been solved, mathematical discoveries extrapolated from magic squares, geometric forms in music and art, harmonic alignments between architecture and the greater stars. She recorded wonderful forms of divination by numbers and cowries and signs, numerological systems for summoning the gods, and humorous permutations of children's games beloved of kings. The old woman in the forest recorded advancements in music, a delightful contrapuntal bar and tone system, music derived from the harmonics of streams and wind and the earth's heartbeat and the flight of birds. She recorded secret ways of extending life, the meaning of bird-cries, the language of animals, ways of seeing a unicorn in broad daylight, ways of speaking to the spirits of ancestors or parents or children or friends who have passed beyond the enchanted mirror of death. She recorded the mystic significance of the fragrance of flowers, the songs of the wind, the songs of history, the music of the dead, the melodies of the interspaces, and ways of making love to produce twins or triplets or a particular gender. She recorded snatches of conversations heard on the wind, conversations that had floated across from other continents. She recorded oral poems of famous bards whose words had entered communal memory, whose names had been forgotten because of their great fame, but whose true names lay coded in their songs. She recorded impromptu poems with measured stresses composed by women on their journey between two kings. She recorded stories and myths and philosophical disquisitions on the relativities of African Time and Space, how Time is both finite and infinite, how Time curves, how Time also dances, how Space is negative, how Space is always populated, how Space is the home of invisible beings, and the true destination of death. She recorded theories of Art and Sculpture, the secret methods of bronze casting, the elaborate geometry and symbolism of the elongation of human features, discovered by an ancient sculptor who was lost in the forest for seven days and who was overwhelmed with visions in which he saw the elongated spirit of his father, sitting in a golden sphere. She recorded forgotten items of meteorological discoveries, calculation of distances to stars as yet unnoticed, and astronomical incidents: the date of a stellar explosion, a supernova bursting over the intense dream of the continent, heralding, according to a king's soothsayer, a brief nightmare of colonization, and an eventual, surprising, renaissance.

EIGHT

Exposing the earth

The old woman in the forest recorded these things in code within her epic narrative of our lives. As she was beginning another cycle of our secret narrative, exhausted from her consistent application and the dissolving bitterness in her heart, a yellow bird flew over her.

She heard the distant noises of men. They were drawing nearer, destroying the trees as they advanced. A wave of anger poured through her being. She got up and hobbled round the hut, dreading the possibility that all her spells and incantations couldn't save her solitude. But then she paused. She heard female footsteps running through the forest, footsteps that communicated despair. And while the old woman smiled at the entrapment of another person in the labyrinth of the forest, it suddenly struck her what her fate would be. Everything dissolved round her. The trees disappeared. The birds, her invisible fence, and her protected outcasts vanished. She saw that in cutting the forest down the community had come to her, had surrounded her; and that after all those years in the middle of the forest alone, she would soon be in the middle of a ghetto, unable to escape. And it was with a strange voice, a voice two hundred and seventy years old, that she uttered a cry – a cry which stirred Dad in his three-legged chair – saying:

'WHAT IS THE USE OF POWER IF I CAN'T FORGIVE!'

Dad, who had returned from the market, and was snoring in his chair, woke up suddenly. He looked around, and spoke his first complete sentence in a long time.

'There are people who are so powerful that no one knows who they are,' he said, and became silent again.

'Like who?' I asked.

He stared at me with dull eyes in which a distant emotion flickered. He seemed to be waiting for a cue, his ears cocked. After a while I realized he was asleep again.

The flies stirred in the room; birds flew in wild patterns round the old woman in the forest. She didn't speak again either, but her great cry had startled the wandering spirit. And the spirit crashed through the forest spaces. Dead leaves and twigs spiralled in its whirlwind. A heat-mist gathered in the wake of its passion. Trees dropped their pods and fruits prematurely. Birds flapped their laden wings, gasping for air.

While the heat gathered, blown on by the wind, Mum – completely unaware of the labyrinth – eventually located the tree-fellers. Possessed by an unfamiliar passion, she strode up to the foreman and said:

'Who asked you to cut down the trees?'

'The government,' replied the foreman, imperturbably.

'Which government?'

'Any one you like.'

'Who cut down the tree that nearly killed my son?'

'Which tree?'

'The one that nearly killed my son?'

'We haven't killed anybody – yet,' said the foreman.

The other tree-cutters laughed. One of them said:

'Madame, leave now. We are busy. This is dangerous work.'

Mum was launching into a tirade when the whirlwind appeared in their midst, blowing the riven earth everywhere, cracking the branches, scattering the men, blasting away their tents. Then the whirlwind found Mum, and obscured her from me, while trees crashed and thundered to the ground, exposing the earth to desolation.

NINE

Birth of the heat

It was nightfall when I woke. Dad wasn't around. Mum hadn't returned. My forest fever had retreated. I couldn't see into the darkness. Intimations of Mum lost in the forest, and Dad dissolved in his silence, haunted me along with the mosquitoes.

The heat of the world was different, and the air was dense. The heat was inexplicable. It had intent, a naked heat, as if some sort of iron veil before a furnace had been rent asunder. It was hot in my blood and when I moved the air made me melt. I was covered in sweat that felt like molten metal. I couldn't move for the heat.

Dad wandered in with a candle whose odd illumination made his head look disembodied. He sat down on the bed, his face like melting bronze. His eyes were large, his nostrils were like bellows, and he breathed the hot air deeply. Touching me on the head, sweat running into his eyes, he uttered his second complete sentence. His words expanded the universe for me and opened all sorts of doors through which many undreamt of beings emerged, rampaging through the world with unintentional fury.

'Our spirits are going mad,' he said.

'Why?' I asked.

'We no longer communicate with them,' he replied.

We sat in silence for a long time. The heat softened the candle, made it bend, till it was like an unfinished question mark. Dad blew it out.

Around midnight, Mum returned. The smell of antelopes soaked by rain clung to her. She brought three strangers who had been lost in the forest as well. When Mum gave them water to drink they fell into a mechanical chorus:

'That forest is terrible!' they kept saying, as if their minds were stuck in a hole.

We listened to them as they repeated the words over and over. As if the words would somehow free them from their mental fever. After a while they left. They stumbled out. They couldn't seem to trust their eyes or feet any more.

Mum was silent throughout. She had sand and leaves in her hair, mud up to her knees, her dress was soiled. I was struck by her puzzled, horrified expression. The angles of her face were more defined. Her eyes were dazed. When I followed the direction of the emotion in her eyes I noticed that she had her precious stones of sleep in her hands. She seemed both confused and afraid. Dad was no longer smiling.

There was a betrayed look on Mum's face. When she came over to me, her back to Dad so he wouldn't see, she uncupped her hands and showed me the wonderful pearls and rainbow-coloured stones of light that she had brought back from her fabulous kingdom of sleep a long time ago. She had planted them in the earth of the forest. She had planted them deep. But now as I looked at them I was shocked to discover that their magical lights had diminished. They were now like ordinary stones. Transparent stones. I didn't understand. Mum was silent, and she didn't say a word the whole night. She too had suffered the lure of the forest. She too had a forest fever. We could not sleep for the curious heat.

TEN

Wrath of the Wandering Spirit

In the afternoon of the next day the Wandering Spirit went past, unleashing a catastrophic heatwave that made women faint, made men gasp for breath, and made eagles fall from the sky. Butterflies flew wildly in the boiling air. The heatwave stunned lizards and spiders, made white snakes come out of their lairs, caused tortoises and cats to collapse on banks of fallen trees, exhausted from the sunstroke. Strange cries of asphyxiating animals came from the forest. The water levels in the wells dropped, and everywhere the people of our area cried about the abnormal heat.

Bottles cracked on the street. The road became a boiling river. Plants dried up. Cracks appeared on the walls of our houses. Everywhere the water was hot, and drinking intensified our thirst, and dehydration left us breathless. Our mouths hung open, our breathing became shallow, and we were unable to speak. Cracks appeared on people's faces. Children playing in the street collapsed suddenly. The air was still. Chickens and goats lay at street corners, jerking occasionally, their eyes fixed and dreamy.

For three days the heat was relentless as the Wandering Spirit passed over the city, spreading spontaneous combustions in its wake. There were inexplicable fires in the market-places. Thatch huts crackled into flames. Stalls burst into smoke. And on the third day the heat intensified over our street in the shape of blazing clouds which turned black as nightfall neared. Stars were in flame that night and the moon was hot and we breathed in the fires of insomnia. We heard pregnant women screaming in the dense heat.

The heat made a furnace of the night. People sat outside their housefronts, their brains stunned, staring at the sky in silence. The heat aged everything; it made the night very old. And for the first time we became aware of a deep silence which had never been there before. The forest was silent and no voices travelled over that air of liquid heat.

Our bodies burned that night. The air made strange popping noises. And even the fireflies had their lights extinguished. Toads and frogs were silent; the owls didn't hoot; but I saw the old woman in the forest floating on a block of ice, while the Wandering Spirit unleashed its innocent vengeance over our lives. The block of ice, white under the moon, melted beneath the flesh of the old woman – and her eyes were very bright.

After she had cooled down considerably, the old woman hobbled to the river bank with the one-legged girl. They fetched water from a secret spring which got cooler the hotter the air became. They made the animals drink. They gave the magic water to their protected outcasts, to the homeless beasts, and the wounded antelopes.

All over the forest, spirits were rising from their

sleep of centuries. Spirits exiled from their forest homes danced on the heated rivers.

The old woman then sent a cool wind through the nightspaces, and it brought temporary relief to the gasping animals. The wind travelled across our street. It was a soothing stream of air that made a little sleep possible, but not many slept that night, for the wind, laden with the heat it had cooled, itself became hot.

Meanwhile the Governor-General was in his white mansion at Government Quarters, fanned by three servants. His wife lay semi-conscious in the living room from the heat which had conquered the electric fans. The Governor-General had completed the first draft of the rewriting of our lives. He put down his pen, ambled to the bay window, looked out, saw the night with its orange tinge, the stars white hot in the sky, the moon with its shade of red, and he began to contemplate the continent. He pondered the passage in Ovid's *Metamorphoses* which spoke of the chariot of the sun-god, ridden by his wilful son, and how the chariot, veering close to the earth, scorched the trees, turned the land to desert wastes, disturbed the waters, and came so close over Africa that it permanently burned the skin of the inhabitants, altering their colour for ever. The heat invaded the Governor-General's brain and from the waves of dizziness came the question which he uttered out loud to his wife, who had now found the ultimate reason to return to her native land and its cool climate. He said:

'Who are we to believe? Herodotus or Ovid? The historian or the poet?'

'What's Herodotus got to do with the heat, darling?' his wife asked.

'Well, my dear, Herodotus suggests that ancient Greece got its gods and its myths and its philosophies from Egypt, and therefore Africa.'

'The heat, darling, do something about the heat,' his wife replied, indifferently.

'And if we are to believe Ovid then Africans were originally white before the chariot of the sun burned them.'

'Believe what you want, darling, but just do something about this heat.'

'A few cranky anthropologists of course believe that man began in Africa. In that case Africa wasn't so hot in those distant days, and Africans were white. I think I favour the poet.'

His wife opened her eyes, stared coolly at him, and said:

'You didn't hear a word of what I said. This heat will roast us alive. If you don't do something about the heat, I will never speak to you again, my dear.'

But the Governor-General was so taken with his perception that he began to laugh. His servants fanned him, barely stirring the heat; a window cracked; their daughter woke up; another window splintered. Mosquitoes and maddened fireflies came in. The Wandering Spirit passed over the house and in the pantry a bottle of castor oil caught fire. The fire spread round the house, exploding the jars, and burning the well-kept garden of jasmines and chrysanthemums. And while the Governor-General meditated on Ovid's indirect theory of racial differentiation, his daughter, upstairs in her room, was suffering hallucinations in which fire spirits of the air were trying to get into her body through her mouth and between her legs. The servants noticed the fire in the kitchen; panic engulfed the house; the fire spread along the Persian carpets, travelling serenely, burning in a low flame. When the household recovered from their stupor they found the walls and floors charred, they found books burnt with their covers and illustrations intact. But all over the house, as if the fire and ash had given birth to monstrous prodigies, were a host of black butterflies with green eyes, creatures of the god of chaos.

In the wake of the Wandering Spirit houses caught fire, cars burst into flames, and people reported seeing green flares on the lagoon. Some even spoke of thin trails of fire searing the wind. The fire travelled through the air, giving birth to its own kind. And in our room, with Mum suffocating on the bed, and Dad breathing hoarsely on his chair, I dreamt that I saw the fire travelling in a horizontal spiralling line to the old woman in the forest. Then she did something quite astonishing. She seized the fire with her wizened hands, trapped it in her earthenware pot, and buried it three feet deep in the potent soil. And when she returned to her tapestry she gasped at the realization that she had completed a visual story about the fiery spirit awoken on the ninth day of the apocalyptic disturbance of the earth. In what mood had she been when she wove her threads of fire round our lives? Aware of the silent vengeance of the forest spirits and the disturbed balances of the forces of our world, she took up her marvellous thread and began a counter-motion. Her head was yellow under the red moon. As she worked, she sighed deeply, and a wind started at the mouth of the forest and blew across our street. And then, in an exhausted voice, she cried:

'After fire, flood!'

And the Wandering Spirit, released from its dream of centuries, went from city to city, from country to country. And then, because it was permanently homeless, it began to roam the entire world, spreading its erratic heatwaves and spontaneous combustions and curious weather conditions wherever circumstances were favourable. It created droughts, extended desert spaces in lands of rich vegetation, and created roads on which nothing would grow and along which the god of chaos would travel. And it mingled with the other negative forces released in the new times, and found affinities with the pollutions and radiations of the century.

ELEVEN

Burning the future

Later that night, with the heat everywhere, Mum's eyes were bright with terror. Dad was rocking in his three-legged chair. I sensed something come into our room, and I woke up.

'They are burning up our future,' Dad was saying.

'Who?' Mum asked.

'Across the oceans,' Dad replied, cryptically.

There was a long silence. The wind blew in gently, sweeping the heat from our faces. I saw a green light growing bigger beside Dad, and I cried out because I thought the house was on fire. And when I jumped up from the floor, I noticed the smell of the forest and felt the personality of a great animal. In the flash of a moment's clarity I saw the emerald leopard at Dad's feet. Its eyes were like diamonds. As it looked up at Dad its aura diminished. Then its presence waned. And it vanished.

'Somewhere, a mighty leopard is dying,' Dad said.

'It's gone,' I said.

'It will rain tomorrow,' Mum said.

The gentle wind brought sleep. Dad slept with Mum, surrounded by fire, dreaming about rain. I slept on the floor, and dreamt about the old woman in the forest who had been floating on a block of ice.

TWELVE

The secret of the heatwave

In the morning the people of the street said they had seen a single yellow flower floating in the air. It did not rain, but the heatwave lessened considerably; and though it was not cool, it was not boiling either. The water levels rose mysteriously in the wells. Chickens and dogs began to roam about listlessly, searching for food among the rubbish. Tortoises and birds, white snakes and lizards had died in our street from the vengeance of the Wandering Spirit. Tree-cutters had fainted and we heard stories about a leopard coughing among the trees. Twenty people had died in the city from the heatwave.

As I stayed in the room, recovering from the concussive fever of the great iroko falling on me, I saw that the Governor-General's house was not completely burnt. His daughter was still in a state of shock from being surrounded by flames. His parrot, which he had taught to say a few African words, had been cindered in its silver cage. The walls of the house and the carpets were charred. The pantry was altogether lost to the flames. One of his servants had suffered skin burns from rescuing the daughter. Hours later she was still hallucinating, still mumbling about the black devils she saw dancing in the invading fires. The first draft of the Governor-General's rewriting of our lives was intact, but it was covered with inexplicable spangles of gold ash.

And while the Governor-General prepared for the forthcoming elections and the inauguration of the first president, withdrawing his empire from our land, but leaving its vast shadows behind to dog our progress; and while he began to speak seriously of returning to his manor house near Winchester and writing his memoirs, the old woman in the forest went back to an earlier section of her narrative and began to weave into the available spaces a tender myth about how white people were invented.

Dad went to work for the first time in a week. Mum went hawking sardines, candles and oranges. When she returned she told us that Madame Koto, fully recovered from her attack of madness, had begun her journey back into our lives. The great rally preceding the elections had been set for September; Madame Koto was coming back to resume her significant role. But it was not the prospect of Madame Koto's re-emergence that made the day so unforgettable in my life. It was the news that Dad brought back from the world.

When he returned from work that evening Dad gathered us together in the room. He lit a stick of incense, poured a libation to his ancestors, and prayed to the great heavens to protect our little family and the rest of the world.

'My wife, my son,' Dad said solemnly. 'The white people have just exploded a big bomb in our backyard.'

'Not our backyard here!' Mum cried out.

'Don't be stupid,' Dad said, flashing her an angry look. 'The backyard of our country. They call it an Atom Bomb.'

'What's an Atom Bomb?' I asked.

'It's a fire that can destroy the whole world,' he said gravely.

Then he spoke of the explosion which shook the entire continent and made the waves of the Atlantic scream over its vast expanse. He filled us with terror at the thought of what dangerous spirits, what diseases, what earthquakes, what unpleasant destinies, were lying in wait. We listened in complete silence, thinking about the explosion that was going to ambush our future.

When Dad finished telling us about the bomb, Mum began to weep silently. I wept as well. This was the first time it occurred to me that the earth might not continue for ever.

THIRTEEN

Dolores mundi

That night, for the first time, Mum dreamt about the secret agony of angels.

FOURTEEN

Invisible books

There is the story of an African emperor who ordered all the frogs in his realm to be exterminated because they disturbed his sleep. The frogs were killed and he slept serenely till the mosquitoes, whose larvae the frogs fed on, came and spread disease. His people fled and what was once a proud land became a desert waste.

But at least the earth continued.

Dad retold this story in snatches, through his long silence. However, it was not the gradual destruction of the trees, or the news of the apocalyptic bomb, which woke up his spirit. Nor was it the retreating of the heatwave, nor the atomic fumes in our blood. None of these things were truly responsible for Dad's re-emergence from his deep silence.

He came back early from work one afternoon and began to rummage through the books he had acquired and which he used to make me read out to him. The new heat had become permanent in our lives. I saw him bathed in sweat, leaning over, flicking through the books, whose pages were covered with spiders' webs.

'The spiders of Africa have been reading these books,' he said.

Then he made me read to him about an African king who had been saved from death in a battle by a wild boar. He had been told the story as a child and later he was delighted to find it had been written down in a book. While I read, he fell asleep. When I finished the story he woke up suddenly, and said:

'You know, Azaro, when I was a child like you, spirits used to read to me from invisible books composed by our ancestors. I didn't understand them at the time. One day, my son, you will make some of those invisible books visible.'

He fell asleep again and I listened in silence to the stories the wind told. Stories told at odd angles, whose logic required serenity and an open heart to understand. Stories about the many invisible lives who were still living out their passions in the spaces we occupied. The wind told several stories at once, interweaving all the simultaneous strands like many voices singing different songs in harmony. There was a beautiful music to the coolness of the wind after the heatwave; and as I sat immersed in the stories Dad suddenly jumped up from the chair. He put on his boots in a hurry and stamped his feet on the ground, trembling the cupboard.

'Something is calling me,' he said, and rushed out of the room.

I gave him a little time before I followed. Something had finally awoken his spirit. It was only after he had left, his shadow haunted by an omen, that I understood what had woken him. It was the old leopard, coughing in the depths of the sacred forest, its line coming to an end.

BOOK THREE

ONE

The shrine in the labyrinth

Every mood is a story, and every story becomes a mood. In the forest, the wind was full of moods. I followed Dad through the mood of trees about to die. My footsteps were light on the fallen leaves. He went deeper into the forest, stopping now and then to listen to sounds only he could hear. I saw the homeless spirits also following him, listening to the peculiar melodies of his being, curious about his nature. Some of the spirits were mischievous to a point of cruelty. I saw also that angry as they were, none of them wanted to harm him. Dad drew a host of spirits to him as he went from one grove to another, searching for the mysterious animal.

Dad was immune to the forest fevers and the fata Morganas; he was immune to the entrapments of the labyrinth. But he went long distances, from river's edge to groves of cedar, in search of the leopard and couldn't find it. He kept hearing the coughing of the great beast. It always seemed close by, but Dad's madness didn't make him think the beast might attack him. And when he couldn't find the animal whose manifestations had emboldened him, when he succumbed to a feeling of confusion, he lost his immunity to the labyrinth and the forest became a sinister place. The trees and piping birds took on a brooding, watchful menace. I saw my father sit on a fallen tree, trembling.

Not long afterwards he got up and walked round in circles, muttering incantations. And then, as if in a trance, he broke into a clearing surrounded by cedars and baobabs. All around the clearing white rocks rose high, as if there had once been a marble hill in the forest. Blue and yellow flowers grew on the rocks. Water flowed from a crevice. There was a red bird with an old face on an outcrop. The earth was white, the air smelt of happiness and the wind was pure. The forest seemed far away; and the radiant white space was like a paradise within the forest. White flowers with red specks grew everywhere.

And right in front of the marble rocks, like wonderful figures in a vision – were the statues. They were a people with intelligent faces and serene personalities, listening to the great commandments of the universe. They were all standing, and they were all completely still. They seemed alive, but they were still, as if what they were listening to had woven an enchantment around them. Not even the wind stirred them, not even the white snakes coiled on their heads disturbed them. Jewels glistened round their necks. Snails inched up their bodies, turtles were at their feet. Their eyes were alive and vigilant and still, as if they knew their worth and place in history, as if they were aware of everything. They had no divisions in their souls, no doubts, and no fears about anything in the world. The statues were wholly submerged in the mysteries of their times, a race of higher beings at peace in their sanctuary. And yet they seemed perpetually ready for a mysterious call that would sound across the divinity-flavoured regions of space, a people ready to depart their lands for ever. A people who knew the deepest exile. It was as if they had arrived from a distant planet and brought the spirit of the planet with them; so that they were both at home in the sacred grove and ready to depart it at the slightest notice.

The statues stood there, in the white space, with beautiful and elongated faces, elegant scarifications, short arms and seven fingers. Some of them had inturned feet and glass eyes. They were a race of magnificent warriors and at the same time the wisest and most tranquil people in the universe.

There were rows and rows of them, standing in straight lines, with the shorter ones in front and the taller ones ascending behind them. The tallest ones amongst them were as gigantic as the mighty trees around. Midgets, intermediaries and giants coexisted with splendid equanimity.

A faintly roseate mist floated just above their heads as they stood there in complete silence. Birds trilled around them. Running water whispered among the rocks, rare flowers and herbs scented the wind. The statues seemed to move and yet they didn't. Harmonious and mysterious, they might have been sculpted by enlightened strangers to the planet to honour one of the holy places of the earth.

Everyone had heard the great tales of their fabulous healing properties. Everyone had heard rumours that they were the guardians of a secret religion. These were the legendary statues which had been talked about for centuries and which no one had seen.

I stood in complete wonder before the awesome figures. I breathed in their air of enchantment and soaked in their tranquillity. Beautiful spirits danced in the clear spaces. I was overwhelmed by the mood of those silent stones. Awestruck by their dignity. Astonished by the humorous philosophies in their eyes. I was lost in their listening stillness.

The wind surrounded me with their meditations. And then, from among the stones, an unearthly light shone momentarily upwards, and was gone. One of the statues moved, and my heart heaved with wonder. Profound spaces opened up in my soul. And then Dad stepped towards me from the stones, smiling.

'My secret training ground is near here.'

'Here?'

'Yes, not far from here. I have been coming to this area to train for years now, but this is the first time I found this place.'

He sat on the ground beside me. We stared in fascination at the rows of statues. They were like frozen spirits, frozen dreams.

'One legend has it that at night these stones move. They turn into magic antelopes and into human beings, and they perform wonders in this world full of evil,' Dad said.

His words started a saffron-coloured breeze in my mind.

'A more recent legend, born in our times, has it that the people who disappeared from our street turned into these stones. And another legend says that these statues turn into human beings and come and live amongst us as strangers, to see what our hearts are like. They are messengers of the gods, spies of the god of justice. They have their kind all over the world.'

Dad paused again. A flock of white birds circled overhead and alighted on the branches of the low tree in the middle of the grove.

'These stones know the secret of time and creation. That's why they can heal. In the olden days people used to set out on pilgrimages for this place. They came with their sick and their dying, and they were cured. Priests of old religions used to conduct initiations here. This place filled them with wisdom. It was also an oracle. Some people believe that after God created man he moulded these stones, but he didn't breathe life into them. Their spirits are pure. Centuries passed, and we forgot about them, and no one has seen them since.'

TWO

An ambiguous old woman

Dad had hardly finished what he was saying when we heard an agonized cry near us in the forest. The birds flew up in the air, not in confused motion, but as one. They circled the air as the cries continued. In another direction, deep in the forest, we heard a tree crashing down, sending the reverberations of its death all along the earth. The cry pierced the air again, louder, as if the agony were in some way connected to the fallen tree.

Dad stood up and, without dusting the back of his trousers, set off in the direction of the voice. I went with him along the paths. The cry kept receding. Dad stopped twice, wanting to go back to the sacred grove. But the voice kept moving away and we weren't sure if we were merely following an echo. We went further into the forest, passing a flame tree in full blossom, till we left the magnetic field of the sacred grove and came to an overhang of dense creepers which formed a cave of vegetation near the forest path. A voice drew us into the green cave of lianas and leaves and we saw an old woman lying on the ground, with a yellow lantern beside her. She was very old and was covered all over with pustules and sores. Her jewelled eyes were set deep within a face that had mushroom-like growths of flesh. She was old and frail and she stank. Her clothes were disgusting and her general appearance revolting. Her nose was sharp, almost beak-like; and her voice was horrible and rasping, full of rabid bitterness.

'Go away! Go away before I curse you with my diseases!' she cried, in the voice of an old witch.

Dad was taken aback by her ugliness and her pustules. Her voice opened up a vision of worms in my head. Her right foot was bleeding. Dad was frightened by this apparition, this creature uglier than the fetishes that repulsed evil from the night-spaces of our ancestors. But he leant over to her and said:

'Do you need help?'

The old woman spat a foul mouthful of bile at Dad, and shouted:

'Go away, or kill me now! Run before I turn into a leopard and eat you up!'

Dad stayed still. The wind rustled the leaves. Night came slowly into our midst. After a long silence, the old woman said:

'Hunters are trying to kill me.'

'Why?'

'They thought I was an antelope.'

'An antelope?'

'There was a white man with them.'

'We didn't see any hunters.'

'No hunters?'

'No.'

The old woman tried to get up. Dad moved, hesitated, then helped her up.

'I am an old woman,' she said, her voice mysteriously losing its rasp. 'I can't walk. And I have far to go.'

'Where are you going?'

'To my house.'

'Where?'

She pointed with her bony finger. There was another silence. A soft wind changed the air. We heard someone singing from a distance. The air changed our minds. I fetched her crude walking stick with the forked top, cut from the branch of an orange tree. The old woman hobbled slowly, with one diseased hand round Dad's neck and the yellow lantern in the other. We were very silent as we went up the path. We walked for a long time. Bird noises kept following us. The old woman didn't speak for a while, but her presence filled me with words. Strange philosophies shimmered from her bird-like face and her peculiar green eyes. She kept looking at me.

She took us round in a wide circle. We passed the cave twice. And when we came to it a third time she gave a mischievous cackling laugh, and I noticed a silver egg at the mouth of the cave. I was about to speak when she stopped Dad, asking to rest a little. Then she turned her face to me, and said:

'Did you know, my son, that in the olden days there were colours which human beings couldn't see?'

I stared at her, confused. I didn't see the pustules any more. Her smell had become almost fragrant. For a second I saw the little girl in her old face.

'In the olden days,' she continued, 'people could

see angels. Now, they can't even see their fellow human beings.'

She gave her cackling laugh again and indicated to Dad that she wished to carry on with her journey. She didn't speak, but her presence was a mood of a thousand stories. We passed trees with clusters of red cobwebs, trees with birds nested in their trunks. We went deep into the forest, past all known boundaries of its limits. Dad asked no questions. The woman hobbled on in obvious pain and when Dad lifted her up he grunted, and said:

'You are very heavy!'

'I am an old woman,' she replied.

'How far are you going?'

She pointed again.

'Not far,' she said.

We walked for a long time. We went round in complex patterns, till we came to a stream.

'Across,' she said.

Dad hesitated. Then he turned to me.

'Wait here for me,' he said. 'And if I don't return by nightfall, go home.'

The old woman gave me her yellow lamp and said:

'Don't take it home. Leave it at the edge of the forest.'

'Dad, I will wait for you,' I said.

'I won't be long,' he replied.

I watched him step into the stream. I watched his back rippling with the weight of the old woman. The crossing was difficult, but he held the old woman high and he bore her across without getting water on her body. When he waded out on the other side he turned to me. I couldn't see him clearly. He shouted something which the stream carried away, and then he disappeared into the forest on the other side.

THREE

Dialogue with an unhappy maiden

I sat with my back against a tree. The lamp shone its spectral light all around. I watched night moving closer to me from across the stream. Shadows of trees slowly merged. Blue mist rose from the forest. An owl circled the tallest tree, and perched, and began to hoot. Water gurgled softly. Invading night was green. Far side of the sky was a blaze of gold and pink which I had never seen before. Red moon. Yellow stars. The forest spoke in many accents. I waited for a long time, sitting there, weaving in and out of a dream in which I saw Dad carrying the old woman over long distances, to another country beyond the boundaries of men.

And when I was awoken by a noise I couldn't identify, I looked around and saw that the forest had changed. The lights were different. A twilight penumbra had descended on the world. I felt as if I had been spirited to another country. With the universal dimming of the lights, the forest became populated. When I heard the cowhorns, the pipes, and the drums of people bustling down the forest path, I rushed and hid in the bushes. The forest was now darker than the sky. The music went past, and I saw people with cloven hoofs, dancing along the path. Dancing to the boisterous music.

They were a fascinating crowd of twilight people. They had weird faces. Incomplete faces. Or faces with too many features. Some were without noses. Or without ears, or teeth, or hands. Some had a combination of too many noses, ears and teeth. A few were distinguished with an excessive number of legs. Maybe they had the farthest to go. Most of them talked in nasal accents as if they still were not used to their noses. They were like spirits who had borrowed parts of the human anatomy.

Not all of them danced to the music. I heard some of them sniffing the air, saying that they could smell something nasty. Then I realized that many of them were without eyes and they depended on those with eyes to do all their seeing for them; and there were those without ears who relied on those with ears to do all their hearing. They danced past, playing their sweet music, arguing, talking from their noses. Many had feet facing sideways and backwards. Some of them were without toes. I glimpsed their long necks and their painted faces. A lot of them had eyes at the back of their heads like a race of people who only remembered, who only looked back towards the past. Some of them had feathered arms like birds that have forgotten how to fly. Others had heads with porcupine quills, as if their thoughts would always be spiky. I noticed a few with long up-curving toenails and crustacean legs. The more learned among them wore glasses.

Some of the women had children growing out of their backs. Some had tuberous legs from the infernally long distances they had walked. Some were sliced in half as if when they lived they were never complete. One woman had three hands and a sagging chin. Their eminent women bore flywhisks, their praise-singers rattled castanets. The horde of them danced past me as if they were returning from an uproarious meeting. Or going to a fantastic party of spirits. Or as if they were looking for dreams to enter as a way of making their existence known in the scheme of things. I hid in the bushes, concealing the lamp under my shirt. But I had no need to do that because the lamp burned very dimly, regulating its own illumination.

The nocturnal beings danced past in their weird and splendid attire of lace, bangles, cowries and jewellery. Then the wind blew along beings with beetle voices. They were gibbering about Madame Koto's return, about the baker's child who was so intelligent that certain spirits were jealous of her, and about the sign-painter's daughter who looked more beautiful every day because she was soon going to die. I listened as they gossiped about Latifa Malouf of Mali who sold delicious peppersoup to travellers and lived under the silk cotton tree at the crossways near the Futa Jallon mountains. They said she would fall ill in three days time because of her pride. The voices, in their eerie susurrations, talked about the sensational party of Miss Rolufo Matumbe of Swaziland. And they compared notes about the fabulous masked ball in honour of Mr Harold Macmillan, prime minister of England, which was attended by many spirits who had borrowed the bodies of his friends.

The voices went past. The path became silent. I was about to emerge from the bushes and resume waiting for Dad under the tree, when I heard someone crying. I waited and saw the most beautiful little girl in the whole world. She was dressed as if returning from a wedding feast. And she was weeping about how she had been betrayed by her future husband with whom she had made a pact before birth in the spirit world. He had just gone and married the first woman that allowed him to make love to her. When she went past I came out and sat in the silver glow of the old woman's lamp. The girl tiptoed back and sat opposite me and said:

'I saw you hiding.'

I didn't say anything.

'Who are you waiting for?' she asked.

'My father,' I replied.

'Where did he go?'

'To the old woman's house.'

'Did he leave a long time ago?'

'Yes.'

She smiled and gave me a piece of bread which she took out of her pocket. I was hungry and every time I tried to put the bread in my mouth it fell from my hands. When it fell on the ground the third time I saw that it was covered with ants.

'Follow me,' the girl said.

'Where to?'

'To my place.'

'Where?'

'Across the river.'

'Do you have a canoe?'

'Three canoes I have. I live in a great city. We have

light there and life is easy. There is no death and
there is no wickedness. Everyone is happy in my
city.'

'I'm waiting for my father,' I said.

'How can you wait for a father who leaves you in
the forest?'

I was silent.

'PUT OUT THAT LAMP!' she commanded suddenly.

I tried, but the lamp wouldn't go out. She began to
weep again. Then she took out a little flask from her
pocket.

'You have a big pocket,' I said.

'Everything we need is in there.'

She was about to pour some wine into my mouth
when I heard someone calling my name.

'Is that your name?' the girl asked.

'No,' I said.

She stared at me.

'LOOK!' I said.

She turned. It was Dad. He seemed weary and he
came slowly towards us.

'That's my father,' I said to the girl.

'Who are you talking to?' asked Dad.

I turned. The girl had gone.

'Didn't you see her?' I asked Dad.

'Who?'

'The girl.'

He stared at me.

'No,' he said, and sat down beside me.

His breathing sounded exhausted. After a while,
he said:

'I crossed two rivers and climbed a white hill and

came to a sacred spot with statues just like the ones we saw today. Exactly the same.'

He paused.

'Water flowed in the rocks of the white hill and when we came to a tree full of white birds the old woman told me to put her down. She went into a bush and didn't come back. I looked for her and then I waited. Then I thought that maybe she didn't want me to know her place. So I returned.'

'How did you find your way back?'

'I don't know. I don't even remember. It's as if I have been walking and dreaming at the same time.'

There was a long silence. The wind blew words in my ears and I said:

'You crossed the same river twice.'

'You mean I stepped into the same river twice?'

'No.'

'You mean I stepped into two rivers at the same time?'

'No.'

Dad pondered me, and then he said:

'Rivers sometimes change their course, my son, for reasons we don't understand. Is that what you mean?'

'No.'

He stared at me as if I were ill.

'You're confusing me, my son,' he said. 'Let's go home.'

We rose. He carried me on his shoulder and I held up the lamp so that he could see the road ahead.

'The old woman told me many things,' he said.

'Like what?'

'She said we are going to suffer the future of our

mistakes in advance. She said black people are the colour of fertile earth. She has heard about our family.'

We went on in silence. The spirit of the whirlwind passed us on the way and didn't say anything. The spirit of the whirlwind had a mean look on his face and I feared for the people he was going to visit. Dad tried to find his way back to the sacred grove so we could rest there for a while before we went back home. We went round and round, following the path which led us to the cave of leaves, but we couldn't find the marble hill and the white grove of statues. He didn't know it, but the old woman had closed the invisible gates of the labyrinth. We were never going to find that magic grove again in the same way.

FOUR

The vanished rock

The lamp made the path clear. There were no voices
in the forest air. Even the crickets were silent. We
came to the place where Dad had first buried the
carpenter whom he was accused of murdering. The
grave was torn as if a giant snake had been thrashing
about beneath the earth. Or as if a tree had been
uprooted from the spot. We left the lamp at the edge
of the forest. We got home safely, slept, and woke
up to a new day of fanfares and Madame Koto's
disastrous return.

And so it was only much later that we realised
what we should have noticed at the time, as we left
the forest. The black rock which Dad had used to
mark the carpenter's grave had vanished. We should
have noticed that.

And because we didn't notice the disappearance of
the rock, we were not prepared for the catastrophes
that were coming.

FIVE

A silent coda

The catastrophes came in the guise of lovely music and bright colours in our street. There are colours that human beings still can't see. Dad often says that we can no longer see all the colours that our ancestors saw. There is a kind of music that is so beautiful that it speaks of imminent death. We didn't recognize the music when we heard it.

In just the same way, we didn't hear the new silence in our lives.

When they began to cut down the trees in earnest, the forest fell silent for ever. It may be that it was this silence which really began the upheavals which would flood our lives and terminate many of our stories. The silence drove many of the spirits mad. The spirits began to drive us mad. And then we became a people that could open up colours which human eyes had never seen before, and that could conjure melodies which human ears had never heard before, but also a people that couldn't see up ahead the seven mountains of their unique destination.

BOOK FOUR

ONE

An angel redeems our suffering in advance

Madame Koto returned to our area with a fanfare of bells, kettledrums and praise-singers. On the day she returned an angel flew over our street to redeem our suffering in advance.

There was much music and celebrating at Madame Koto's infamous bar. We saw her troupe of women, all in red wrappers and white blouses. There was much feasting. We heard that two goats and a pig were slaughtered as sacrificial offerings.

Mum was very lucky that day. She went out hawking and returned early with all her goods sold. Twelve times that day she bought provisions from wholesalers and sold them rapidly. She came back with presents for us. I got a new pair of trousers and leather sandals to protect my feet from the blistering road. Dad got a new jacket – a little tight under the arms, but it gave him some dignity. And later that day, inspired by the mysterious wind of good fortune, Mum replanted her precious stones of sleep in the forest. She replanted them near a shrine, in the hope that the sacred earth would regenerate their powers.

Everyone was kind that day. There was laughter

everywhere. The mild sunlight and the cool wind opened our senses to the hidden joys. It was a Saturday. The children dressed in their best clothes. People were able to look their enemies in the eye without bitterness and without the horror of confrontation. Madame Koto sent her women to our various rooms with paper plates of fried goat and stewed rice. It was her way of announcing her return. It was also her way of getting the community to participate in her gratitude at being cured of her illness. We were all so well disposed towards everything that we ate her sacrificial food and suffered no negative consequences. Dad smiled a lot that day. Mum prepared the tastiest chicken dish. After we had eaten, I went out to play on the first of the many days of little miracles.

It was a time of respite from antagonisms. The sun washed the air clean of enmities and bad dreams. The constellations were in harmony. And in all the realms of existence the battles between opposing mythologies seemed in abeyance. Supporters of contending political parties mysteriously found themselves drinking together and sharing jokes. Even the blind old man was friendly that day.

The blind old man had been absent from our area for weeks. Such was the nature of his powers that we hadn't noticed his absence till we saw him stumbling down the street in his black hat, yellow sunglasses, red cravat and white suit. He had a peculiar smile on his face, revealing that most of his lower teeth were missing. He seemed confused as he wandered home alone, feeling everything a little frantically with his sorcerer's cane, tripping over the accumulated rubbish. Then he surprised us by walking right into our compound and tapping his way to our door. We followed him. He came back out of the compound, and went back to our door again. We were astonished to hear him say:

'Someone has changed the world around!'

He stood at our door with a bemused expression on his face. We were too amazed to say anything. It wasn't until he said 'Someone has taken my house away and I can't find it,' that we understood.

But before we could go up to him and help, he began to laugh a little hysterically. It was as if he were confronted with greater and more tranquil powers than he had ever imagined. It was as if they had scrambled up the world and made him the butt of a divine jest. With his free hand clutching the air, he staggered from our compound. He went to the housefront and stood in one spot. He turned round and round, chuckling. Then, jabbing the air with his sorcerer's cane, he said:

'I don't recognize this place!'

Propelled by the serenity of the sunlight, we rushed to him, and led him to his compound. But before we got there his followers emerged from the house and led him to his secret chambers.

Two hours later he re-emerged with a red flower in his lapel. He was guided along by a tall woman of strange beauty. Together they went everywhere, from house to house, greeting everybody, asking heartfelt questions about their children, their jobs and their health. The blind old man tipped his hat at women like a perfect gentleman, gave sweets to the children and remembered everyone's names from the sound of their voices. He also remembered details of illnesses, deaths, and pregnancies in the family. He asked us about them, offering help. He congratulated those whose lives had improved in some way. He spoke warmly to the strangers in our midst. People laughed at his jokes.

Later he brought out his accordion, set up tables and chairs in front of his house, and played rather haunting tunes for us. He played melodies that he swore he had never heard before, melodies that seemed to dream themselves out from the accordion. The air carried the strains of his harmonious mood over the street. Concentric drinking circles formed around him.

The blind old man astounded us with his unsuspected generosity. He bought beer and ogogoro for the crowd, and ordered that everyone be fed to bursting point. Inspired by the sunlight on his face, he kicked about joyfully in his chair and played the accordion with the facial expression of a wise lizard. Squeezing out delightful tunes and variations, felicitous cadenzas and counterpoints, he positively bristled with artistic ecstasy. His accordion made us very happy that day.

He seemed possessed by the very spirit of music and played the instrument with the abandon and jerkiness of an inspired puppet. The music spread a delicious enchantment over our reality. It spread a golden hue over the liquid bleating of goats, over the disembodied cries of babies, and over the jagged faces of men and women. The music touched our ordinary reality in unusual ways. It touched the kites in the air made from newspapers. It touched the birds that circled the kites with what seemed like envy, but which must have been curiosity. It touched our faces and softened the angles of our suffering. And the luminous spaces within us shone out through our perspiration, catching the light in ways that made us wonder.

And so, for a heavenly moment, the blind old man's music restored our faith in the democracy and justice of time. His music got so infectious that we started humming tunes a moment before he actually stumbled on them, as if we were in perfect harmony with the possibilities of his inspiration. This was the same blind old man whose eyes filled our nightmares with terror at the things he really saw. He was happy as a condor, playing as if he were riding the invisible humps of the wind. It didn't even seem odd to us that he should be the one to so deepen our joy with music that could only have come from celestial realms.

We drank and sang so much that day under the auspices of an auspicious enchantment, that we didn't get drunk on the alcohol. We only got happier. There were no quarrels and there was no violence. There was only much merriment and much laughter at the frightening faces the blind old man pulled under the influence of his musical discoveries.

TWO

'The instinct in paradise'

The angel, flying over the city, filled us with fortitude enough to last through the suffering that was to come, and touched the Governor-General with a sudden perception of the beauties of the continent. Standing at the large bay window, whose frames had been repainted after the inexplicable fire, he said, to the empty room:

'I could live here for ever.'

Outside the window he saw an African child sitting on the charred lawn. He had never noticed the child before and the sunlight made the burned grass take on a golden hue. The Governor-General, struck by a vision of African sunlight over the splendour of an English countryside covered in snow, left the window and went to his study.

'I suppose it's time to leave this country,' he said, as he sat down to work on a new draft of the rewriting of our lives.

And as he wrote, his mind dissolving in words liberated from bureaucratic jargon, his eyes filled with an inexplicable yellow light which he would for ever associate with the best years of his life. He heard very faintly voices singing in golden harmonies from the servants' quarters. He was so moved by the singing (which seemed to him so sublime he didn't for a moment connect it with his servants) that as he pressed on with the rewriting of our existence he paused, looked up, saw a yellow moth circling his head, and wrote a sentence which completely took him by surprise. Startled by the revelation which his mood had brought out of him, he got up, and poured himself a whisky. Watching the moth, listening to the singing and to the creaking of spirits through the vast empty rooms of his great white house, he read the sentence again, and let out a long sigh.

'WHEN YOU BEGIN TO FALL IN LOVE WITH A PLACE THAT YOU HAVE WOUNDED IN SOME DEEP WAY, MAYBE IT'S TIME TO LEAVE,' the sentence read.

The singing grew louder; a harmonic chorus of female voices joined in; and the tinkling of bells sounded faintly beneath the voices of a heavenly choir in the remote distance of his servants' quarters. He had never been there. He had never seen how they lived. And as he contemplated the sentence it suddenly occurred to him that though he had been in the continent for fifteen years he didn't have the slightest idea of the true nature of the place.

The thought troubled him and I saw him get up and sit down twice, as he thought about the ritual noises of the African night that always kept his daughter awake. Then he remembered the ceremony he had attended in a village deep in the jungles of the southern creeks when he was made chief by a tribe in return for a favourable decision in a fierce boundary dispute with another tribe. He remembered the smell of chicken blood and the sweating barechested

African men. His face colouring, he re-experienced the lust awakened in him by the virility of the men and the sensuality of the antimony-charmed women and the powerful smell of the ancient trees. He also recalled an occasion when his wife fainted. They had driven fifty miles at night through the primeval forests on bad roads. She had spoken of seeing ghosts along the roadside and spirits in the faces of the insects crushed on the windscreen a moment before she passed out. And then there were his daughter's hallucinations. Her horror of being possessed by fire demons. Soon afterwards they had her sent home to school in Winchester.

He no longer heard the singing, for it had become part of his spirit and his future yearnings. He was so moved by his own feelings, which suddenly occupied such unsuspected depths within him, that, with the yellow moth still circling his head, he began writing things about our lives which he thought he was inventing from ignorance but which on reflection he felt to be truer than the things he would have written if he had known the soul of the land. He wrote his most lyrical passages about the benevolent spirit of the nocturnal continent. He suddenly became very hot. Sweat crept out all over him. He felt for a moment as if a gigantic being had occupied the space he inhabited, the space that was his body. But as he wrote he stopped being aware of the occupation, the heat, and of the sweat, which the singing intensified. He wrote his purple passages about the abounding generosity of the land, its abnormal fertility. He wrote about the innocent eyes of the old, the old eyes of the young, the incomparable sculpting which suffering and forbearance made of the African faces, and the sensuality of the air. He poured out a symphony of words about the docility of Africans and their awe of the white man, about their myth-making natures, their praise-singing souls, their touching obedience, their trusting natures, their immense and ultimately self-destroying capacity for forgiveness, forgiving even those who wounded their destiny. He rhapsodized about their love of music, their unscientific thinking, their explosive laughter, their preference for myth over reality, for story over fact, for mystification over clarification, for dance over stillness, for ecstasy over contemplation, for metaphysics over logic, for the many over the one. He praised their polygamous thinking and their polygamous gods, noted their excessive compassion, their indiscriminate kindness, their unholy abundance of feeling, their terrifying piety, their regrettable preference for the spoken over the written, their talent for languages, their abominable mathematics, their excessive interpretation of things, their penetrating directness, their deplorable habit of treating all events as signs meaning more than they do, their tremendous and saintlike capacity for suffering, their philosophical fatalism, their transcendent optimism, their irrepressible sense of humour, their childlike sense of wonder, their infuriating naivety, their oblique and magic-working art.

The Governor-General paused in his writing. The yellow moth flew towards the door. He smelt fireflies in the air. He tried to resume writing, but found that the unique mood had left him. He had taken his passage up a vertiginous crescendo of feeling entirely alien to him, and the mood had deserted him just before he reached the musical peak of his perceptions. For a moment he realized that the singing had stopped. Its absence filled him with restlessness. He got up and went to the door. When he opened it the yellow moth flew out and soared into the ripe golden sky of that unique Saturday.

The singing started again, as if under the command of an imperious conductor, and the Governor-General followed it down the stairs and outside. Without knowing why, he wandered towards the servants' quarters. The yellow moth fluttered behind him. The Governor-General stopped. From a distance, he peered into one of his servants' rooms. Through the crude window he saw a group of African men and women with white cloths on their heads, and six candles alight on the table. He was surprised to see them singing in the cramped room. The beauty of their singing caught him in the throat. He saw their glistening faces and poignant eyes. He beheld the gentle fever of their celebration and the intensity of their expressions. And he might have moved closer to get a better glimpse into the lives of his servants if he hadn't instantly become aware of being stared at, of being studied. His mood changed and a vague feeling of dread invaded the nape of his neck. He turned round suddenly and startled the yellow moth which circled the back of his head. For a moment the Governor-General felt a rush of hot blood to his brain. He felt dizzy, as if he were falling from an elevated space.

When he recovered his dignity, remembering that he was in charge of a colonized nation, he noticed the same African child he had seen earlier. The child was still sitting on the lawn, surrounded by a yellow glow. The Governor-General looked up and noticed that the African night, moving silently with its immense indigo cloak, had come upon the land. There were still a few golden showers of light in a far corner of the sky. The boy sat immobile, amongst the shadows of the charred lawn. The Governor-General moved towards him. When he was close enough he stopped and stared into the boy's face, and was startled by the absence of awe in his eyes.

Confused by the persistence of the yellow moth, disturbed by the notion that the moods of the country were making him superstitious, and struck by the serene eyes of the African boy sitting in a yellow glow, the Governor-General stumbled back into the house, followed by the moth. A sense of magnificence quickened his heart. And with a rich sense of well-being rising up within him, he continued his writing, taking it up at the crescendo without even a moment's doubt, and he wrote about the possibility that there were angels in disguise among the wretched of the earth, angels who were spies of God, witnesses of suffering and injustice and the arrogance of the victorious. He talked about unearthly personages in the most unlikely places on earth. In the midst of a paragraph in which he discoursed on sewage problems, poor hygiene and the people's indifference to sanitary conditions, he found himself writing about angels in Africa, writing about the unnamed ones, who seem to be human, with eyes that penetrate the human spirit and see into the full nakedness of the heart and conscience. Then his mind dissolved into an indigo space as, unknowingly, he wrote the following problematic lines.

'What happens to Empires, to those centres of power that set out to dominate the world? Rome, Greece, Egypt? Rome is now a glorified theatre of ruins. Greece is a faded place, with no active memory of its astounding past. And Egypt is a necropolis. They conquer the world and are later overrun by the world. Because they set out to dominate the world they are condemned to live with the negative facts of their domination. They will be changed by the world that they set out to colonize. They shrink, and their former glory becomes an angry shadow. Is that the fate of imperialists – the inevitable dissolution of overreachers? Is it possible that those we colonize will later overrun us? Are we too to suffer the fate of all overreachers – the inevitable etiolation of the spirit? These people we call barbarians, will we not, like ancient Rome, find that they both devour and regenerate our powers?'

The Governor-General paused again. He was unaware that an angel, all celestial fire and gold, was poised just above him. It hovered in the window behind that opened out onto a sky of African blue and onto the charred lawn from which the African boy had arisen, transfigured. The Governor-General's mood deepened. His thoughts had wandered into an unknown place. Novalis might have had this place in mind when he noted that 'instinct is the genius in paradise'. And, touched by the enchantments of that unknown place, the Governor-General began writing again. He wrote that in moments when the wind changes, bringing beautiful night on its wings, he felt like an African himself and could understand the hidden stories in the fragrance of orange blossoms and agapanthus. Soaring and lost in himself, he wrote that in the beginning the creator spread the great jigsaw of humanity and human genius amongst all the peoples of the earth, and that no one people can have the complete picture alone. He wrote that:

'It is only when the diverse peoples of the earth meet and learn from and love one another that we can begin to get an inkling of this awesome picture. Call it the picture of divinity, or humanity if you want, but like the magic powder that Africans sometimes allude to, this great jigsaw has been distributed amongst all of us; and one aspect of our destiny on this earth may be to discover something of that grand image or music of our collective souls, of our immense possibilities, our infinite riches. No one person or people has the final road or the great keyboard or exclusive possession of this jigsaw of humanity. Only together, as one people of this earth, facing our common predicament and redeeming love, can we make use of this universal gift, this map of our earthly journey and glory.'

Much later, in his native land, the Governor-General was to be quite frightened when he came upon that passage. He had no idea what had made him write it, no memory of when he had written it, or how. And when his memoirs came out to a modest critical reception, he would much regret the fact that he had allowed the editor of the small publishing house to cut out that passage which he felt constituted the most inspired fruit of his colonial service.

I watched him that day, and I saw him that night through the eyes of the yellow moth. I lay in the darkness of our small room in the ghetto, while he wrote feverishly about our lives in the white spaces of his colonial mansion. I saw him trying out ways of putting Byron's lines about the second dance of freedom into his own words, without much success, as he sweated in his study. His inspired mood had deserted him and the singing had stopped. The moth had circled away from him towards the open window. It had flown out into a sky magnetized by an unusual saturation of the yellow dust of angels.

THREE

A beauty bordering on terror

The magnetic field of the angel as it flew over our city enveloped the old woman in the forest with a humility deeper than wisdom. The suffocating animals had recovered in the wake of the heatwave; she felt their presence amidst the trees around her hut. She had seen the herbaceous plants recover their intensity of green; birds were piping among the dense branches.

The forest breathed a new fragrance. For the first time in many years she awoke into a day of tender sunlight without despair or bitterness in her heart. I could see her bafflement at the music which came from the settlements on the other side of the forest. The music and the singing roused in her memories of feast days in her village when elders spoke of the holy man who had seen an angel at night and who knew the precise date and hour he would die. She remembered them talking about how the holy man had called everyone together to make preparations for the special day. In the midst of her solitude the old woman found her hut now crowded with ancient presences; she saw holy men in shrouds bearing gifts for an invisible king. She went outside and looked up at the sky for signs of a visitation. A cat brushed past her foot. And then, in a startled moment, she saw a white and yellow form floating in the air above her hut. It was a form with mighty wings, dazzling like the brightness of pure moonlight. In a moment the form was gone.

Then she heard voices in the trees. Hobbling to the edge of the forest, she saw women with white dresses fleeing down the paths. For a moment, her eyes seemed to fail her. She watched as the intensity of the women created a marvellous turbulence in the wind. The leaves stirred. Then the women released a beautiful cry in unison and their bodies rose from the ground and they ran on the air of tender sunlight. Their transformation was accompanied by an explosion of yellow dust which struck the old woman blind. She hobbled back to her hut, her hands feeling the air. But her heart was serene. A beautiful terror glowed in her spirit.

When she got home she lay on her bed. Her mind was full of visions of angels whose wings had been a little stained by human blood, the blood of the innocent dying. Her mind was rich with the vision of angelic presences in human forms, of angels baffled by the intensity of human suffering.

She lay on her bed till her sight returned. I watched her through the eyes of the cat as she hobbled out and began her most extraordinary weaving. She wove scenes of frightening beauty, beauty bordering on terror. Painstakingly, and with a dexterity unusual for her age, she wove her most lovely section about the good people who survive terrible times through innocence and patience and through transformations. She wove idyllic landscapes and hillsides with yellow and blue flowers. Beautiful men and women were lying on the grass with a golden glow around them. Above them was a shimmering sky. She wove charming designs for future African cities. She wove the rich dream of a city, with magic water spouting from fountains. The inhabitants were radiant in the higher realization of all their sleeping possibilities. She wove villages with houses made of blue mirrors. Trees with palatial interiors. Serene rivers running alongside well-made roads. Trees in bloom along the streets. Flowers in the middle of lanes. She wove another city with seven sacred hills as its centre of pilgrimage. She worked all through that splendid day.

In the afternoon, as we were listening to the blind old man's music, and as the Governor-General spied on his servants, the old woman wove herself into a tranquil hallucination. In this hallucination she created the forms of angels flying over a future city, taking into their beings some of the dust and atomic radiation of our human history, taking in the flurry and chaos of our restless spirit. She wove scenes in which angels entered human beings or passed through them and emerged a little confused about their momentary humanity, while the human beings were terrified at their own sudden angelic qualities, their moods of a golden eternity. The old woman created a mesmerising section in which goats were turning into men, in which men were half-transformed into angels, their black wings bristling with a deep yellow glow. It dazzled with the confusion of angels. Angels who had the feet of women; one wing eagle, the other angel. Their faces were puzzled and enchanted. Their eyes were horrified and full of wonder. Around these scenes of redemption by beauty, this terror of angelic presences, were scenes of carnage, poverty, war, corruption. And containing it all were golden weaves, a mellow frame like an eternal summery dawn.

The old woman worked all through that day. Her sight failed her and recovered. Turned moon-white and then green. Lost in her visionary mood, she created the intermingling of humans and angels. The angels were weighed down with the debris and the failures of the human spirit. And the humans were raised up by angels who breathed alternative dreams of a beautiful future into the disturbed air.

And it was only when she was exhausted, with tears pouring down her face, clearing her vision, that she saw something which astonished her. She saw that in her inspired mood she had woven angels of many colours. There were blue angels. Flaming red angels. Black angels. Yellow angels. All her colours were mixed up as if her dyes had been poisoned by the air. She saw all this and got up, screaming. The girl with the wooden leg hurried over and led her into the hut and prepared for her a strong draught of herbs which put her into a profound sleep. In the depths of her sleep she was encompassed by the many-coloured angels she had woven.

That evening I saw an angel of a colour human eyes have never seen as I got drunk on the blind old man's wine. Everywhere along our street people were drunk on the mood of angels.

FOUR

End of an enchantment

The spirits of the land were peaceful in their spheres. The air was fresh. And there was a yellow cloud in a far corner of the sky. The mood of angels lasted several days in our lives. We seemed to have discovered a paradise lurking in the heart of our wretchedness. The people who write history always concentrate on great events and neglect the days when unsuspected bliss, like an enchanted dream, shines out from the lives of human beings.

There was much music in those days. Strangers increased amongst us. And everyone looked beautiful. But no one looked more beautiful than Madame Koto when she appeared in public on those days of forgiveness. Who can forget the splendour of her gold-bordered wrapper. Her silk blouses. And her astounding hairstyle which had been specially plaited into a pyramidal glory.

She reappeared amongst us like an undeciphered sign in the middle of our good days. A fanfare of talking drums announced her fresh ascendancy. Her praise-singers rendered all manner of epics about her legendary power and generosity. But then the music from her bar grew louder. It spread a coarse revelry up and down our area. And then our drunkenness, which had been full of light, gradually turned overbearing. The louder her music sounded, the more the serenity of the lights retreated. And the days that were joyful dreams changed imperceptibly and turned unpleasant when the first blood of fighting was spilled. Because two strangers argued about politics.

People sometimes say that happiness is the holiday of the spirit, the lovely dreaming of the nerves. But after the mood of angels there came a yellow karmic dust which settled everywhere over the continent, creating unpredictable effects which the historians took to be spontaneous events. We lingered too long in the holiday of our spirit and in the lovely music of our days. And we didn't notice when it all changed. We didn't notice when the dance became a stampede, when the peaceful songs turned rousing, when the musical instruments spoke a different language, issuing crude commandments to the brain and hands. We didn't notice when the mood darkened, obscuring the profound joys that were intended to outlast all the suffering that was to come.

II

BOOK FIVE

ONE

The story of the Rain Queen

Madame Koto appeared to us again on the third day of the angel and her moonstones shone brightly round her neck as if they were on fire. Her eyes also shone and her skin was oily and smooth. She was massive. Her plaster cast had been removed and her bad foot was still swollen, but her face showed no pain. Her pregnancy was entering its final stages of ripeness and she floated around with the dignity of a great ship loaded with exotic gifts. She walked with the aid of a crocodile-headed walking stick, she had gold bangles round her arms, and all about her lights glittered as if she were wearing mirrors.

The whites of Madame Koto's eyes were so white they seemed like moonstones cleaned for the advent of a new vision. And when we stared into her eyes we were transfixed by their milky death-white beauty. She seemed to have changed profoundly since recovering from her madness. She stared at the world with a gaze at once serene and deathlike, as if she had swum in the nightmare milk of the abyss and had seen visions that reside only within the beings of inscrutable gods.

Madame Koto burned and was silent in her

maternal beauty. She burned fiercely and the intensity of her presence, blinding us with its ice and fire, seemed like a great farewell.

All around her was the sweet staccato music of her praise-singers, a music so piercing that it seemed to speak of an imminent death or an abnormal birth. Just as the rainbows in the sky during the music of gentle rains speak of mighty elephants giving birth deep in the forest.

Madame Koto was silent as she went amongst us, drawing crowds of children and curious adults. But all through that day we heard rumours, fuelled by the arcane syncopations of the talking drum, that she was planning the most fabulous of wedding feasts. We didn't know who she was getting married to. But we heard that the great event would take place after the elections, whose results had already been decided in advance in all the realms of manipulated reality.

She was silent in the midst of her flaming beauty. But she distributed bags of sweets to the children as the air turned sour. The dark clouds returned, sailing across our skies like the fleet of an invading navy. The music from her bar had poisoned the sweet music of the days.

I am not sure at what point it all changed but one morning instead of music we heard the crackling of loud hailers. The politicians had returned and they blared out their contradictory promises over our air – while malnutrition devoured the children, while poverty crushed the hopes of the inhabitants, while the women grew haggard from the sunstroke, the crippling domestic duties and no freedom.

It was Dad who put the last idea in my head. He

came back from carrying loads one evening and sat down on his fabled chair. Mum was sweeping the room. Dad stared at her grim implacable face. Then he broke another of his long silences, and said:

'We are destroying our women.'

Mum stopped sweeping, and sat on the bed. Dad sighed.

'Why did you say that?' Mum asked.

Dad was silent. His eyes were dim in the candlelit room. After a while Mum got up and said:

'Men are nothing but talk.'

She resumed sweeping. When she had finished she gathered the pots of soup from the cupboard. Just as she was about to leave for the kitchen, Dad spoke again.

'Have you ever wanted a wife?' he asked her.

Mum came back into the room, dropped the pots, stood over Dad, and said:

'Why do you ask these questions, eh?'

Dad was silent for some time before he said:

'Someone told me a story today. It made me think about all sorts of things. There is a powerful Rain Queen in the southern part of our continent who has sixteen wives.'

Mum didn't say anything. Dad didn't continue the story. The silence made me restless.

'Is Madame Koto a Rain Queen?' I asked.

Mum and Dad stared at me contemplatively for a long while. The fireflies sizzled in the room, circling Dad's head. Outside we heard the loud hailers again, blaring their promises into our nightspace. Mum sighed. Dad sucked his teeth in contempt. I got up and went to the door.

'Come back!' Mum said.

I stopped.

'Let him go,' Dad said. 'The road is calling him.'

'Let the road call someone else's child,' Mum replied.

I stayed at the door, my nose suffused with the bad air that the politicians had brought to our compound. It stank so much that Dad ordered all the windows be opened.

'We will die of mosquitoes,' Mum said.

'Better than to die of the bad smell of those politicians,' Dad countered.

'I'm hungry,' I said.

'Azaro, if you keep quiet and sit still,' Dad promised, 'I will tell you the story of the Rain Queen.'

Mum went out with the pots, and Dad went to help her cook. I sat in the room, oppressed by the midges, the mosquitoes and the political bad smell. My stomach rumbled. I caught a fleeting glance of the old woman. She seemed to be at the window, staring at me. I went to the window, looked out, and saw nothing. A large frog croaked from the rubbish heap outside. A lizard scuttled up the wall and it stayed in a far corner, watching me. I had the dim suspicion that someone, somewhere, was watching me from the lizard's eyes. The lizard was very still. Its stillness made me notice a spider in another corner of the room. Midges circled my head, a constellation of fireflies flitted everywhere, and for a brief moment I saw the Governor-General standing at the bay window of his huge white house, a black pipe in his mouth, contemplating the nation whose sleep was about to be altered.

Mum and Dad came back with the food. I ate hurriedly, washed the plates and sat down. My back was against the bed. I stared at Dad, and after a while became aware that I wasn't the only one staring. Mum stared too. And behind us, up on the wall, so did the lizard. Dad cleared his throat, his expression remaining the same, except that his eyes took on a faraway gaze, as if he too could see people with whom he had a mysterious affinity, people living their lives somewhere else, unaware that they were being watched by distant eyes. And when Dad's gaze had reached its best point of focuslessness, as if he had suddenly flown in spirit to the southern part of the continent, he said:

'The powerful Rain Queen lives in a mighty hut deep in a forest. She lives under a great tree that is two thousand years old and which bears powerful, poisonous fruits. There are many Rain Queens in the world but she is the mother of them all. She knows how to talk to rain, she knows the language of the spirit of the whirlwind, she can make clouds turn black, she can command lightning to strike, she keeps the secret of thunder in a white pot, and she has sixteen wives and many children. She is very old and very powerful. She can enter into the dreams of nations and continents. She has something to do with every great thing that happens in the lives of her people. Her spirit is feared all over the world, feared by people who have never even heard of her. She holds a great feast once every seven years. The feast usually means that something incredible is going to happen somewhere, or that it has already happened but no one knows it yet. But before she holds the feast she waits for a sign, an omen. Often the sign will take the form of a wonderful animal appearing in front of her hut. Once a giraffe lowered its head into her door. No one knew how it got there. Another time a camel was found sleeping near the communal well. Many years ago a white man came with gifts of gold and emerald beads. And people even say that there was a time when the spirit of their great god spoke through the mouth of a two-year-old baby. The feast she held after that particular sign was so fantastic that they still sing about it today, in a hundred versions, all over the continent. Great events don't just travel to people's ears through the mouths of men. Sometimes they travel through dreams, through the invisible cables in the air, or through the whispering mouths of spirits.'

Dad paused and looked at us through eyes that momentarily blazed with a prophetic intensity. Then he returned to his focuslessness, and soared away to the wonderful south.

'Not long ago men and women from several lands, from distant continents, from strange places in the universe set out on a pilgrimage to her famous shrine. When they began to arrive one by one people marvelled at the fantastic gifts they brought. They marvelled at the different kinds of human beings there are in this world. When these amazing people began to arrive the Rain Queen knew that this was no ordinary sign. In fact this was the sign she had been told to watch out for many many years ago. When the pilgrims left, she held a quiet feast. And during the feast she made the startling announcement that her time had come to leave the earth and join her illustrious ancestors. But she presented a riddle to her people. She said that from birth it was foretold that when her time to die came, she would have to choose between eating the fruit of the ancient poisonous tree or going up the highest hill and, without food or water, climbing the ladder of the gods into the realm of illustrious beings. Till this day no one knows what choice she made. That is my story, and it is true.'

When Dad finished his story he shut the window and put out the candle. That night I dreamt that Madame Koto was a Rain Queen whose time to die had come. I saw her burning in the flames of her moonstones with a red angel standing behind her. Then I saw the angel's enormous wings enclosing her as she burned, her eyes bright, in complete inhuman silence.

TWO

How Mum paid for my careless words

I was playing in the street the next day when I saw
ghosts pouring into Madame Koto's bar. I didn't
recognize any of the ghosts. I followed them but
when I entered the bar I found the place quite
empty. One of Madame Koto's women came in from
the backyard and saw me and drove me out. I told
Mum about the ghosts, but she hit me on the head
and made me promise not to utter a word of what
I'd seen ever again. I told Dad about the ghosts and
he said:

'She is going to throw a feast.'

I saw Madame Koto that evening. I saw her
burning in her unnatural beauty. She waddled up to
me, encircled by seven spells of protection and a
perfume which could repel all evil. She seized my
hand and then, in a man's voice, she said:

'I am soon going to give birth.'

'You are soon going to die,' I said.

Uttering a twisted cry, her face contorting into a
mask so ugly that she brought the night closer to my
eyes, she let go of my hand and staggered backwards.
Swiftly, drawing her spells about her, and banishing
the waves of approaching madness with a fantastic

movement of her arms, she regained herself and gave me the most eerie smile.

'Your mother will pay for what you said,' was her response.

I wasn't moved. Then, suddenly, a sharp pain cut through my head. For a moment the darkness was flooded with a blinding flash of lightning. And when the darkness returned I was standing alone in a hot space in the street. Madame Koto was gone. Not even her perfume betrayed her vanished presence.

That night, while we were all asleep in a land with too many dreams, my mother began to rave and it took six men to hold her down as she fought with the tigerous strength that madness gives. She howled all night and drained our compound of energy. The men were exhausted, their eyes scratched, their chests lacerated, their wrists sprained from the supernatural effort of holding Mum down. Foaming at the mouth, her eyes bulging, it was as if many insane spirits were fighting for dominion within her lean body.

My mother went mad while Madame Koto burned in her new beauty. They stuck a spoon in Mum's mouth to prevent her biting off her tongue and in her elemental fury she left precise indentations of her teeth on the metal object. Dad refused to bring in a herbalist. His stillness grew more fearful as he regarded Mum with his dark eyes. For an entire day Mum was insane. The politicians returned with their trucks and bullhorns, their traditional attire, their dubious powdered milk and their extravagant promises while Mum screamed about strange things in strange languages. I watched her contort on the bed, kicking feverishly.

Then, astoundingly, she burst from the bindings of hempen ropes and began destroying the room, tipping over the cupboard, hurling the bed at the wall, throwing the centre table to the far corner of the room, and tossing clothes towards the ceiling. She developed a sudden obsession for the staring lizard and pursued it across the walls, throwing her shoes at it and missing. And in the afternoon, when the heat reached its most unbearable intensity, Mum quietened down and began to sing a dirge in tones so vertiginous that we sat around her wondering what demon had entered her spirit. I watched Mum's eyes swimming round in their sockets till only the whites were visible.

And when she began to mutter again, fighting the rising tide of insanity, she broke into the familiar language of her ancestors, and spoke about a hot black rock growing inside her womb, growing hotter and vaster. She spoke of ghosts who had missed their way and who had wandered into her body and who were confused about their destination. She muttered about drums pounding in her head. And when she spoke of a leopard growling in her heart, releasing a flood tide of ancient desires and dreams, Dad's expression changed. No longer was Dad's stillness potent. It had emerged from its lair.

In the evening Mum broke into torrential prophecies, shouting about hanged men in distant continents and others who suffered injustices inflicted on the beauty of the skin, shouting about women who were turned into animals by the sheer pressure of the unnumbered days, about burning towers and liquid currencies bursting up from the dark sleeping earth, about eras of extravagant corruption, incredible devaluation of currencies, murders by governments in broad daylight, assassinations and wars, worms on the living flesh of children, about people walking around breeding colonies of diseases and rage, about marketwomen storming the government houses, about poor nations whose entire lands and seas and minerals and skies had been leased to foreign powers for two hundred years, about earthquakes which would level cities leaving only children below the age of seven; and when she began to scream of the dreadful time of karmic balances, the assault of old religions, when she broke into her torrent of prophecies and nonsense none of us were surprised that it began to rain outside, that it began to pour, that rain gushed down in an avalanche, a deluge, battering the rooftops, disintegrating the houses, and flooding the streets.

When the rain reached its cataclysmic height, and most of us cowered close to the floor, terrified of the abnormal fury of the storm, and while Mum lay quiet on the bed, her mouth moving, her words silent, Dad sprang to life, uttering his powerful incantations. He became electrified, as if his spirit had finally been prodded from sleep. Seizing Mum by the waist, he tossed her on his shoulder, and ran out into the storm, wading thigh-deep in the stream of the road, shouting in his mighty voice.

I followed him, and saw how small he was beneath the torrential sky, beneath the low street-long cracks of lightning that split everything open, revealing visible and invisible realms. The lightning opened a way for Dad through the forest. Still growling, as if he had turned into a beast, he took Mum to a place where five paths met. There were sacrificial plates of food at the mouth of every one of them. He laid her down on the waterlogged ground beneath the thousand-year-old tree, and vanished into the forest, his voice ringing out through the labyrinth drenched with rain.

The torrent obscured Mum from me and the crash of thunder over my head sent me scurrying back to the street and to our compound. I stayed in the devastation of our room. Many hours later, rising out of myself, I circled the air and saw a silver form floating over Mum. It was the old woman of the forest. And when Dad returned from his futile search for the old woman's hut, he found that Mum had disappeared from the crossroads.

The lightning created new roads in the air that night and the old woman took Mum's spirit flying into its crevices, to the miraculous centre and source of lightning flash. And when the incandescence flooded over our street, blinding the earth and trees with explosions of light, I saw Mum neck-deep in the secret springs of the millennial shrine and heard her cry out in a purified voice.

Not long afterwards I heard Mum and Dad coming down our street. Mum was covered shoulder-downwards in a white cloth. Her hair had been cut low, her face bore multiple cuts and bruises, her eyes were calm, and she was singing a dirge which was as sweet a tune as any mermaid ever uttered from the great rivers.

The rain had stopped when Mum got home. When she stepped into the room her eyes registered profound displeasure at the chaos she beheld. She flashed Dad an angry glance, which told me that she had no recollection of her fury. She did not even remember her madness as a dream. It was all my fault, Mum's suffering. I hated Madame Koto so much that I wanted her to live.

THREE

Vigilance

We did not speak to Mum about her brief madness. We tried not to look at her as if she were a freak. But we watched ourselves, we watched what we said, we were careful about our gestures, we hid all the mirrors for a time, and Dad resorted to all kinds of methods to make sure that we were discreetly vigilant. There was no need for any of it, because Mum's one-day storm had passed for good, and we had survived one more of Madame Koto's bewitched transferences.

I kept Madame Koto's threat to myself, but I changed my wish. At night I prayed for her beauty to burn her up into golden cinders.

FOUR

Ghosts of narratives past

Madame Koto had indeed returned and there was no way to avoid it. In the classic manner of the powerful, through the agency of Mum's ravings, she sent word round that she had survived her nightmare ordeals and had made terror her ally.

She sent us a basket of onions as a present. I threw them out, and on the same day they sprouted in our backyard. I uprooted the bewitched onions and ran to her bar and threw them in. As I fled I heard her laughter all around me in the wind.

It was a special day for Madame Koto. The power of her flaming spirit had sent word round to all the realms of her affiliations. And that day, as if our street had become the centre of the world, as if a shadow religion were being born in our midst, we saw the most amazing pilgrimage of people to her bar. They came as ghosts first, a legion of shadow beings.

I saw the ghosts of sacrificed animals. I saw the spirits of the unborn. I saw the host of spirit-children who were chained to one mother and to one place, a confluence of several histories. It was as if from their lives must come the resolution of so many crossroads, and cross-histories. They all came in silence, shadows without bodies, spirits without memory, ghosts without dreams. They melted into Madame Koto's bar and hung on the walls or floated in the air.

I saw them all and was afraid that my time had come and that my end was assaulting me in visions of last farewells, and homecomings – which is what a pilgrimage also is. I waited for these ghosts to leave, but they stayed. And it was only later I realized that they had merely travelled in advance of themselves. Their substance was yet to catch up with them.

The next morning, I saw the real people pouring into Madame Koto's bar. They were revenants. It began with a man who was half-spirit and half-human. He had the trickster god's smile on his face. He wore clothes of many colours, checked trousers, a bright red shirt, a yellow hat and carried a white umbrella. He was very tall and thin and I recognized him as the last man Dad fought outside Madame Koto's tent in the twilight of the early years. I was so struck by his return that I stopped to watch what reception he would get. He had hardly stepped into the bar when two midgets went past me. They too were headed for Madame Koto's bar. Then came the man who could remove his eyes. And the spotted albino couple who could exchange their features, and the yam-headed woman, and then the toothless man who had an eye at the back of his throat which looked like a bright marble when he yawned. Then there was the short man whose head resembled a camel's. I couldn't understand why all these people were returning to the bar after their long absence. And while I stood there puzzling, two blind men with sunglasses came up to me and asked the way to Madame Koto's bar. They said they had been travelling for a month.

'Why?' I asked.

'We got a message,' they replied.

'What message?'

'Why do you want to know?' they asked querulously.

'I'm interested,' I said.

They became impatient with my questions, and so I described the way. Looking up at the sky, as if the land was above, they went towards the bar. And then I recognized them. They were the ones whose sight improved the more they drank.

The people who poured back to Madame Koto's shrine came slowly at first. They came, most of them, with their musicians, who bore xylophones, accordions, guitars, koras and improbable drums on their backs. They came alone or in groups. They came with glittering robes and emblems of power, with staffs, crosiers, shields, standards, pennants, mast-heads and flags with indecipherable emblems. And they came, all of them, as if the story of the birth of our community was being replayed.

Then they came in droves, in torrents, in crowds. They filled out the bar and had extraordinary celebrations outside. Their acrobats did somersaults in white robes, turning over and over through hoops woven from elephant grass. Their jugglers circulated bright red eggs in the air. Their musicians performed strange lovely melodies with haunting harmonies, their faces ghostly with antimony. They transformed Madame Koto's bar into a fairground. And they all came bearing gifts. We heard rumours about the gifts they brought, and we were astonished.

They brought monstrous lobes of cola-nuts, golden cowries, basins of rich Sudanese sweets, cages with aquamarine parrots, monkeys with red hats and yellow three-piece suits, gramophones, magic stones which turned light into rainbows, bronze stools, a baby camel, a white mare, a fetish with a demonic androgynous smile, a cow without a tail, a bull with its head painted red, a chicken that laid stones instead of eggs, bales of lace cloth, a basketful of snails, tortoises in green buckets, red and brown sunglasses, hats and headties, dane guns, machetes electrified by lightning, eels, singing fishes, a dead shark painted gold, dogs with blue eyes, cats with an iridescent sheen on their fur, and sculpted messengers of new gods made out of black rocks which glowed in the dark.

Apparently, they also brought silver bangles and taut-skinned drums, giant calabashes and antelope horns, the teeth of crocodiles and golden ropes, sand from the Nile and rocks from the site of the great Egyptian pyramids. They brought the earliest models of telephone, ballpoint pens, varied electronic gadgets, and electric light bulbs. They brought maps of future countries, documents signed by the Governor-General relating to secret economic pacts between the colonizer and the colonized – trade bargains, military dependence, monopolies – documents the Governor-General thought he had destroyed. They brought papers with the signatures of future heads of state. They brought lists of future events, coups, executions, scandals, wars and uprisings. They brought newspapers with future headlines about the numberless massacres of rioting students, the economic collapse of the nation, the diversion of national funds to private accounts in foreign countries. They brought photographs of the key players in the four-year war that was being obliquely dreamt into being by the nation in advance. They brought aerial photographs of future oil sites and details of future trading partners. They brought papers relating to future models of military equipment and military technology, papers relating to the construction of the houses in which future heads of state would live, and extensive maps of the ghettoes with all roads leading out of them drawn in red. They brought many other gifts, gifts seemingly unconnected with the bearers; and the bearers themselves were all strangers from the past.

Slowly, I began to recognize them beneath their transformation, ghosts of narratives past. There were midgets who had become a little taller, tall men who had become a little shorter. Former barmaids of Madame Koto who had grown fat with complacency. Thugs who had become politicians. Assassins who had become priests. There were witches and wizards with shining skins and wall-gecko eyes. Dogs and goats came as well. Cats on strings. Peacocks. People with no legs. Wrestlers and perfect gentlemen. White-haired magicians in black capes. There were mermaids in high-heeled shoes, of dazzling beauty in the daytime, but ambiguous at night. There were animals that had turned into men, and walked uncomfortably with their hoofs in big boots. I saw them all. Contact with Madame Koto had transformed them into individuals with influence in many spheres, transformed them into spies for the dominant powers.

All levels of society were represented. There were truck pushers, metalworkers, clerks in government offices, night soil men, road sweepers, messengers, street traders, policemen, thieves, murderers, bankers, all those who were the eyes and hands and ears of the ascendancy, protected under the vast wings of sorcerers and secret societies, party chiefs and business tycoons. I saw them all, the early denizens of Madame Koto's bar. They had all changed. The bar too had changed beyond recognition. It had become a fantastical place of many spells.

Many of Madame Koto's prostitutes started coming back too. They had become boutique owners, powerful marketwomen, hoteliers, restaurateurs. Women who had long left her service, but who had not left the long arm of her influence, also returned. Many of them were covertly affiliated to her great underground organization. I saw the legendary marketwomen with dreaded eyes and wads of wrappers round their monumental frames, women who smelt of dried crayfish and much-handled money. I saw the women who had been started out by Madame Koto in their own independent lines of business, and who were now bar owners and cash-madams, all converts to her secret religion. And there were people whom I didn't recognize, who seemed to have come from another planet, or from regions of the earth where there was no sunlight.

They had all made long awkward journeys of one

kind or another, weighed down with gifts. They had left the turbulence of their private lives to come and pay their respects to Madame Koto, as if they had heard of her forthcoming feast in advance. In fact, they were all on a mystic pilgrimage back to their beginnings.

I was surprised to see our landlord among them. He too had changed. Now he collected his rent through thuggish intermediaries. He never deigned to come himself any more. He ran gambling houses on the edge of the ghetto, and owned huge portions of land which was now a marsh but which later would become the site of massive chemical-producing industries.

Things seep back from the future into the present; the past presses everything forward; and the future makes things search for their lost origins.

FIVE

The black rock of enigmas

The return of all these people puzzled and worried us. Inhabitants of the area gathered at the street front of Madame Koto's bar wondering what this new invasion of the past signified. It turned out that it wasn't only those from the past who were returning. There were beings I had never seen before. People who were indeed complete strangers. Odd pilgrims. Celebrants. We watched them silently. We watched them as night fell, as the tumult and the celebrations grew noisier. We watched them sacrificing monkeys and sheep. We watched the fearful shadows cast by the great fire of their sacrificial rites.

Their activities held us magnetized. Suspicions and forgotten bad dreams came amongst us. We watched the women who had become chiefs and title holders, the men who ruled places in the country so remote from the centre that they never encountered the national census or taxation.

It was only when Dad cried out in horror at something he had seen in Madame Koto's backyard, something illuminated horribly by their giant fire, that I began to understand. Dad had seen the sinister black rock that he had used to mark the carpenter's grave in the forest. And when he saw it, we all saw it too. There it was, in the backyard, bristling with an infernal life. Its pitted surface kept quivering. It glowed a curious yellow under the flickering light of the flames. It fizzed and crawled, as if it were animate, or as if peculiar life forms were trapped and writhing within its implacable density.

SIX

A secret chain of dream worlds

And then it occurred to me that all the people from near and distant places, who had received an impulse computed in direct relation to how long it would take them to arrive here, all these ghosts and revenants, all those who were strangers amongst us, who listened to our heartbeats, who knew the inclination of our politics, our hunger, our dreams and our rage – they had all come answering the call of a forthcoming spirit-child birth, a triple birth, one for each sphere.

I have heard it said that there are two shadow worlds to every reality. I have also heard it said that every possibility is a reality existing simultaneously with the real.

A nation was being born in our area. Somewhere else an avatar was dying, and another one was ready to take her place in an endless secret chain of dream worlds which, at the right time, explodes into a new way, a world dream. And the dreamers are often wholly unaware of the forces they are bringing into our lower world of the earth, for great truths take time to manifest in our leaden reality. And when they do manifest, their effect through time is never entirely pure.

SEVEN

Where does a birth begin?

Where does a birth begin? It begins with a death. Things have to vacate the space we haven't properly used, in order for new things to be born. It begins with a death, and that night we heard plangent dirges in the air, foretelling a death in advance. Meanwhile Madame Koto floated in the incense and cedar wood smoke of her ritual atmosphere, burning in her beauty. Meanwhile, the yellow dust of karmic angels grew in her spirit.

There was much revelry and parrot squawkings from the bar. We heard many voices. Human voices. Animal voices. Voices of the dead who had borrowed human bodies to attend the homecoming. Even the nasal voices of spirits who never get used to the restricted noses of human beings.

There were many languages too. Languages totally incomprehensible to us. Languages whose occasional word we understood. Languages from the extreme reaches of the earth. The languages of Inuits and Pygmies, of ancient Greece and Babylonia, of Celts and Indians. Languages of the dead and the unborn. Languages of power and dreams. But the revenants had no trouble understanding one another in Madame Koto's bar.

I stood amongst the onlookers. We were all silent in the face of such a powerful display of alliance. I could occasionally understand the language of the dead, the spirits, and the half-humans. These numinous pilgrims from the underworld of our history had come to pay their respects to the great Madame Koto. Whorehouse owner. Power broker. Priestess of a new and terrible way.

They had all come to celebrate this woman who had managed to transform herself completely under the gaze of our history. They came to ritually infuse her, to show their extensive allegiances on the night before the great rally, and to widen our world for the birth of their ascendancy. They came to honour her, to seal the pacts of secret organizations for the satisfactory division of this world's territories.

They came, and stayed for two days. As always we were on the outside, looking in at a bewildering reality.

EIGHT

The last feast

On the third day Madame Koto, wearing a crown of rock-beads, held a great feast. It was an extravagant affair. Five bulls, three cows, seven goats and countless chickens were slaughtered, cooked and served. Whole areas of our street were filled up with collapsible chairs and tables. Throughout that evening it was as though a market-place and a bazaar had materialized in the street.

It was a feast of monumental proportions. Chicken bones, skulls of dead antelopes, broken beer bottles were scattered and strewn about the place. Whiffs of oriental melodies, haunting pipe organs, speaking of last suppers, floated across the yellow clouds of twilight. The guests were rowdy and drunken. They argued about divisions of power, tribal rivalries, territorial control. They quarrelled about their loyalties, their achievements, their interpretations of the new African way, age-old disagreements surfacing. The air resounded with the clash of their myths and ideologies.

Madame Koto tried to include everyone in the feast. That evening she sent for Mum, to ask her forgiveness before the moment of the great rally. She sent bowls of rice and aromatic chicken and antelope meat round to all the rooms, in all the compounds, asking for our forgiveness and support. No one replied.

As night approached, the rowdiness of the guests mysteriously diminished. Only the drunken musicians kept up their performances. Sitting at different tables, they played their conflicting music, competing with one another, answering dirges with praise-songs, assaulting threnodies with hunting songs, attacking the epic cycles of the seasoned kora-players with the withering satires of the harmonica-weavers, undermining the mnemonic feats of dynastic musicians with songs of lust and songs of work. Their different kinds of music fought one another in their hidden ideologies and world-views. They warred with music, carrying on where the main guests had left off. They sang of death and power, conquest and courage. They sang of illustrious kings and heroic families. They brought to us the rich river of all our songs, histories and philosophies. They salted the air with proverbs. They sang of birth and initiation, but they did not sing of love. They sang of politics, but they did not sing of the poor and the suffering.

I did not see it myself, but it was said that as night swept over from the diminishing forest a yellow bird flew across Madame Koto's head and shat on her crown of rock-beads. But I did notice when the musicians fell silent, as if the wind and the night were cancelling out their music, banishing it from the air. Some say that when the yellow bird flew off into the darkening sky one of the guests from Bamako cried:

'A BAD OMEN!'

I heard the silence which followed. Soon the wind

was all I heard as it blew over the guests, their eyes both drunken and aware.

Madame Koto, who was standing holding a bowl of stew, sat down and then stood up again. Some of the women rushed over to clean the birdshit from her crown, but Madame Koto made a gesture which stopped them. Then she began to make her speech.

She spoke, but her words were silent. She cleared the rusty organ of her throat. She spoke again, but her words were still silent. A curious premonition spread over the guests. The night became deeper. The wind whistled softly over the trees. And then the oddest thing happened.

The women closest to Madame Koto started singing and, without reason, she began to weep.

At first, no one moved. No one comforted her. The women sang and Madame Koto wept noisily, banging her arms on the table, throwing food on the ground, her bangles rattling. The women stopped singing and then she became still. She wept in silence, her face contorted, tears glistening on her oily cheeks.

The lights were kind to her. The lamps heightened the sadness of her ripe beauty. When she stopped weeping she got up and tried to speak again. She opened her mouth but instead of words a great gust of animal pain poured out and she held her stomach and staggered backwards, falling over a chair. She got up again, limping. Her women rushed to her, surrounded her, and led her to the house, while rainclouds gathered above us all. As they led her away a musician, striking up on the kora, began to sing, in a voice that pierced our chests, a single line of a proverb, over and over again:

'If you look back, pilgrim, you will twist your neck . . .'

And when the musician stopped singing, Madame Koto was gone. There was a brief silence in which the wind whispered insurrective words over the air, words which Dad would later pluck from the spirit of the times.

And the monkeys that had been spared sacrifice because of some unique quality they possessed – the talent for mockery, or prophecy – and the peacocks and the birds in domed cages, all began to gibber and squawk. I could not understand their language. But a wind of madness started up from their horrid noises and all the guests were struck silent by the premonitions flying about in the blue darkness of the feast.

Not long afterwards, a message came from Madame Koto. The message travelled round the guests and their faces changed at the prospect of their long journeys home. Madame Koto had insisted that the guests carry on feasting without her. She charged them to continue with their momentous task, their great work: to multiply their influence and power over the many spheres.

The party ended abruptly. Those who were drunk, who had eaten too much, and who had a long way to go, became aware that their pilgrimage was over.

That night Madame Koto remained alone in her room, with her illness worsening, and her foot erupting with pain. And while the agony of her pregnancy approached the unbearable, the guests outside soberly gathered themselves together to depart for their distant homes.

NINE

The wind whispers insurrective words on the air

On that third night the visitants left. They came with gifts and left in silence. They returned to their shadowy worlds where history is a perpetual wound that grows on the faces of the people, and where good dreams for the future barely stir the wind or the dust. They returned to their crepuscular worlds where suffering, centuries old, had coalesced into severe religions of many roads and many ways. Each way crying with questions. Each road drawing blood from the feet of men and women, pilgrims who know not why they travel, what they seek, or what the golden doors of the grave hold for them.

The visitants also left lethal shadows in the spaces sifted by the aroma of forest herbs. They had come with eyes of impenetrable indifference. They did not notice the rest of us; they did not notice those who are always on the outside, looking in. Within the computation of their gaze, we did not exist. They would rule segments of our world for a long time and never see us. Their shadows would lurk in our air, locked in pockets of our consciousness, awaiting a terrible exorcism.

And when the visitants left, our world would not

be the same: dust from their terrible dreams would always trouble us. That evening Dad began to speak for the first time of revolution. It was a word he had plucked from the air. It was a new word and I saw strange stars in the sky whenever he uttered it. Throughout the evening, whenever he commented on the visitations we had all witnessed, he used the word as if it were a new punch he had invented. He kept punching the empty spaces of our room, muttering gibberish, firing up his spirit. When we asked him what he was doing he began to speak of preparing for a higher fight, a greater struggle, transforming all the lessons and techniques of boxing into the realms of true revolution.

That night, when he was silent, when Mum paced up and down the darkened room, with the smoke of mosquito coils dense in the air, I heard the spirits who wandered through our living space passing the word to one another. I heard them muttering it, making songs out of it, playing with it, shortening and lengthening its syllables, handing it over from one voice to another, till the word floated on the air, as in a barely audible choir. And then everything fell silent as Dad spoke again.

'Revolution. It takes time and one second.'

I didn't understand him. He never mentioned the word again. It was as if he somehow understood that it was necessary to utter the word, to release it into the air, and then to let it descend into a potent silence, like a seed into the fertile earth, to die in order to be reborn with power and direction. It was as if he needed to utter the word, let it grow in the air, let it take on voice and life, and let it float in all the realms of reality, weighed down and gathering force like a rain cloud, till the word found its perfect conditions to be real and right in its manifestation. Then, and only then, as technicians of the fighting spirit, would we rise for the wonderful battle and the storming of the high walls of deadly and selfish powers till our lives had been changed into something beautiful for ever.

When I lit a candle there was a sweet sadness on Dad's face. I knew he was thinking that he might not live to see the day when we would be free enough to join the great transforming men and women of the earth.

TEN

A river of contending dreams

That night, while we slept, I found myself circling
Madame Koto's room. Her spirit drew me inwards. I
spun in the vortex of her illness, her erupting
nightmares, her agony. She was alone in a mint cool
place, silk beneath her, graven images all around her,
and five red candles alight in silver niches. At the
heart of her solitude I saw a vision growing.

She dreamt that her children had stabbed her from
behind while she was walking through a silver forest.

Then she dreamt that she was giving birth to a
nation. An unruly nation, bursting with diversity. A
bad dream of a nation, with potential for waste and
failure as great as its enormous resources, its fabulous possibilities. She did nothing to alter the dream.
She could affect our sleep, and work powerful spells
on our innermost natures, but could not transform
her dream into something higher. And we who
tuned into the resonances of her spirit were infected
with this failure to change our dreams. And because
of her we took our dreams as realities, our realities as
dreams. We read our omens as prophecies, which
became facts. Those who cannot transform their bad
dreams should be rudely awoken.

I tried to wake her up, screaming the word

revolution into the vents of her spirit. But I became aware at that same moment that the people of the fertile land were also dreaming the nation into being, and not questioning the nature of their dreams. They were dreaming their futures in it. And I was knocked about in the wordless multitude. The river of dreams was without direction. The dreams were too many, too different, too contradictory: the nation was composed not of one people but of several mapped and bound into one artificial entity by Empire builders. The multitude of dreams became a feverish confluence of contending waters. The fever affected the dreamers, made their dreams more intense. All those who dreamt the nation created it even as they dreamed – all those who wanted their gods to prevail, their tribes to rule, their ideas to become paramount, their ideologies to wield the lash, their vengeance to be made manifest, their enemies destroyed, their crop yields greater than all others, their houses the biggest, their children the most powerful, their families the masters, their clans to gain the eternal ascendance of fame, their affiliations to rise the highest, their wars to be fought, their secret societies to gain the golden seat, their souls alone to know contentment, their mouths alone to taste the rich honeycombs of the land. They all created the nation as they dreamt it. All those who dreamt such narrow dreams imprisoned us who came later in their fevered steel webs of selfishness and greed.

ELEVEN

Contending dreams (2):
god of the insects

My spirit was reeling from the violence of the dreams of the new nation when I found myself in what I thought was a cooling place. I found myself in the great white house of the Governor-General.

The Governor-General lay asleep in his spacious room. He was dreaming that Africa was inhabited not by human beings but by a monstrous variation of black insects. The insects hindered his complete domination of the continent. In his dream he was surrounded by a jungle where primitive drums tapped out the ritual signals of cannibalism. Deeper into the jungle he went, till he saw his daughter bound by natives in a clearing. He screamed, and his dream changed. Then he saw the black insects everywhere, gigantic in size. They had the faces of his servants and watchmen. They had horrid wings and wore big boots. The insects descended on him and he fired a shot from his double-barrelled rifle, and the air cleared. He turned over on the bed.

With the blood leaking out of the numerous places on his body where the insects had bitten him, the Governor-General then dreamt of a luxurious road over the ocean, a road that was fed from all parts of

Africa. A macadam road of fine crushed diamonds and sprinkled silver and laminated topaz. A road that gave off the sweet songs of mermaids and nereids. Beneath this marvellous road there were dead children and barbarous fetishes, savage masks and broken spines, threaded veins and matted brains, decayed men and embalmed women. It was a road made from the teeth and skulls of slaves, made from their flesh and woven intestines. In the Governor-General's dream this was a heroic and beautiful road, a milestone in the annals of human accomplishment.

There was a gigantic sign at the mouth of the road that read:

HEART OF WORLD

It was indeed a splendid road. It had been built by the natives, supervised by the Governor-General. He dreamt that on this beautiful road all Africa's wealth, its gold and diamonds and diverse mineral resources, its food, its energies, its labours, its intelligence would be transported to his land, to enrich the lives of his people across the green ocean.

Deep in his happy sleep the Governor-General dreamt of taking the Golden Stool of the Ashante king, the thinking masks of Bamako, the storytelling rocks of Zimbabwe, the symphonic Victoria Falls, the shapely tusks of Luo elephants, the slumbering trees of immemorial forests, the languorous river Niger, the enduring pyramids of the Nile, all the deltas rich with oil, the mountains rifted with metals apocalyptic, the mines shimmering with gold, the ancestral hills of Kilimanjaro, the lexicon of African

rituals, the uncharted hinterland of Africa's unconquerable spirits. He dreamt of taking Africa's
timber-like men, their pomegranate women, their
fertile sculpture, their plaintive songs, their spirit-
worlds, their forest animals, their sorceries, their
myths and their strong dances. He dreamt that the
natives would transport all these resources tangible
and intangible, on their heads, or on litters, walking
on the great road, in an orderly single file, across the
Atlantic Ocean, for three thousand miles. He dreamt
of having all these riches transported to his land.
Some of them would be locked up in air-conditioned
basements, for the benefit of Africa, because Africans
did not know how to make the best use of them, and
because his people could protect them better. He
dreamt of having them in the basement of a great
museum, to be studied, and to aid, in some obscure
way, the progress of the human race.

He dreamt of the great road on which all the fruits
and riches of African lives would be directed
towards sweetening the sleep of his good land. He
did not dream of the hunger he would leave behind.

At the end of this momentous road, there was
another sign, which read:

BRAVE NEW DARKNESS

An insect flew above the Governor-General's
sleeping form. It settled on his eyelid, and drew
blood from his vision. The particulars of his dream
changed again. In the new dream he became a
luminous god who needed to drink souls and suck
blood in order to regenerate the human race. He

became a radiant demiurge who needed the impure to maintain his purity. He became a sun-god who had to devour the primitive in order to create paradise. The blood of the continent was the precise elixir needed to sustain his divine status in the universe of humanity. In his dream he sucked out the blood of the natives of the continent and he drank in the very soul of the continent itself. Then he spun a fine golden web which divided and enmeshed the mighty land. Then he infected the natives with his deism. He made them his worshippers. He made them want to recreate themselves in his image, and to suck the blood of their own kind, for the benefit of his divine status, and for his people across the mythic ocean.

His dreams shocked him but he made no effort to change them to something better. Those who cannot transform their bad dreams which might become real, should be rudely awoken.

The Governor-General dreamed on. And while he dreamt, the karmic dust of angels lay waiting in the universal chambers of Time.

The Governor-General's dreams sowed misery in the realms where dreams become real. But he lived long enough to witness the first of the ambiguous harvests of the karmic dust of angels.

TWELVE

Contending dreams (3):
good disguised as bad

When the insect had finished drawing blood from his eyelid it flew over to his lips. It was beginning to draw blood from his utterances, when the Governor-General woke up suddenly. He was drenched in sweat that he thought was blood. In his disorientation he saw the white walls covered in black insects. He fled from the house, half-naked, screaming into the night, startling me.

I found myself floating in the air of dreams, circling in the crowded spaces of the atmosphere, till a gentle breeze blew me to the old woman in the forest. She was dreaming of a new breed of human beings. The creator-god was melting down the wicked forms of existing men and women, and inventing better ones, with finer minds and a universal sense of humour. She dreamt good dreams that were disguised as bad ones. She dreamt of the chaos to come, of the short reign of colonial domination, of the fevers and the awakening spirits which would break out on the nation. She dreamt of the suffering to come which would either waken people to the necessity of determining their lives or make them dependents of world powers, diminished for ever. She dreamt of new forms of government, based on the old, open to inspiration from all over the world. She dreamt of new fictions and a new poetics, new ideas sprung from the old earth of our ancient philosophies and traditions. She dreamt many years in advance, into the new millennium, when the ambiguous gifts of karmic angels had enfeebled the former world powers and when the salvation of the earth would be in the hands of the righteous peoples of this world, unknowing custodians of the best secrets of life. She dreamt of an age of fire, when the sun had moved closer to the earth and burned through the protective atmospheres. Her dream made my spirit hot.

THIRTEEN

The angel and the shrine

I spun higher on the currents of the dreaming land. I kept trying to get back into my body, but I found myself again in Madame Koto's room. She had been awoken from her bad dreams by a crackling candle. Awoken into a deeper dream. She heard a heavenly voice singing an intense melody behind her. At the same moment that she looked back, and twisted her neck, she realized that she was staring into the terrifyingly beautiful eyes of a yellow angel.

Madame Koto became aware of the abnormal heat of her space. The yellow angel stared with radiant eyes at Madame Koto's fetishes and masquerades. It stared at the great female image with red stones for eyes and reflecting sunglasses, a machete in one hand, and peacock feathers sticking out of its head-dress. The blood of animals and countless libations glistened on its body. The angel gazed at this image of a secret religion.

Madame Koto was so terrified at the incandescent presence of the angel that, not knowing whether she was awake or dreaming, she cried out, and backed away in horror. But the yellow angel embraced her with its flaming wings of gold. Madame Koto turned her head away, her heart bursting into flames.

A moment later, she was alone. She was on her bed. Her body bristled with the low crackling flames of gold ash. She slept with her head buried under the pillows, her neck twisted, weeping in silence.

FOURTEEN

Resilient ash

I slept badly that night. My head ached with feverish afterglows.

I saw the angel hovering over our area, disturbing the spirit of the blind old man, who would later come out in yellow pustules.

The angel lingered over our street, subtly altering our dreams, planting unconquerable alternative ways deep in our souls, sprinkling resilient ash over our sleeping bodies, strewing the white powder of music and beauty in our hearts, and spreading unknown regenerative powers in our blood – so that we might survive all the suffering that was to come.

FIFTEEN

The ambush of reality

In the morning the golden glare of the sun woke us up. I noticed that Dad had changed. His spirit, about to be broken by the suffering to come, had become purer. The gold-ash staining his face from his prison experience had changed into a green furry growth. Mum too had become different. She had somehow become more fiery, and more concentrated.

In spite of the fact that the golden glare of sunlight woke us up, it wasn't going to be a normal day. Normality had long ago fled from our lives. A new fever would now run in our veins and in our days.

As we prepared for the new day, we heard the talking drums, the loud hailers, the flourish of instruments, the clash of metal, and the piercing voice of the dawn-criers telling us that the event had arrived. Powerful nightmares and unresolved histories had accelerated time. Before we knew it the moment of the much-delayed rally was upon us. It ambushed us in the midst of our dreams.

III

III

BOOK SIX

ONE

Draw a deep breath for a new song

I am a spirit-child wandering in an unhappy world.
Draw a deep breath, for my new song is pitched to
the wings of those birds of omen, birds that fly into
new dawns, changing with their flight into the forms
of future ages.

TWO

Call of the political rally

After a great dream often comes great chaos. The failure to follow the best dreams of our lives all the way to the sea might be one of the secret agonies of angels.

With the call of the rally another new cycle launched itself in our universe. Without knowing it we entered an era of implacable chaos. While we slept we had strayed into the groove of time where the raging heart of our problems took the form of nightmares. The nightmares came alive amongst us.

All through the afternoon of the new day Dad went round bewildered by the low green growth on his face. He was also confused by supporters of the Party of the Rich. They had overrun the streets. They were everywhere, in terrifying numbers. They poured out from the familiar houses. They materialized, from all over our area, like a previously invisible army.

They had been sleeping amongst us, seemingly innocent. And now, with the call of the rally, they thundered on the roads, singing war songs. Trucks and lorries, grinding up and down our streets, blared the party's anthem. And crackling loud hailers urged us all to vote for the party, the only party that would guarantee stability and prosperity. We had heard those promises a thousand times before. We had heard them from thugs.

Up and down our area there were clashes between warring factions. People bolted their doors. Children were forbidden to go out. Those who had heard about the troubles in advance had fled to their villages. Very few of the people we knew stayed to witness the violence of the new season. But Dad, spoiling for a fight that would redefine him, went about the place denouncing the party, calling them cowards and bullies for using threats to compel people to vote for them.

It was a day of noises. Drums and trumpets fuelled the energies of party vigilantes. Gangs of thick-necked men ran everywhere with flags in their hands and political banners that spoke of victory in advance. The road was exhausted that day with all the footfalls, all the thudding and pounding. Crowds of women, wearing the matching dresses of the party, poured up the street, gathering supporters, singing party songs. We heard rumours that the rival party, the Party of the Poor, was staging a rally of its own nearby. We saw vanloads of fierce-eyed police-men and soldiers in battle fatigues. They came to control the events, to manage the crowds, and to combat any opposing factions. They came with guns and whips, batons and tear gas.

In the afternoon, as we sat in the room, listening to the noises of terror all around, Dad said:

'The strangest things will happen today.'

We were silent, listening to the hundreds of footsteps pouring in one direction. We listened to the organized chanting of marketwomen, to the fury of party henchmen and street-runners.

Dad said none of us should attend the rally. He sat in his chair, his muscles straining his shirt, his eyes shut. The green growth was clear on his face. He kept working his jaws, trying to contain his insurgent energies, sweating. Mum was silent. Flies buzzed in the room. It was a little dark. As I sat there, watching Dad, something came in through the door like a luminous breeze. After a while I heard a voice, in an enchanted whisper, say:

'The rainbows are coming.'

It was Ade, my dead friend. I looked around the room but couldn't see him.

'The six-headed spirit has been asking after you,' he said, with sublime mischief in his voice.

'Why?'

'Why what, Azaro?' asked Mum.

'Because you owe him something,' replied Ade.

'Lie!'

'I've never lied to you, my son,' said Mum.

'You're going to see my father today,' came Ade, obliquely.

'Where?'

'On stage.'

'Performing?'

'No.'

'Doing what then?'

Mum towered over me.

'Breaking the planks.'

'Why?'

'Azaro, what's wrong with you? Are you talking to yourself again?'

'No.'

'Yes,' Ade said, in delight, trying to confuse me.

'Why?' I asked again.

'Why what?'

'Why will your father be breaking the planks?'

Mum gently placed her hand on my cheek. Dad turned his huge head towards me.

'So that the birds can escape,' Ade replied, eventually.

'Escape to where?'

'Shut up, Azaro,' growled Dad.

'To the sky, to the stars, where they belong.'

I was silent.

'But your father will see blood today.'

'No, he won't,' I said.

'Yes, he will,' Ade said.

Mum lifted me up and turned me round in the air.

'If you're going to talk like that – GO AWAY!' I shouted.

Mum lowered me, held me tight and began whispering sweet words in my right ear.

'Go away!' I cried. 'Go away.'

Mum held me tight, whispering gentle words, surrounding me with warmth. After a while I sensed in the new silence that the spirit of my friend was gone. But I listened hard, waiting to see if he would speak again. I shut my eyes, deep in my listening. I heard a distant wind raging over the trees. I heard all the political noises and all the cries. And then I heard fourteen feet, moving against the direction of the single-minded crowd, coming towards our house.

'People are coming here!' I cried.

'What people?' asked Dad.

253

'Women,' I said.

'What women?'

Then I heard that sweet impish voice again.

'Women who will vanish,' Ade whispered to me.

'I don't know,' I said.

Mum put me down, went to the door, looked out, and saw nothing.

'Azaro is talking rubbish,' she said.

I waited for the footsteps; I waited for Ade's elusive spirit-child voice. We sat in silence. I ached from all the buffeting in my sleep. I felt bruised all over, but there were no signs of bruising.

Ade didn't speak any more. My feet yearned to wander. The songs of the road were calling me. Suddenly there was a knock on the door. After a moment, the Photographer came in, with his lizard-like head and suspicious eyes. He was carrying his camera and his black bag of photographic equipment.

'Why is everyone quiet in here?' he asked. 'And why is the room so dark, eh?'

No one said anything to him.

'The world is full of strangers today,' he said. 'I saw them bringing truck-loads of supporters. I think there is going to be war, eh?'

Dad stared at him darkly. Mum offered him beer. He drank contemplatively. The silence lasted till we heard footsteps outside our door. Then in came the rowdy voices of the seven women who had followed Mum on her campaign to free Dad from prison. As if we had seen them only a moment ago, they entered our room without knocking. They were arguing noisily. They had come to ask Mum's support for one of their husbands who was a trade unionist and who had been imprisoned for taking part in a strike against the government. Dad listened in silence, without moving. The Photographer perked up instantly, offering to go with them and publicize their new campaign.

'But only after the rally,' he said. 'Or I will lose my job.'

The women showed no interest in him. Mum went to the bathroom to get changed. When she came back she seemed like one prepared for battle. Without a word, like a soldier who is grateful to repay in action an outstanding debt, and with the seven women still arguing about the best method of carrying out their campaign, Mum set out with them into the street quivering with events. The Photographer hurriedly finished his drink and rushed out after the eight women.

'They won't get far,' was all Dad said, grumpily.

I watched him in the silence. I watched him twist and contort in the chair. I watched him as he suddenly began to groan. He stayed in an inexplicable agony, for an hour. I lay down and fell asleep to the noises of the rally, the echoing voices, the harsh war-songs, the clanging of metal against metal, the rude banging on doors, the thundering feet, and the frenzied drum-rolls beating out the syntax of a violent language. Suddenly I heard Dad cry out. I jumped up and saw him sweating. Muttering something about the leopard, he came over to me, and growled into my face.

'If you leave this room today I will flog you with my iron belt, you hear?'

I didn't know he had one. I nodded. He strode out of the room, locked the door, and took the key. I didn't wait long before I crawled out through the window.

The road was calling me into its fevered dream. The road sang all around me, waking from its sleep, with eruptions everywhere. The road called to all of us. I heard its call with a special lust.

I set off down the street. Houses and stalls seemed smaller. My eyes were misty with odd things that kept breaking on my vision. Answering the call of the rally, I followed the crowds to the place where our nightmares were becoming concrete in the hard world of objects.

THREE

The dead carpenter

Without any idea where the rally was being held, and confused by the numerous routes the crowds took, I followed a group of women who seemed to be going for the spectacle and the prospect of sales. They had trays of provisions on their heads and children tied to their backs. The main road was packed with people, all pouring in one direction. There was chaos all around, as if an alien army were in occupation, or as if a civil war had broken out.

Light glinted on metal. Dense smoke pervaded the air. The crowds were in such an intense state of expectation that I heard the sizzling of their hopes and desires, the churning of their hunger.

Further up the road, in the midst of a dense crowd, I saw the dead carpenter. He was taller than almost everyone else, glowing in his white suit, waving his fists in the air. I saw him shouting. The crowd jostled him. I struggled to get to him, but the crowd pushed me across a gutter that ran alongside the road. By the time I got back to the main stream of the crowd, the dead carpenter had disappeared from view.

At an intersection, I saw Madame Koto. She was

257

resplendent in her gold-bordered dress, and surrounded by fierce women and noisy men. After a night of fitful sleep, with a pulled tendon in her neck, she couldn't move her head very much. She shouldn't have gone out that day, but the call of the rally, and the central role she had manipulated for herself in the festivities afterwards, made it necessary for her to go out into the changing world. She had a white towel round her neck. Her forehead was creased with agony. Her eyes had deepened, and her head was held high in the stiff dignity of pain.

FOUR

The great rally

The evening made the faces of the crowd into masks.
There was a light wind and the universal commotion
of traffic. Madame Koto got into a van with her
protectors; the van drove through the crowd, cutting
a path through the density of bodies.

People were talking about how their lives could be
improved, their dreams steaming within their spirits'
agony. I felt dizzy at the sheer number of people and
terrified by the heated smells of their intolerable
lives.

Madame Koto's van disappeared among the
bodies. Further up I saw Helen, the beggar girl, and
her troupe of beggars. They were huddling in front
of an unfinished bungalow. She showed no sign of
recognizing me. She had a vengeful glimmer in her
eyes. Her appearance had changed; she was dressed
entirely in red and looked more like an incarnate
goddess of war. She looked sad and wasted, ill and
lean, and more beautiful than a woman can be,
among so much suffering. When she saw me, as if I
were a sign, she made a motion to her band of
beggars, her much multiplied companions. They set
off down a side road and I followed them through
the maze of bodies, through the labyrinths of streets

in the ever-expanding ghetto. I followed them till I had the feeling that I was lost. Darkness was falling over everything, and wide-eyed I wandered into another terrain. I wandered into a space crowded with thousands of people. I had wandered into the rally.

High above the crowd, there was a large wooden platform with microphones and bright lights. Hundreds of cars were parked all over the place. The crowds jostled and fought. The air was turbulent with a million voices, shouts, songs, chants and blarings from loudspeakers and bullhorns. Soldiers with guns paraded the edges of the crowd. They also had batons and canes. Policemen with riot helmets and guns and horsewhips were there too. Everywhere I turned I met a wall of giant bodies. People who were so tall that their beards were like darkened leaves of a tree. There was absolutely no escape from the crush and crowding. I was tiny among giant beings. I found myself struggling for space with people's feet, raw and bleeding, ridden with road-worms, eaten by the salt rains and acidic contents of marsh roads.

As it got darker, the crowd seemed stranger. They seemed like alien beings, visitants from other spheres, dense retributive spheres – so solid and impassive were their bunched faces, so intense and dull were their bulging eyes. The darkness made them hybridous. Men with twelve arms, women with four heads, adults with six feet, all wearing different shoes. I saw midgets crawling between the legs of the crowd; I saw pickpockets and thieves robbing those too intent on the events unfolding up on the great stand.

A bizarre fiesta was in progress all around. All types were present: carpenters, stock-fish sellers, cloth traders, boisterous hawkers, undiscovered witches and wizards, old men and women, young men and girls, marketwomen, fishermen, butchers, mechanics, builders, truck pushers, indeterminate members of secret fraternities, layabouts, beggars, thugs, thieves, journalists, prostitutes, soldiers, and men so hungry that they brought starch-bread with them and ate with angry motions of their jaws as they watched the proceedings on the great lighted stage of the rally.

The darkness made us anonymous, made us amorphous, dissolved our faces and bodies. I felt my mind melting into the stream of anonymous beings. My feelings were no longer my own. The impulses that flowed swaying through the great animal of the crowd, flowed through me, and dissolved my emotions in a brackish tide of barely restrained fevers. There was darkness everywhere. The darkness made us anonymous. But the lighted stage conferred individuality on the people gathered there, dressed in the splendid attire of the party. The flags of the party flew high, spotlighted. Its banners billowed in the wind, displaying its emblem of power. The standards, too, were proud in the wind.

'WE WILL CONQUER THIS COUNTRY!' bellowed one of the men into a microphone.

The loudspeakers crackled. His voice dissolved into the screeching volume, as he continued:

'VICTORY IS OURS ALREADY. WE HAVE WON. WE

BRING POWER TO THE PEOPLE. WE BRING WEALTH AND STABILITY. THOSE WHO VOTE FOR US WILL ENJOY, THOSE WHO DON'T WILL EAT DUSTBINS!'

A loud cheering spread out from the front of the crowd. The crowd amplified the cheering, modified it, hissed against it, dissented, agreed and shouted till the road began to rock gently beneath us. No one noticed.

The loudspeakers behaved oddly. It was as if ghosts had entered the instruments and were playing mischievous games with human voices. Speaker after speaker came to the microphone, made long speeches, sweating under the glaring lights, and we couldn't understand anything they said. Their words changed before they reached us. We heard things that insulted our hunger, and derided our patience. We heard them call us fools for trying to exercise our right to democratic choice, for trying to be discriminating. We heard ourselves called idiots for expecting the other party to represent an alternative. I was no longer sure what party was holding the rally; I seemed to be at several rallies at once, an underworld of negative rallies.

The politicians on the stage were all dressed in similar attire, they sweated, and none of them made sense. And they all spoke as if we were not particularly important to the results of the elections. It soon became clear that – for the speakers – we didn't exist. We, the crowd, were the ghosts of history. We were the empty bodies on whose behalf the politicians and soldiers rule; we were not real. We could not communicate our desires save by the intensity of our cheering or hissing. We were shadows in the world of power; the mere spectators of phenomena, the victims of speeches. We were meant only to listen, never to speak. We were not meant to feel or to think or argue or dissent. Assent was all we were good for. And our faces, which the night made masks of, finally found their true identity in the world of power; we were statues, rows and crowdings of sculpted bodies. We were bodies without urgencies. From the viewpoint of the stage, that is how we seemed.

Crushed among the torsos of men, I found it difficult to see. I had to be carried by a neighbour who recognized me. Then I saw, for the first time, the bizarre theatre of politics, the magic tricks of power, the power of illusion. The stage was arrayed in lights, as if a great magician was about to perform wonders for our hungry consumption.

Oh, the host of dreams in the yellow lights of the air, the illuminated midges, the fireflies, the moths and the shadows of the multitudinous gathering. And on the stage – politicians with sunglasses and animal-headed walking sticks. They were surrounded by sorcerers in white smocks and feathered headgear, amulets round their necks. The sorcerers kept waving flywhisks, uttering incantations.

Party candidates came forward and spoke into the microphones, drenching us in amorphous decibels. The crowd rocked; the neighbour who had been carrying me on his shoulder put me down; and the chaos of the crowd soon separated us. I pushed my way through the nobbled knees of adults and I came to a wiry tree and climbed up its branches and sat there, perched, looking over the crowd of five thousand heads, watching the stage. And then, suddenly, a blast of hot air knocked my head backwards and I saw a host of birds flying madly through the atmosphere. I felt myself falling. When I opened my eyes everything had changed. Everything had become inexplicably hotter and darker, more intense, as if the collective dreams of the hungry were about to combust.

FIVE

Shadow beings in all the empty spaces

I could see the stage more clearly now and could make out the forms of shadow beings and spirits who saw us but whom we couldn't see. I could make them out in the spaces between the people on the lighted platform. Then I noticed that there were shadow beings in all the empty spaces, and even in the spaces that we occupied with our bodies. The shadow beings were part of the crowd, tangential to everything, yet living their lives in spaces filled by a thousand pressured bodies. The realization made me cry out, but no one heard me. Lights flashed on the dais, and I saw the Photographer perched on a wall. Then for a while I didn't see the shadow beings any more. Instead I noticed Madame Koto on the stage, amongst the resplendent politicians.

Then I saw the blind old man with a host of sorcerers, and I became aware of the focus of his role. He had an enchanted flywhisk and charms round his neck. And he was orchestrating certain events backstage. His true role was supreme; he was a political sorcerer and controller of phenomena. While the clouds gathered above us, turning yellow in the darkening sky, while they erupted, exploding not rain but dark air, I realized that the blind old man was holding our spirit in check, holding back the rain, filling the spaces with dread darkness, filling our bodies with the dreams of his party's domination.

On all spheres the ascending powers were waging their battles for our consent. In the spirit-spaces the blind old man was unleashing a host of fears and shadows and forms that whispered submission into our bodies. Meanwhile the other sorcerers fought off the counterspells of the other political party, fought off their rain-bringing powers, diverted the blasts of thunder they hurled at the dais. They sent out protective shields to repel the lightning that flashed over the platform, aimed at the presidential candidate. And they sealed off the spaces so that no demons could slip into the bodies of the politicians and fill their heads with nonsense, and make them start to say the wrong things on stage.

And while we gathered there, ordinary citizens in the presence of invisible powers, all the higher spaces around us were battlezones of insurgent disembodied fires. In the air, I saw the forms of witches and wizards, sorcerers and herbalists, manufacturers of reality, dreamers of spells and rallying songs. They were all in violent confrontation, hurling blasts and counterblasts at one another. I saw the shadow bullets, the air of fire, winged lightning and spears of spirit-substance. I heard the jagged words and the animal cries.

A whole new domain erupted before my gaze. And the battle for reality, blazing over the quiet

spaces above our heads, took some time before it
became manifest on the level of concrete things.

SIX

The insurrective laughter
of the dead

On the stage, discreetly amongst the new rulers of the new age, stood the Governor-General. I recognized him immediately because of the invisible black insects clinging to his body. He looked so innocent in his grey suit. I saw him scratching himself, unaware of the black insects. Then I understood why sometimes, without willing it or even knowing, I found myself in his dreams or his nightspace. For he too was a manufacturer, a retailer of phenomena. It may be because of his presence on the stage that the impish spirits of our nightspaces came awake.

The Photographer had somehow moved closer to the stand. I saw the flash of his camera. Spirits took form in the flash and gathered round the Governor-General. They climbed on him, investigated him, and studied him. The spirits looked curiously at his striped tie, and fell about laughing when he came to the microphone and made a short speech about something which we missed altogether. The spirits would have continued their exploration of his body-smells and shadow-smells, but for the flourish of drums which startled their impish investigations. The crash of cymbals and the blast of trumpets announced to us all that the extraordinary spectacle meant to seduce us into assent had begun.

Midgets with fiery paint on their faces, in lines of sixes, came dancing on stage. Their machetes burned with antimony. After them came the beautiful women of the land. They were half-naked and they sweated. They had ruffles on their ankles and party armbands on their wrists, and they danced with a splendid sexual vigour under the hungry gaze of the crowd. At first, the crowd went wild. The midgets jumped up and down, the music flourished, the loudspeakers screeched, the women danced and flags of party symbolism were carried past by masked figures. A man rode a white horse on stage and blew fire over the heads of the crowd.

'Will all this nonsense feed us?' an angry voice said below me.

The question was unanswered. The moment of grand spectacle had arrived, sowing the whirlwind of wrath. The great rally and the battle for our future had called forth the spirits of the whirlwind, the storm spirits, the spirits of extinct beasts and the shadow beings. They were amongst us. They had come to attend the rally that had shaken the land and unloosened the trapped resentments in the air.

The organizers of the rally then brought on the dancing farmers with their giant yams, pawpaws, massive plastic fruits, symbols of future plenitude under the party's rule.

The crowd fell silent. Then from places in the crowd came strange, isolated laughter. People turned to look at those who were laughing. The dancing farmers seemed both embarrassed and happy to be on stage with their plastic harvest. Their dance took the form of a fertility ritual, and a woman crowned with fruits was at their centre. Those who laughed did so even harder. The laughter was so chilling that it created silence and empty spaces all around. The laughter made the stage look desolate and bare, made the whole spectacle look garish and cheap.

The dancing farmers left the stage. An announcer came on and introduced the next event. Certain members of the crowd laughed at the introduction. The boneless dancers, who could twist their bodies into knots, as if they were made of rubber, came on and performed to the intoxicated uproar of those who laughed. The boneless dancers, with their curious beetle faces and small eyes, performed their unique act, contorting themselves, forming letters of the alphabet, which became the name of the party. No one found it funny except those isolated groups who laughed with bizarre vigour, laughing as if they had no chests, their laughter coming out in uninterrupted bursts, as if they had unlimited air in their lungs.

Then came the firebreathers and the fire-eaters. They jumped up and down the stage. They swallowed the flames on the ends of brands and torches. They spread fire over their bodies and danced in ecstasy. And the weird members of the crowd fell over themselves with laughter, caterwauling in a hilarity that was both exuberant and joyless.

Then came the somersaulters from the salt-creeks. They wore red skirts of raffia and red shorts. Their faces were painted red and white. They did brilliant turns, tumbling over one another. And as they did these extraordinary feats, the strange members of the crowd, who had silenced the rest of us with the sheer insanity of their humour, laughed so hard that they destroyed the balance of the intrepid performers.

One of the somersaulters began with a cartwheel, did two extravagant turns in the air and, with his concentration broken by the odd laughter, landed on his back, lay still for an amazed moment, jumped up suddenly, and began to turn and twist in every direction, as if he were trying to straighten out the queasy disjointedness of his being. Soon he was seen chattering up and down the stage, pulling the queerest faces. Everyone thought he had gone mad. He was quickly whisked from the platform, while the laughter grew worse.

At first I thought that the dreaded spirit of laughter had come amongst us. But as the announcer came on to apologize, and the accompanying laughter turned into something quite fierce, I noticed that all those who were laughing were impeccably well dressed. They wore white hats, white suits, black ties, unimpeachable blouses, proper headties, with gold chains and cowries round their necks. They all had one thing in common: they didn't sweat. Also, they looked too healthy, too rudely healthy, too radiant and well turned-out. Their features were without pain. They were too perfect to be alive, too perfect to be at the rally. They were like people who had no doubts, people who were absolutely certain of their futures. They seemed too well fed and too clear-headed to find anything funny. I thought I recognized the dead carpenter amongst them.

I was trying to get a better look at him when the

agile drummers and the masquerades on stilts came on stage. They danced to rousing tunes neutralized by the laughter from the homogeneous group. The drummers found themselves playing out of harmony, out of tune, and the masquerades on stilts danced awkwardly, with fear in their movements and bewilderment in their steps. They were hurriedly ushered off. Religious leaders, in full regalia, came on and prayed for peace and harmony, while the laughter continued uninterrupted, infectiously sowing insurrection.

The blind old man, waving his fan of eagle feathers in frenzied movements, was in a feverish rage at the edge of the stage. It was only when he turned his blind face towards the crowd, making authoritative motions with his hands, as if banishing waves of madness from his vision, that I began to understand. We had been listening to the terrible laughter of the dead.

I saw them now through the eyes of the blind old man. They were in the front row and on the walls. Some of them stood alone, but most were in groups. And they were scattered everywhere in the crowd. They kept laughing. The dead found everything funny. They laughed at the politicians in their stiffened dignity and forced affability. They laughed at the politicians and their promises, their claims about the glories of the past, the glories to come, and the blessings of their paternal rule. The dead laughed hysterically, raising dark winds around us. They laughed at everything that happened on stage. They laughed at the religious leaders, the rituals perverted to political ends, and at the soldiers who came on stage to appeal for calm. They laughed at the Governor-General who said something in a strangled voice about the future greatness of the country and the hope of continued co-operation in business and culture.

The dead laughed very hard indeed, and the dead carpenter was chief amongst them. I saw children who had died in our street. I saw the adults who had been felled by malnutrition and diseases, by political thugs, and hopelessness. I saw those who had perished in the war in Burma, perished in prisons and road accidents. I saw those who had died of malaria and fear, poverty and milk poisoning, typhoid and rumours, yellow fever and superstition, gut-worms, tape-worms, illnesses of the spirit, madness, famine, drought, weariness, too much acceptance and too much hope. I saw those who had withered away under bad harvests, who had been crushed by cruel laws and enshrined injustices. I also saw those who had died of too much love and too little love, and those who had died under the stars, without a home anywhere on this wide earth. And the more they laughed the more the dead increased amongst us.

The head priest of a renegade church stepped forth to the microphone, and said:

'POLITICS IS NOT A LAUGHING MATTER!'

And the dead drowned him out with their unconquerable hilarious response. It must be said that the rest of us, the living, did not find the events funny. We did not find anything funny at all. The wind turned cold and lashed us with the embers of an undying fire. The heat turned unnatural. A nameless rash broke out within us at the laughter of the dead. It was troubling, but the dead found our solemnity and our impassivity unbearably funny. It was very odd that the dead should find the living funny. But everywhere I looked I saw the dead amongst us, staring at us with wondering eyes, as if they found the fact of our passivity and mental laziness unbelievable and strange. The serious cast of our faces, our acceptance of the intolerable conditions of the world, the shabbiness of our clothes, the hunger in our eyes made them collapse into tears of laughter.

The laughter of the dead created chaos amongst us, stirred our emotions, intensified the rash in our brains, confused the politicians, sent the blind old man into paroxysms of fantastic rage, reduced the mountainous Madame Koto to tears of despair, and made the Governor-General come out in a beetroot-coloured flush. The bizarre laughter of the dead made the sides of our faces nearest our eyes come out in a furry heat. The heat wandered around in our brains. It crawled on the nape of our necks. It made our eyes twitch. It wriggled between our ears, and sizzled at the top of our heads. The cooling winds made us even hotter.

An irritable dark energy bristled amongst us. Then there was a moment's unaccountable silence. Out of the silence came a host of insects, flying beetles and midges, chattering cockroaches with dark wings. They flew over our heads in the darkness. The dark energy faintly illuminated the heads of the crowd. Then suddenly, it seemed as if the whole world was there at the rally, listening to the dark wind over our heads, waiting for something to happen. Thunder-clouds drifted across the faintly yellow sky. I heard the queer syllables of the dead, rousing the silence, and stirring the air with unborn turbulences. Something cracked in the distance and I found the silence of the crowd immensely terrifying. I had started to climb down from the tree when one of the politicians came to the microphone. The loudspeakers blared, and the weird antiphonies of his translated speech started an insurrective murmur.

'THUNDER IS COMING!' someone cried from the crowd.

I looked back and saw a host of white birds sailing through the air. The loudspeakers screeched again, and the politicians looked distressed. The white birds had risen from the brains of the dead. They flew amongst us, flapping their wings in our faces without disturbing the air. The birds became dark thoughts of thunder forefelt. And then, as if their thoughts were as one, the birds rose, turned luminous in the night air, circled the crowd three times, and vanished into the sky. When they vanished, the world became diminished.

SEVEN

The silence of Tigers

The loudspeaker cleared, and we listened to a politician's long-winded speech. The dead listened intently without laughing. The politician spoke for so long that we forgot what he was saying and we ceased to hear him altogether. He went on at such length, turning empty phrases round the microphone, fingering his beads, sweating intensely, that his speech drew the heat to the surface of our skins. He spoke for so long, forgetting what he began with, wandering down circuitous routes of improvisation, stopping off at a hundred speeches we had suffered before, that the sheer length of his utterance nearly made us break out into spontaneous revolt. He made no sense at all. He seemed to be speaking an alien language whose words denied our reality, whose proverbs intensified our hunger, whose grammatical deconstructions filled our heads with empty spaces in which an old rage began to simmer.

It is impossible to tell what might have happened if the politician had been allowed to continue any longer. For by the time a party functionary had been sent to drag him from the microphone our silence had grown immeasurably deep. The heat that his speech had created threatened the rally itself. As they led the politician away he was still talking, still making his speech. Our silence had destroyed him. It is possible that he is still making that speech to this day.

To fill our minds, where restlessness was turning dangerous, the announcer rushed on stage and made the briefest possible introduction to the most famous musicians in the land. The crowd was silent. The musicians shuffled on stage and encountered the cold blast of our silence. The leader of the band made a joke which got no response. Our silence blew over him in chilling gusts of wind. Hurriedly, they fumbled with their instruments. The loudspeaker distorted their fumblings. Abandoning further jokes or preambles, the musicians struck up their most popular tune, with the hope of warming our mood.

EIGHT

The dance of the dead

It was a night of deep amber. Birds circled our heads unobserved. The smells of the forest blew amongst us. Indigo lights rose from our silence.

When the most famous musicians in the land struck up their most popular tune, the hidden dead rose from the earth. The spirits living in the space in which we were now crowded woke up from their trance and saw us. They must have been amazed to see us occupying their space without intruding on their shadow world. The dead populated our midst. And we, the living crowd, also had the crowding of the spirits, the angry dead, the unjustly dead, the serene dead amongst us. They woke up, gyrating to the most catchy tunes of the land.

On stage the musicians performed with leaden solemnity. Their faces were stiff as they stared out into the unresponsive crowd. As they played, increasing the vigour of the drums, the pierce of the guitars, the colours of the maracas, the mood of the accordions, the strangest thing happened. We, the living crowd, were silent and still and unmoving, but the dead began to dance in mad fervour. They danced their dread dance amongst us. They danced through us. They danced on to the stage and danced over the musicians, marvelling at the instruments, tampering with the sounds, perplexing the spirits of the musicians, distorting the music. And when they began to change the music into a madness-making sort of chaos – the peculiar groups of the dead amongst us began to laugh again.

The new laughter of the dead created chaos everywhere. It confused the politicians, made the musicians falter, causing them to play discordantly. The discordant music began to wreak havoc on the loudspeakers. The discord jangled our nerves. Female dancers were ushered on stage and they danced rigidly to the odd distortions of the music.

I watched the triple realities on the stage with terror. I watched as the musicians strained against the new resistance of their instruments. The depth-less thud of the drums. The lifeless screeching of the guitars. The dull wailing of the tambourines. And even the whining of the loudspeakers. The instruments began to produce the sounds of the anguished gyrating imps, the syllables of the dead, the ominous indigo hum of the awoken spirits. Music and spirits collided. The musical instruments became somewhat dead, heavy, unresponsive; the dead became more festive.

While the half-nude female dancers weaved and writhed in a somnolent daze, the dead jumped about on stage, laughing wildly. The spirits and imps, with their bat-like faces and their ill-proportioned bodies, danced with frightening and fantastic mobility, contorting their frames, and swinging round the women, who did not see them.

As the music got worse, the awakened spirits grew

weirder. They laughed grotesquely in their celebration, their awakening.

The politicians watched with consternation the half-empty stage. Madame Koto's face was swollen. The blind old man was transfixed. The Governor-General seemed in a daze, rooted to that ghostly mood.

NINE

The forgotten power of laughter

The laughter of the dead infected our mood and suddenly we couldn't stop laughing at the broken music and the rigid dancers. The laughter of the dead broke through the protective seal of sorcerers and controllers of phenomena. I learned, one moment before the bizarre fiesta changed, that the manufacturers of reality had no power over laughter.

As the spectacle on stage reached its weirdest moment, I saw a flash from the Photographer's camera, and heard one of the sorcerers – attired in a black robe, with glittering magic stones round his neck – point a crooked finger at the Photographer, and shout:

'That man is a demon, he is evil! Catch him!'

The Photographer fled from the edge of the stage into the crowd, spreading waves of frenzy over the great gathering.

Then the mood of dervishes and the spirit of the whirlwind descended upon us.

TEN

The rally turns into a fantastical riot

There was a crashing noise on the platform. The planks had broken and the musicians, dancers, politicians and manufacturers of reality all disappeared into the quivering hole. Musical instruments splintered our ears with high-pitched noises. Loudspeakers came tumbling down. Policemen and soldiers at the edges of the stage froze for a long moment. And there was a brief silence, during which I clearly saw the dead carpenter. Yellow flowers sprouted from his head. I saw him pulling up the planks and scattering the equipment with wild energy. No one else seemed to see him. And when the brief silence passed, one of the greatest rallies of our times turned into a blistering riot.

Voices screamed everywhere. Police whistles blasted our ears. Soldiers released a round of gunshots into the sky. All those who had fallen through the stage began to scream in the black hole, that underworld of phenomena.

Below me, there was the sheer cacophony of wailing women and the cursing crowd. I heard a man saying how dangerous it was to get too close to the powerful. He was not too close to the powerful himself, but the crowd poured over him, stamping on his body, breaking his legs. Everyone was fleeing in a hundred directions. Soldiers were hitting people with batons. Birds were squawking over us. Lights were flashing in our faces. Children were screaming. Everything was changing. The world was widening and waves of heat kept blasting us.

The first to emerge from the wreckage of the stage was the blind old man. He was feverish with rage. All about him the great wave of the crowd became a heated beast, tearing everything, attacking soldiers. Then they descended on the platform and wreaked their rage against anything they could lay their hands on. The wreckage of the rally was truly frightening. A storm had broken on the proceedings: the criminals released from prison, the thugs, the beggars and the marketwomen all went entirely wild. Destroying things. Shattering the windscreens of parked cars. Tearing down the banners and flags of the party. Burning vehicles. Ripping down stalls and sheds. Their noises raged through the night. The supporters of one party turned on the other. Soldiers shot into the crowd, killing two women and three men. Thunder growled above. Below there was the din of stones against glass, of clashing metal, the rumble of collapsing walls, the cries of people trampled underfoot, the wailing of those stabbed in the eyes, the swell of angry voices, the lambent caterwauling, the faces broken by fists swung in any direction. The fury of the crowd attacking itself. I saw it all from the tree. I saw the riot scattering a thousand heads in a thousand directions.

The riot broke the tree on which I perched and I fell to the ground and many feet trampled on me. I kept twisting and turning. When I managed to get up, a red night with spirits appeared before me. I saw masquerades on white horses. Masked faces clubbing people. Soldiers whipping the women. Angry men setting on the police. Gunshots creating furious gaps between the crush of bodies.

As I struggled to walk a man snatched me up and I found myself on horseback. When I turned to look at my rescuer, I screamed. He had five heads and ten glowing eyes. I fought him, unable to bear the fact that the five-headed spirit sent by my spirit companions to bring me back to the land of the dead was still intent on me and hadn't given up. Screaming out Dad's fighting name, I kept hitting the five-headed spirit. His horse rode through the crowd, trampling on people.

The five-headed spirit rode furiously through the mass of bodies, then we entered an indigo realm. I saw the dead carpenter in front of us. I called out his name, I shouted that I was Ade's friend. I begged him to help me. The dead carpenter turned his yellow-flowered head to me and laughed happily. Then he jumped on the horse. The collision sent me flying. I landed on the chest of a wizened old man. When I looked back I saw the dead carpenter battling with the five-headed spirit. They fought themselves into other realms.

Beneath me I heard deep coughing. I got off the old man on whom I had landed. He lay there coughing strenuously, beating his chest. For a while I couldn't move. The wizened old man turned to me and, after another bout of deep-chested heaving, said:

'They are destroying Africa!'

He lay there, quite still. Then he sat up straight. When he lit a cigarette I recognized him. He was the herbalist who had ritually washed Madame Koto's car a long time ago. He was the one who had prophesied that it would be a coffin. He seemed very drunk. His eyes bulged. He didn't appear to know whether he was alive or dead. His serenity seemed to protect us. The crowd thudded around us without harming us in any way. He smoked his cigarette for a while, staring at everything with tranquil eyes. Then he said:

'I had this dream. A white man turned into a tortoise and asked me to give him my land. He had a gun. I fought him, and he shot me through the head.'

He stopped speaking. I was transfixed. He began to cough and did it so violently that a bullet popped out of his mouth. He turned the bullet round in his hand. The bullet glittered through his phlegm. Then I noticed that the wizened old man was covered in blood. I noticed that he had three eyes. The third eye, in the middle of his forehead, was bleeding. I fled when I realized that I had been listening to the dreams of a dead man. He ran after me, shouting my name. I fled into the tangle of rioting bodies.

My head ached. An insistent din pierced my ears. Everywhere I looked, the world of spirits was in turbulence. I saw men with the heads of chickens. Goats with the boots of soldiers. Horses with women's heads. I banged my head against a wall to straighten out my vision. And then I really started to see things. A priest in a red smock, carrying an image of the bleeding Christ, weeping about the world's distortion of his message. Red creatures with massive bellies. Red human beings, looting shops, drunk on stolen wine, screaming into the flames. Red insects in the night air. I blinked, and found myself in another space, floating above the eruptions. Floating above the Governor-General, the future Head of State, and their entourages. They were fleeing into the night. Crouching beneath crumbling red walls. They were exiles from reality. Afraid. Surrounded by red spirits. Led on by the dead. Stumbling along in the gutters. Their heads low as they made for their vehicles.

A special host of spirits followed the Governor-General. They marvelled at the illuminated yellow dust of angels growing in his body. The august group of leaders got into their cars, but the crowd smashed the windscreens, and turned the cars on their sides. The policemen lashed at the crowd. Whipped the possessed women. Clubbed down the enraged men. But the Governor-General and the future Head of State managed to get through the tumultuous crowd to a convoy of soldiers, who immediately formed a protective cordon round them. The leaders were ushered into a police car and, sirens blasting, sped through the crowd. Mowing people down. The car soon gained the main road, and was free of the insurgent crowd. The car had six outriders on motorcycles, with sirens wailing. Closest to the speeding vehicle were two-headed outriders with silver boots.

ELEVEN

Adventures into chaos

The red crowd poured past me towards the city centre, their fury unabated. They went on an insane feast of destruction, wrecking everything they touched. They rampaged for every child of theirs that had died of malnutrition, for every humiliation they had suffered, for hunger too long endured, for every prayer unanswered, every dream betrayed, every mosquito bite borne, for every night of insomnia, for their relentless poverty, for their roofless huts, for the rewriting of our lives, the rain leaking into their dreams, the long years of unemployment and bad pay, all their despair, all the insults of being powerless, all the frustrations of being unheard.

Floating in the air, I raged with them. They were angry at everything, at the walls around their lives, the many rigorous laws that pressed down the poor and lifted up the rich, the tight narrow spaces crowded with too much history. They were also raging at all the suffering, all the waste, all the betrayals, and all the failures to come.

Not one person escaped without bleeding. The barbers, signwriters, marketwomen, truck pushers, sellers of trinkets and oranges, they all bled, they all suffered blows, lashings, cuts, and falls. The fury of the crowd was so intense that I feared everything would spontaneously combust. Cars were set alight, houses burned, and people ran around with fires in their hands. The intensity of the people's anger, the raging of spirits, the shrieking of the dead filled the world with harsh lights.

Looking at everywhere with strange eyes, I witnessed the ritual passage of an old god reborn. The god of chaos, with uncountable hands and five thousand heads. Where did all those hands come from, those hands beating the air like withered wings, those hands hitting, burning, tearing down roadsigns, setting petrol stations on fire, looting the jewellers and the banks, smashing the windows of government houses, invading Independence Square? The god of chaos rode through us all, whipped our minds. At Independence Square we laid out a burning altar to the god, and made it one of his homes.

Where did all those feet come from, the calloused worm-eaten feet, beating relentlessly on all the doors of the earth, rousing the nightmares of the road, trembling the land, shaking open the abyss, widening the pits, starting cracks in the fortunes of others across the seas?

Where did all those faces come from, masks of the new god, hardened faces, beautiful faces, undefeated faces, raw and bony faces, crafty faces? Where did all those eyes come from, flaming eyes, trancelike eyes, clear eyes of young girls, wild eyes of thugs, the defeated eyes of the fallen?

I saw them all, saw them possessed by the moon-madness of the new god, their bodies inhabited, their hearts occupied by spirits goading their rage. I saw women with handwriting on their necks, men with fierce scarifications. The fury of the crowd became so incandescent that I feared witnessing a metamorphosis, a mass transformation. I saw the bodies begin to give off yellow lights. The yellow glow filled everything, but it was more intense where the stampede was fiercest.

TWELVE

The procession of higher beings

Murderous cries were rending the air. Petrol tanks burst into flames. The road heaved. I blinked. All the redness vanished, the rioting human beings disappeared. For a long moment, all I saw in the darkness was the awe-inspiring procession of higher beings. I saw majestic spirit-kings and their courtiers. Famed warriors with their attendants. Ancient and illustrious philosophers with their disciples. Mighty figures in golden robes, riding liveried spirit-horses. Mythical beings. Representatives of the gods. The great mothers. The masters of the great African underworld. The dazzling plenum of the unborn who would lead special lives. The shimmering stream of noble personages, each with a blue and serene radiance. They moved with dignity, and with grace, distilling gold lights about them, followed by silvery birds.

I saw the higher spirits as they moved over the scenes of rioting. Their priests waved censers that gave off the aroma of their wondrous philosophies. I saw them riding, walking, sailing past in the air. They were silent. They moved with solemnity and lightness, as to an important convocation. They went over us, seemingly unaware of our existence. I beheld these splendid beings. The ancient and future mystics. The political philosophers of the ancient worlds. The strategists of Timbuktu and the thinkers of Songhai. The Kings of Great Zimbabwe. The Pharaohs of ancient Egypt. The lawmakers and the intense dreamers. All those invisible beings whose achievements spread enlightenment from Egypt to ancient Greece. I beheld them all. They filled the air with lights of topaz, emeralds, diamonds, aquamarine. Mists of gold and yellow swirled about them. They poured over us in colours that human eyes have never seen. Colours seen in dreams but never remembered.

Enchanted by their procession, I began to follow these higher beings. To see where they were going. But a knock on my head stunned me from that realm. Then I found myself in the middle of the road. The rioting was all around. Cars sped past me, stoned by the crowd. I fled from the road. Felt my head bleeding. I began to cry. I called for my mother, but she didn't hear me. Women with black hoods bore down on me, and I ran away from them, and lost myself amongst a group of urchins who were looting a shop. I saw the policeman who many years ago had locked me in his house as a substitute for his dead son. I fled again: I seemed to keep running into my past.

There was a weird smell in the air. Further on I saw a man whose coat was on fire. The road heaved again. Convulsions rent the air. The road swayed, arched its back, and became a feverish snake. Everything shook as if there were an earthquake. Pits opened as the road seemed to wrench itself up like a maddened animal. Cars drove into houses. The air, the moon, the people, the objects of the world, all began, it seemed, to hallucinate.

Is the world capable of dreaming, as if it were a whale? Are the objects and the particulars of this world – beings? Can a thing be a table or a brick to us, and yet be a living thing in another realm? I don't know. But the world was in a hallucination that night. The world was dreaming itself. And all of us who were possessed by the new god dreamed the world as a fever, changing it even as we dreamed it. We had broken the spirit-barrier. Higher energies burned in us. We were everywhere that night. We had awoken into an unholy rage and had crossed over the barrier of ordinary awakening. We had entered the fullness of power and spirit. A thousand suns flamed in us. Charged with the intoxication of the new god, we became chaotic gods ourselves. Our bodies, unable to withstand such intensity, began to howl for cooling sleep.

The road became a stream and lashed us with its burning waters on that night of six hot moons. I saw the six moons, all clustered beneath a golden glow. I shouted, pointing upwards. Then I saw them again. The ancient Chaldean astronomers. The soothsayers of ancient Greece. Dream-interpreters of ancient Babylon. Omen-readers of Damascus. Magic-workers of Mesopotamia. Sumerian guardians of mysteries. They were an illustrious and tempered host. Masters of the art of hiding their greatest discoveries in time. They travelled over us, unmindful of the confluence of moons.

We who had burst our spirit-barrier, had we materialized in another realm?

THIRTEEN

Night of wondrous transformations

Then it occurred to me that in other realms, new
worlds were being dreamt up, were being born. New
things were emerging from the turbulence of people
speaking the only language that is understood – the
language of violence. On other spheres new realities
were coming into being. On which sphere was I? It
seemed I dwelt in several of them at once. The
different spheres seemed all superimposed, existing
concurrently within the same space. All this confused me. I wandered amongst the rioting people.
There were six hot moons in my head.

As I wandered, utterly lost, I saw Helen, the
beggar girl, coming towards me. She was alone. She
seemed too beautiful to be alive. She flashed me a
gentle smile. Mysterious. Full of meaning. Then she
vanished.

When Helen vanished, the road changed. The
stream stopped flowing; mosquitoes enraged my
ears. A jackal-headed masquerade, on a white horse,
rode past me. Its hoofs thundered the ground. My
head swelled. The road changed into a snake again,
lashing out with its tail. Its cratered back was like an
old sea-monster. Then the snake changed back into a
road. A flash of light struck me in the eyes. I saw a

host of enraged women, singing old warsongs, hell-bent in their rage on changing the world, and altering reality. They bounded towards me like an avenging army. A conquering battalion. Sweeping everything aside. Worshippers of the new god.

The women were terrifying to behold. I fled round the compounds, till I emerged at the rally again. In the dark men, meek in their ordinary lives, were tearing down remnants of the stand. Women were amongst them, hair in disarray, blouses torn, wrappers in shreds, cuts and bruises on their faces.

Then the heat of the six moons got to everything. The rage and heat of the rioters got so much that their frames cracked. Their bodies changed. Their spirits burst out of them stunned. And as I watched men changed into spirits, and spirits into men. New human beings manifested amongst us. Amidst a crackle of electricity in the air, a pantheon of gods came alive. They descended on our fury. The mercury heat of the spirit intensified. In that fog of night, that forge of incandescence, with acrid smells all around, I witnessed frightening transformations. The skins of the beggars cracked. The granite muscles of political thugs crackled. And with the sound of rushing lava I saw men turning into bulls, into horses, into tigers, their skins bristling, aflame in the night. I witnessed men turning into jackals. I recognized them instantly as worshippers at Madame Koto's shrine.

It was a night of sorceries. In the wild crowd I saw men with dread hoofs and almond-shaped eyes. They stood upright, their fingers thickening into stumps, as they changed into hippos. I saw the

half-men, half-beasts, part time human beings, manufacturers of reality, themselves remanufactured. I
saw women burst into new shapes, into antelopes
and great feline creatures. Into ravenous anteaters.
Into jaguars and lionesses. Into beings with jagged
teeth and diamond eyes. I saw women turn into
smoke, into spirit-wisps, into gigantic birds with
golden talons and aquamarine wings. They swooped
over me, raging into new elements. Men became
dwarfs. Became hunch-backed. Became long thin
monsters with vertical eyes.

The night of sorceries steamed my flesh. The
transformations galloped at me. Birds with shredded
wrappers round their sharp talons flew over me,
knocking me down with their lashing wings. I
scrabbled on the ground, and ran towards the
houses.

Near a tree I saw Sami, the betting shop owner
who had run off with Dad's money a long time ago.
I saw him changing into a giant rat, as if he were
merely taking off his coat, tearing off an outer layer
of human identity. Even as a rat his face was still
familiar. When he caught me staring at him he
uttered a monstrous syllable, barely human. I ran
again, no longer carried by my feet, but by a hot
wind. The bad dreams of politicians were wreaking
havoc on the earth. A tree burst into flame and a
yellow star pulsed in the remote regions of ash-
flavoured space. New realities were being born in the
birth-throes of a new nation.

At the main road I saw the wild women again.
Their voices were intensely chanting new things into
being. Widening the spaces for better realities.

Extending the womb of the world. I recognized some of the women. They were the endless toilers of the earth, the strong-willed marketwomen, the women who worked all life long in salt marshes, the seven women who had followed Mum on her campaign to free Dad, the hawkers who trod the endless dream of the roads, their brains sizzling under the undying language of the sun. They were the perpetual mothers, the great virgins, the somnolent widows, mothers of priests and criminals, mothers of the endlessly poor, mothers of beggars and cripples, prostitutes and cloth-dyers, mothers of the strong and the timid, the cunning and the weak, all intoxicated by the incarnation of the new god.

I saw the wild women, but I didn't see Mum amongst them. The women poured towards me, and I feared the most frightening transformation of all. I waited for the cracking of the skins, the acrid stench, and the sudden conflagration. I held my breath, transfixed, waited for the women to trample me into the fevers of the road.

Then something happened. The spaces widened. The hard reflections of burning cars on half-broken windows flashed in my eyes. I heard a cry. Everything changed in my vision, and I moved sideways into another reality. The women who rioted, wild and barefoot, started changing forms before my stunned gaze. As the women got more violent they began to mutate into giant butterflies. They changed from the head first. Their feet shrivelled and disappeared. Their arms, beating the air, spread out, and became wider. Their faces became smaller. Their clothes fell from them and their wings became the exact pattern of their wrappers.

As the women ran towards me, their faces lit up by the fires, they changed into large butterflies, lifting off into the wind, wings frantically beating the air. Those that changed sowed disarray amongst those that were unchanged. Suddenly, I saw them all transformed, clothes first. They were utterly changed in that air of bark and fires and herbaceous sorceries.

It was astonishing to see it all. To see how the women's feet at first still touched the earth; and how the next moment they were in the air. It was amazing to see the girls in white dresses, walking serenely towards me, leaping into butterfly forms. They all took off, flew up into that sky of six moons, and circled the chaos below three times, emitting poignant cries.

Then the seven women swooped down on me. They seized me with their soft pincerous claws, and soared up into the sky. I tore at their wings, and they dropped me. I fell slowly. I fell through the procession of higher beings. I hit the ground and rolled over. The lights changed in my eyes, my spirit knocked from its centre. I lay there, on the ground, feeling as if something had moved out of me, or as if something had moved in. I felt all mixed up. It was as if my feet were where my hands should be. As if my head had gone into my body, or as if my body were all scrambled up. I couldn't make sense of anything. I didn't know if I was still a human being. Or if I had changed into a butterfly, a bird, a fox, a spirit or a mixed-up song. As I lay there, my mind dissolving in the brown lights of a new terrain, the six moons become one. I saw the seven butterflies flying up into the air. They flew up higher and higher. Then they became seven new stars, fluttering in the night sky. I watched the stars pulsing.

FOURTEEN

A sympathetic invasion

After a while, I noticed that the world was quivering, as if a sympathetic invasion had been unleashed. The whole ghetto was covered in little blue and yellow butterflies. They beat on our faces, and they clung to our bodies. I found myself so completely covered with these butterflies that I felt I had woken into a nightmare. I screamed and kicked. When I opened my eyes, the air around me was thickly populated with little winged creatures. It occurred to me that the butterflies all over me were in fact devouring me. With all the energies embedded in my fear, I cried out, and jumped up from the ground.

Hitting out at the bristling horde of soft-winged creatures, I ran screaming, my brain on fire, my eyes hurting, and blood seeping out from a thousand places on my body.

Flailing, crazed, lashing out, I ran blindly through that dense air of transformations. I ran till I couldn't see anything. My rage and horror had burned out my sight.

IV

BOOK SEVEN

BOOK SEVEN

ONE

I flailed my way into a cool terrain

As I went on running I flailed my way into a new
terrain where the air was cool. Gentle spirits serenely
floated about their business. Girls in white shifts,
kaolin on their feet and antimony on their faces,
glided about with great ease, as if they were dreams.

I ran through a world of shadows. There were
shadow beings everywhere. Everything was alive.
The objects in that realm shone with eyes. The lovely
cross had an eye at its centre. The earth had eyes, the
trees had eyes, and the river had eyes too. There
were pretty young girls everywhere. They had three
eyes, rings in their noses, hair beautifully plaited.
The girls looked happy and more at peace than I had
ever known people to be. They didn't notice me or
see me. I ran through them without disturbing their
shadows.

I had run into a world of mirrors and dreams. The
earth was a brown mirror in which I wasn't
reflected. I cast no shadow amongst the shadows of
that world. Within me there was great heaving. All
around me there was great serenity.

There were no butterflies in the air. There was no
rage and no rioting. There were no artificial lights.
There was no darkness either. And everything in that

world had a sun at its centre. The trees. The images of an unimaginable god. The great river with its many tributaries. The young girls of quiet beauty. The babies that could fly. The animals with intelligent eyes. They all had suns. Everything blinded me. I saw not with my eyes, but with my whole body. I seemed to be covered in eyes, to be as full of eyes as I had been covered in butterflies.

It was also a world in which everything was in blossom. A blossoming world. The trees, the plants, the people, and even the lights were all in white and golden bloom. I was moved by the gentle beauty of the place.

All around there were voices in the air. Voices without bodies. It was as if I were hearing all the voices, all the speeches of several worlds. The stream of voices followed me wherever I went.

TWO

I enter the realm
where thoughts are voices

Had I entered the realm where the dreams of human beings are real, where their thoughts are voices? Was I listening to the whispered thoughts of the world, to the interior monologue of the earth, to the soliloquies of the road? Had I entered into the road, into its ambiguous underworld, the underworld of our dreams? I didn't know where I was and didn't know how to get out. I didn't know if I was in my body or if I had strayed into a universe where all things as yet unborn live their natural pace, a realm where the dead pass through. Neither was I sure if I was simply wandering in the vast living corridors that lead beyond the famished road to new beginnings.

Was I amongst the living or the unborn? Was I amongst those who live a secret life of serenity on this sphere while they sleep or suffer and strive in the world of human beings?

How many lives do we live simultaneously?

In that realm I saw Helen. The beggar girl. She was dressed like a queen, surrounded by shadows. I saw her walking along the river. Then disappearing into the great clear mirror of the air. I also saw Mum. She was with six women I recognized as her sisters, though I knew she had none. She looked right past me. Not registering my presence or my gestures. When I tried to touch her I touched the air instead. Then I saw Dad. He was riding on a great black horse. I tried to follow him. But I found myself intermittently breaking into the world of human beings and then coming back into this peculiar realm. My being came alight and turned off. Like a human beacon.

I found myself wandering through images of workers mangled in machines. People electrocuted by the new mode of electricity. Houses collapsing on poor tenants because of cheap building materials.

The terrain changed. I wandered in the nocturnal harmattan glow of peaceful villages. Pumpkins and five-fingered cassava plants flourished in the backyards. Old men rode ancient bicycles along the meandering forest paths. I came to the forest of shadows. I met a man who was hallucinating about his favourite palm-wine. Still searching for a dead tapster. Further on I encountered the stuttering spirit of a grim man. His machete was still bloody with the murder of an outcast. I fled from his humourless presence into a flare of forest lights. I caught glimpses of famous tribal gods.

On that night I also met the blind old man. He was wandering around in the darkness with his arms outstretched.

'I'm going back to my village!' he cried.

He was covered in glowing yellow pustules. They were so alarming that I fled again.

In that wonderful realm I met a one-eyed man who wanted me to read Homer to him in Greek.

Women who wanted me to write love letters for them on the leaves of baobab trees. Letters to their departed lovers whom they hadn't appreciated while alive. They wanted me to take their messages through the forest. I met people who wanted me to do nothing except listen to their stories of ancient times when the gods lived amongst human beings. When heroes ventured out beyond the village gates, beyond the seven forests, battling monsters in faraway lands. Heroes who turned into sunbirds when they died. Or stories of women who sowed havoc in eight villages because of their supernatural beauty which they had been given by twilight gods because they would never bear children for men. The stories aged me. I met white men marooned in the underworld of dreams. They wanted to know if the atom had been split. Or if the solution to world peace had been found. Or if the eternal secret of life had been discovered in the busy laboratories. Or whether the true author of Shakespeare's works had finally been uncovered. They also wanted me to carry messages across the seas. To their loved ones. They gave me the addresses and the names of their wives, children and mistresses. The messages were mysteriously erased from my memory the moment I left them. The addresses vanished from my pocket.

Further on I heard voices plotting to assassinate Madame Koto. I listened to their frantic dialogue.

'Fear?'

'No fear.'

'Kill her.'

'Why?'

'She now believes in love. This is a weakness.'

'So?'
'She betrayed us.'
'I know.'
'She confessed too much.'
'Revealed our secrets.'
'She wants all the power.'
'To become a goddess.'
'To rule us.'
'Make us servants for ever.'
'Turn us into animals.'
'Chickens.'
'Goats.'
'Rats.'
'Sheep.'
'Cows.'
'For sacrifice.'
'To take our power.'
'And plant our heart in her rock.'
'To increase her life with our blood.'
'To turn us into beasts.'
'Not even into peacocks.'
'Or sunbirds.'
'But maybe into bats.'
'Kill her.'
'Yes, let's kill her.'
'Before she becomes a god.'
'Let's go.'
'Let's go to the old man first.'
'Fear?'
'No fear at all.'

The voices moved away. The wind took their places. I wandered puzzled into other voices circling the air.

'The white people turned our children into slaves.'

'In broad daylight.'

'And made our people work to make their coffee sweeter.'

'So they could build roads that are never hungry.'

'We didn't even threaten them with death.'

'And they haven't been taken to any court on earth or in heaven.'

'To answer their crimes to God.'

'So now we suffer.'

'In broad daylight.'

'With our roads that are hungry.'

'And our history weeping.'

'And our future full of question marks.'

'And our people seen as inferior.'

'And our case unheard in any court.'

'On earth or in heaven.'

'And the great injustice forgotten.'

'On earth and in heaven.'

'Meanwhile we carry on struggling.'

'With our hands tied.'

'And our history in chains.'

'With tears in our souls.'

'And laughter on our faces.'

'And love in our hearts.'

'On earth and in heaven.'

The words lingered. Flavouring the air. After a while I heard the voices ascending. Spiralling away. Like birds returning to their homes in the sky. There was an orange glow of silence. The breeze was gentle on my face. I sat by the roadside, like an orphan. I felt at home. Here the thoughts and dreams of humanity are real. Real as the shadow of a tree in an oasis. Then I heard a sweet voice speaking. The familiar sweetness of the voice pierced my heart. It was Mum's voice. She was talking to the six sisters she didn't have.

'My dear sisters, last night I saw a host of yellow angels. They were weeping high up above the world. When I asked them why they were weeping, they said: "We are sad because you human beings don't know how magnificent you are. How wonderful. How beautiful. How blessed. You came from Love. And it is to Love that you will return. You make a complete mess of your ideals. You turn your good dreams into living nightmares. You turn the garden into a graveyard. Terrible things you do to one another. You can make heaven real in your lives, instead you prefer to live in your own hell, your ignorance. You do not use your light, but delight in your darkness. That is why we are in agony. Love is your mother, Humanity. Light is your father. Life is your gift eternal. And all three are one. You have forgotten the original river, the seven mountains, and your royal destiny. And so we weep. You are made from an immortal dream. Rise up, and reach for your precious inheritance." That is what the angels told me.'

I listened as Mum's six sisters talked in lovely harmonies about the agony of the angels.

The breeze changed. A harsher wind took over. There was silence. I waited for Mum's voice to speak again. I waited to hear her invisible sisters speak. But they didn't. The harshness of the wind impelled me to move on. I got up from the roadside. Like a pilgrim with a happy destination in his heart, I set off along the road that only voices travel.

I came to a building made of mirrors, crowned with a golden cupola. I wandered into a clearing and listened to other voices talking calmly into the night. I had no idea where the voices came from. I didn't know if they were thoughts, or whispered words blown over oceanic spaces by the gods that make audible all the secret intentions of men and women.

'They are not like us,' said one.

'William Blake may have said the black boy's soul is white, but, to be honest, they are not really like us,' said another.

'They eat dirt.'

'Snakes.'

'They smell.'

'So do we, but they smell different.'

'I don't like the difference.'

'They have no history.'

'No past.'

'So they have no future.'

'Do they dream?'

'They bleed. I don't like their blood.'

'They must be kept in their place.'

'Can't let them have anything over us.'

'They are the younger brother of the human race.'

'Are they of the race?'

'Maybe not. Maybe somewhere in between.'

'Between dust and brain.'

'Infiltrate them.'

'Spy on them.'

'Find the strong ones among them and make them like us.'

'Not the strong. Destroy the strong among them. Find the weak. Make them like us.'

'Not like us.'

'Divide them.'

'Use them against themselves.'

'Make them our eternal servants.'

'Our distant workers.'

'They have no talent for order.'

'No sense of responsibility.'

'For their own good keep them down.'

'And out.'

'But how do we manage to remain human after this?'

'That's our children's problem.'

'For how long do we do this?'

'Do what?'

'Keep them down?'

'As long as necessary.'

'Do you think there is a God watching us, monitoring our intentions?'

'There is no God.'

'We are now the gods.'

'And anyway if there is a God, he most certainly will approve.'

'But will we pay a horrible price for this? I mean can our children ever face the truth of what we have done, and what we will continue to do? Can our race live with the guilt?'

'Guilt is for the weak.'

'But can we live with the truth?'

'As Pilate said, "What is truth?"'

'Besides, it is for their own good. In a thousand

years' time they will thank us for bringing them the future.'

'Our future.'

'But what about sleep? How do we sleep in peace through the centuries?'

'Wandering amongst the spirits of the mothers of slaves.'

'Trapped amongst them.'

'Wandering in this inferno of history.'

'Where everything is remembered.'

'Eternally remembered.'

'I don't know.'

'I don't know either.'

The words faded away. The voices ascended. No wind came to clear the air of their words.

THREE

Assassination of a Rain Queen

I wandered much in that realm of a hundred
thoughts and dreams. I kept trying to find my way
back into the hard world that I had made my home.
Then I came to a place where someone was telling a
story of an elephant that was killed. They were not
so much telling the story as performing it. I listened
to how the elephant appeared. How it crashed about
in the undergrowth, felling trees in its rage, stamping
on mud huts. Trampling on people. Bellowing in the
most horrid way. I listened to how the elephant fell
into a pit and how the people finished it off with
dane guns and spears. Then the storyteller, rendering
the death of the elephant, released a powerful cry
which blew me to another place where my father
was riding a black horse.

I followed Dad. Soon I found myself becoming
blind among the objects of that crepuscular realm.
When my eyes cleared, I had surfaced into the
familiar world. Into the rally that had gone wrong.

There were clashing supporters everywhere. Burnings and wailing all around. Anguished voices.
Children being trampled. Men being whipped. Soldiers shooting at the moon. A man appealed for calm

over a loud hailer. Thugs descended on him and beat him with it. Each blow became an ugly sound.

There were screams in the air. Cars on fire. Party flags set alight. Stampedes. Women dragged to corners, screaming. There was a man whose face was slashed with a broken bottle. Blood poured from his lips. I even saw the Photographer in all that madness. He had climbed a tree and was calmly taking pictures. I called to him but he couldn't hear me; and I couldn't get to him for the awfulness of the commotion.

So I ran where the stampede took me. I found myself lost again in another realm where a table was continuing its dream as a tree. It had sprouted little branches and green buds. The table frightened me. I ran on, flashing simultaneously in two streams of time. In one stream of time I saw images of the nation's troubles in advance. Oil wells drying up. Valuable gases burning out on the city air. I saw the era of the great national squander to come, and the dissipation of its fabulous wealth. I saw coups and wars and animals eating the corpses of men. In the other stream of time, I walked the tributaries that became roads. People were sitting outside their houses, fanning themselves, unaware of the chaos.

I went on for what seemed like hours. It had become dark. I noticed two beggars following Madame Koto. I got confused. I saw Madame Koto hurrying back home. Then the women of her religion were setting upon her, stabbing her with knives that shone under the moon, sticking the knives in her repeatedly and shouting that she was growing too powerful. The blind old man was

317

stabbing her too. Killing her. Because of her public confessions. Because of the change in her heart, her love for the poor and the suffering. And then it was all different. It was people I couldn't make out who were attacking her from behind. Madame Koto might have saved herself if she could have turned her head round, for her assassins would have been petrified by the power of her eyes. But she couldn't. And they cut her open with long knives. I heard one of the assassins saying:

'So you want to become a god, eh? So you love the people now, eh?'

He said it over and over again as they slaughtered her. She didn't fall. They cut into Madame Koto many times and still she didn't fall. They murdered the spirit-children growing in her and she stood there and spewed out all the food and drinks she had consumed that day. Blood and gore and vomit and gristle and the sigh of unborn children burst from her on to her assassins and on the mud and all over her rich garments.

And – yes – at that moment the wind howled. In a flash, a silver crack between spheres, I saw the old woman of the forest staring at her weavings of the rally gone mad and the brutal murder of a Rain Queen. I saw her surrounded by the weird birds of night. When the wind howled, the birds, wings beating in a convulsion of feathers, took off into the air, leaving the old woman in a stunned space.

And – yes – at that moment liverish rain clouds cracked above and thick rain poured down. The inklike water writhed with worms and sardines. The rain washed away the moon and the seven new stars.

Masquerades on horseback released cultic cries. I heard the splitting fissures of a great rock. Potent spells rushed out from Madame Koto's blubbery body. I heard the crackling of spells and the dissolution of sorceries. The downpour drenched the butterflies. I watched them writhing on the road. I saw deformations everywhere. Spells and animistic powers of Madame Koto's spirit burst into the air, unleashing nightmares which ran mad amongst us. Trees cracked and weird birds piped haunting melodies. I heard the bursting of ancient powers and saw the spirits of Madame Koto's unborn children wandering about the street, stunned at their release into the raw spaces. Madame Koto's spirit floated above her and turned into the shadow of a big animal with anguished noises.

And – yes – caterwauling music started out from the emptiness. Peacocks cried out. The jackal-headed masquerade exploded into yellow flames. How many realities were in conflagration on that night? I was spun around by the forces freed from the spewing body of Madame Koto. And through all this, she still didn't fall.

She stood upright like an indefatigable warrior. Her assassins were petrified by her fast-congealing blood on their faces. Then I saw something quite electrifying. I saw Madame Koto changing into a young girl, and then into an ancient Celtic warrior of great virility. Then into a crocodile-headed priest of Pharaonic Egypt. And then into an old woman of 203 years. When all her transformations stopped, I felt a grip of steel round my wrists. A brief darkness passed across my eyes.

I had been clawed by hands of bone, a living skeleton, hooded with shadows, sharp-jawed, long-toothed. Yellow pustules glowed all over his face. I gave a cry of horror when I recognized the figure of the blind old man. He was raving above me. His eyes were yellow. He was raving confessions of murder. Screaming that he had killed the daughter of a goddess. With his vice grip round my wrist, he kept begging me to lead him home to his village. Scared beyond my wits, I led him through the chaos and the violent rain.

The blind old man was possessed by a feverish insanity. He stumbled. Uttered terrifying confessions. Wailed as if an inferno blazed inside his spirit. Dragged me about the place. He staggered this way, rushed another, fell, brought me down on him, got up again. His evil grip kept crushing my wrist.

Then a wave of howling women poured over us, almost trampling us into the ground. The blind old man squealed pathetically. As he fell, he let go of me. I fled from him, and wandered confused over the battlefield of enraged bodies. Later, when I saw the blind old man tramping into a marsh, intent on dying, bellowing out his desire to return to his peaceful farm in the village, and calling my name with the voice of a nightmare bird, I went blind again and fell on my hands and knees and crawled through the upheavals of that scabrous night.

As I crawled, a large cat brushed past my face. Its tail tickled my nose. I sneezed, and the night became a little clearer. I got up. With my arms outstretched, I followed the form of the big cat. As I went, with great cries and noises all around me, I stumbled on a gargantuan body lying at the roadside. It was like a beached whale. I kept trying to get round it, but couldn't. I tried to climb over it but felt how every time I touched it, thick liquids bubbled up from its flesh. Then the rain came down harder, beating magnified tattoos upon everything. The rain washed away my blindness and I saw the body not of a whale or a great horse but of a woman with her head turned away, one eye open, staring at me.

'Get up!' I said.

The head turned ominously in my direction. The woman stared at me without moving, without breathing. Her face was swollen and full of folds. Blood gushed out of her belly.

An intermittent light shone on the unholy sight. The woman's eyes were wide open and her face was contorted. White moonstones gleamed in her hand. The string had broken. The moonstones were red in that dark night. The woman wouldn't budge when I prodded her. It was when I pushed her, trying to get her to move, to stand up, that I noticed she was lying in the thick puddle of her own blood. Then, heaving a volcanic sigh that knocked the senses back into my head, the woman seized my hand, shoved the moonstones in my palm, and fell back with a grating death rattle.

The moonstones burnt my palm and I dropped them. They sizzled on the rainwater. And when I realised that the woman was Madame Koto I screamed for the world to come and help her, but no one heard. I went on screaming, for the body of the legendary Madame Koto kept growing in my mind.

Soon I was overpowered by the fury of the rain,

and the smell of damp burning rubber, and the stench of Madame Koto's wild blood. I heard someone calling my name from behind me. I turned, and saw nothing. Then I heard my name again, uttered with a ghostly sort of rhythm. When I looked back I made out the spirit-form of Ade. He was standing on a pile of bricks, an incandescent white hat on his head. My eyes were feverish. I went towards him and found nothing but shadows. Then I thought I heard the snorting of a big animal behind me. And when I turned round, I was astonished to find a wild bull with a golden bell around its neck standing astride Madame Koto's body, as if protecting it. The bull bristled with low yellow flames. Its eyes were red.

I stood transfixed. The bull lifted its great animal head. Then it snorted again. Then it kicked. And then it charged. Screaming into the dark universe, I fled into the arena of rioting. I fled past the dead, past the spirits and the horses, in that air emptied of rage. The rain suddenly ceased falling. But gusts of exhausted wind went on blowing over the desolation of burnt cars, broken houses, and writhing bodies.

FOUR

A cooling wind

I fled through the riot, with the heat of the wild bull
on my neck. I ran a clear line in the cool air, past
limping women and masquerades on stilts, and
dancers who still breathed out fire. I ran through the
vertiginous domain of the god of chaos who had
scattered the passions of men and women, torn up
roads, devastated the rally, hurled beams and fire-
brands in all directions of the earth.

I fled over the scattered garbage, the swollen
gutters where dead cats floated, past the broken stalls
and burnt-out cars, and agile drummers who were
still beating out ferocious rhythms of a new ascendancy.

The wind was mysterious and cooling. It cleared
the dead from the air, swept away their insurrective
humour, and vengeful appearance. It blew me past
the crossroads, down our street, towards home. The
wind made all the things of this world stable. It
stopped the transformations. It stilled the dreams. It
calmed the rage. It cooled our spirits. And it led me
home, protected.

The wind protected me from the huge fallen
shadows, the mammoth forms of listening trees, the
lion-headed butterflies, and from the voices of my

spirit-companions of the other world who had been plaguing me ever since the day I arrived on the expanding spaces of the earth.

V

BOOK EIGHT

BOOK EIGHT

ONE

Earthing evil

There are certain trees that seem worthless but when gone leave empty spaces through which bad winds blow. There are other trees that seem useless but when felled worse things grow in their place. In ancient times, according to Dad, wise men had a special place for the statues of the god that earths evil things in our interspaces. They were kept outside the village gates because they were too powerful. The statues were ugly. Their ugliness warded off greater evils. There is a kind of evil, a bearable and human evil, which prevents bigger evils from being here.

There is always some kind of evil on earth. Poisonous herbs and wicked people and diseases and earthquakes. Some say there is no greater breeding-ground for evil than when a people's reason falls asleep, their dreams unencumbered, and when the air seems clear.

Dad says that sometimes we are more awake in our dreams: we hear what the spirits are whispering, we see what the gods see in our lives, we become what we really are.

When Madame Koto died we slept as if the boil

of time had burst. We slept as if time had been undammed. Slowly at first, and then suddenly, the future rushed upon us.

TWO

The disintegration of myth

Madame Koto died and time changed. Her death altered our lives in ways we could never have foreseen. Her space was taken over by the vicious little monsters of this world: they fed on the myth of her great body. They came from everywhere. We did not recognize them at first. They came to her funeral and then stayed. They drained us of blood.

When Madame Koto died, time accelerated. The hundred narratives of our lives merged as in a great weaving. Time became a flood of brackish waters. Not many of us survived. The gates of our sleep burst open and a horde of previously sleeping demons crept out into the world. They became real, and began to rule us.

The time of miracles, sorceries, and the multiple layers of reality had gone. The time when spirits roamed amongst human beings, taking human forms, entering our sleep, eating our food before we did, was over. The time of myth died with Madame Koto.

Her body festered for seven days in her secret palace. Poisonous flowers which give off sweet smells, herbs which cure blindness, onions and salamanders, grew on the myth of her great body.

Hardy leaves of rhododendron grew from her armpits. The yellow dust of angels which had been germinating in her spirit burst into little golden maggots. They grew fat in the heat of her funeral chamber.

Night and day, for seven days, her ministrants strove to disinfect her body. They scrubbed it with carbolic and the juice of banana plants. They washed it with fermented palm-wine and tar soap. They soaked her in a mighty tub full of herb-marinated alcohol and rubbed her over with palm-oil till her complexion turned ripe and beautiful, glowing in her death as if she were merely asleep.

But as soon as they had finished with the cleansing of her body, decomposition set in again. The yellow dust turned into maggots, herbal seeds sprouted on her belly, and her eyes grew bigger for having seen so much.

Her eyes kept growing and her followers became possessed by this terrible faculty, for with her eyes' expansion came the diminishment of their sight. Her eyes grew so big that her followers became convinced she was seeing more dead than alive.

I saw her eyes growing in my sleep. The rest of her body got smaller. I was struck by the expression in her eyes. It was the expression of one who can't speak, who sees too much, and who can't express what they see. It was horror. And self-disgust. Her eyes swelled with bitterness. They turned purple. Then they turned yellow. And they became so disgusting that her ministrants dreaded their daily cleansing of her body.

Her followers' eyesight diminished and they

began to see only the festering of her myth, its dissolution. They saw, with horrified eyes, the decaying of her ritual images. Her statue of a goddess started to crumble to dust in the space of a few days. The dust infected her followers with fevers. Her peacocks became ill. Green liquid dribbled from their eyes, maggots infested their feathers, and the smell of advanced rot emanated from their living flesh. Many of them died. Madame Koto's moonstones vanished with the secrets of their self-illuminating powers. No one knew who took them. Her room gave off a fetid stench. Her bar stank. All her clothes, possessions and ritual objects were covered in vibrant mould, continuing the potency of her myth.

Her domain shrivelled; her followers became ill; her camp divided; and most of the people associated with her fled and disappeared. The great black rock, whose sinister life compacted the force of her myth, cracked one night. We heard hellish cries escaping into the air of our street. How many lives, how many spirits, demons, djinns, had been trapped in that rock of old powers? I had no idea. But all night we heard hellish cries from the heart of the rock encircle our area.

THREE

The yellow growth

During the heat and silence of those seven days, Madame Koto's body became the womb of worms and slugs, cockroaches and flies. Geckos mated on her brow. A yellow growth accelerated on her fine complexion and on her resplendent robes.

When they found her on the fourth day, she had grown a beard which they shaved off and which grew again during the night. They shaved off her beard three times before the day of her funeral arrived.

FOUR

New rumours change reality

The diminishment of the sight of Madame Koto's followers got so bad that they could not be relied on for the things they said. Things which filtered through to us in the form of ghostly rumours. The rumours changed the appearance of reality. I cannot be considered a reliable witness either, for I suffered hallucinations after I discovered Madame Koto's body. I suffered most because I had been the first to stumble upon her. The days seemed to have merged into one another like successive dreams. Could it have been when I fled home from the rally, pursued by the incandescent bull, that I saw Dad battling with six political gangsters, or could it have been the next day? I could not be sure. And so I can't be certain of the things I witnessed, or the things I remember. But on one of those days, as in a vivid moment of a living dream, I saw Dad fighting with six men at the mouth of our street. Uttering the cries of a madman freed from hell, he knocked three of them out with the new punch he had perfected from the spirit of revolution. He kept screaming that it was men like him who had defeated Hitler. Mum was there too, her wrapper tied tightly round her waist. On her face was an expression I had never seen before. The grim expression of a merciless warrior. She was hitting the men that were battling Dad. Hitting them with a pestle.

Not far from where they fought, hunters were celebrating the death of a rogue elephant. It had fallen into one of the pits the white men got our people to dig for the creation of new roads. The hunters were drunk. While one of the thugs clubbed Dad at the back of the head with a blunt machete, the hunters sang salty dirges to the dead elephant. A thug swung a vicious blow at Mum. The blow glanced off her cheek. She howled and cracked his head with the pestle. Dad pounced on him and kept punching him on the nose till it was all bloody and textured like red paste. Then the other thugs fled, alarmed by Dad's unbounded ferocity. And when they fled, when there was no more fighting to be done, Dad sank to the ground, covered in blood. I had been wailing. The hunters, seeing me crying out in the midst of my fallen parents, rushed over and carried Dad home on six shoulders like a fallen warrior. Mum went home, limping, bruises all over her face.

FIVE

Dad hears lovely melodies

While Madame Koto's body began to smell, my father began to bleed from the ears. And when Madame Koto's body released gaseous aromas of rotting wild hibiscus, Dad's bleeding stopped. Then he started to hear things. He heard voices and the charming melodies of the dead.

The smell which escaped from Madame Koto's body hung over our area for days. The decay of her possessions, the crumbling wood of her images, the dust of her dead tortoises, leaked out into the air and made many people sick.

And when we heard rumours that her body had shrivelled and become so small that it resembled the corpse of an ugly old woman, not many of us were surprised, because the disintegration of her myth had begun long before her assassination.

SIX

The curious stigmata

Mum's bruises hardened her face. Dad couldn't hear most of the things we said to him because of the voices and tinkling bells in his head.

Mum's face became calloused. Her eyes took on the spikiness of bitter herbs. Desert herbs that retain their water through the heat of the hallucinating sands. She began to talk of giving up hawking and of selling clothes instead. She complained about Dad not going to work. She berated me for eating too much when there wasn't enough food in the house. Dad didn't hear her for all the wailings he heard in his deafness.

He stayed in all day, listening to bells and cries in his echoing ears, like one straining at other people's keyholes. His deafness made him appear distracted. He listened intently to all the melodies, and the voices of the universe about us. The things he heard seemed to age him.

Lumps appeared on Madame Koto's body, making her beard difficult to shave. My hallucinations grew worse. The redness in the middle of my palm, caused by Madame Koto's moonstones, began to expand. I was so afraid of this curious stigmata that I told no one about it. I went around with my fist clenched.

SEVEN

'Who is crying?'

On the third day after Madame Koto's death, with
time accelerating around us, Dad heard wailings long
before they manifested in the street.

The wailing puzzled him. It worried him. He
would sit up suddenly in his three-legged chair and
say:

'Who is crying?'

We would say no one is crying. But he wouldn't
hear us. He went on asking the same question over
and over again. He drove us mad with his insistence.

Mum's face became so hard that not even the
shadow of a smile touched her cheeks. She gave off
the weight of a bitter presence. Between them both,
one deaf, the other hardened in spirit, the room
became unbearable. I went out to play and saw the
faces of the women: they were all hard and bony,
their eyes unforgiving. Their bitterness made their
children ill with the bitter milk of their breasts. The
children cried all night long. The men went around
as if they were deaf, or slightly blind, or dumb. They
spoke very little, they didn't recognize anyone, and
they heard no greetings.

Something new and infernal invaded our lives.
Our doorways which had been crowded by Madame

Koto's presence were now empty. The imps of the new era crept into our rooms. They found a corner, installed themselves comfortably, and watched us with hollow eyes.

Meanwhile the smell from Madame Koto's domain filled the air with fevers and rumours. The dust of her disintegrating myth fed the hungry mouths of ghosts. An era was passing away. The blasting heat of new realities blew over from gaps in the forest.

EIGHT

The blind old man's piety

On the fourth day of Madame Koto's death, when the elephant in the pit began to smell, when the hyenas came and reduced its great bulk with their jagged teeth, we heard the horrifying noises of wailing in our street. When we couldn't locate the source of the wailing we too began to ask Dad's question: 'Who is crying?'

The wailing continued for hours. It was only in the evening that we became witnesses to the blind old man's peculiar piety.

He appeared in public, wearing a black suit and tie, a black hat and white shoes. He looked normal enough. He was without the pustules caused by the dust of the yellow angel. It was as if I had merely dreamt them, or as if they were not yet visible. He began to mourn loudly, throwing himself on the ground, weeping at the death of Madame Koto.

His weeping was a mystery to us. While Madame Koto's body stank out the labyrinths of her palace, the blind old man unleashed on us his weird and overpowering mourning. He wept at night, he wailed in the afternoon, he sang dirges in the evening. And while he was mourning in public, and mourning very loudly, he was seizing power, taking over Madame Koto's terrain, swallowing it into his shrivelled body, sucking it into his public weeping.

He mourned in the street. He wept by the well. He shouted at night. And he wailed with his yellow spectacles on his face, so that we wouldn't see his eyes.

NINE

The rewritten riot

On the fourth day after Madame Koto's death, we were banished from the night. The hypocritical wailing of the blind old man mystified us. But nothing astounded us as much as the rewriting of our lives by the new powers of the era.

Far away from the places where our realities are manufactured, it took four days for the most extraordinary rumours to reach us through the dense air of Madame Koto's death. We read the newspapers and missed the rewriting of the upheavals. The bad grammar of our speech probably made it worse. The rewriting had worked so well that we didn't notice what was being rewritten.

It took rumours to awaken us. And our awakening made us doubt our collective memory. It made us doubt our individual memories too. After a while Mum began to doubt how she got the bruises on her face, but Dad's deafness saved him the humiliation of having to question his wounds.

After the rally, which became a riot, I heard it said – and it was written in all the newspapers, with photographs to prove it – that the rally had been an unqualified success. We heard that the rally had ended peacefully, the only sign of trouble being the spontaneous ovation, the tremendous enthusiasm of the crowd, demonstrating their overwhelming support for the Party of the Rich. We heard how the crowds had taken up the chants and victory songs. How they had dispersed peacefully to their homes, singing the party on to triumph.

We heard these rumours with disbelief. We began to wonder if the papers had been referring to another rally that had taken place in the same arena as ours – a phantom rally, a shadow rally, or a rally of ghosts. Then we began to think that the rally we had attended had been the phantom rally. One that we had all dreamed up together. We even suspected that the riot which followed was a collective fantasy, a mass hallucination.

We began to think of ourselves as hypocrites. We began to imagine that we had indeed been peaceful at the rally, that we had colluded in our cowardice by inventing the alternative ending, the disruptions, the burnings, the rage, the ten people dead. The papers said nothing about the deaths.

We saw an interview with the future Head of State. He praised us for our tremendous show of support. We saw photographs to prove it. Our faces beaming, our expressions intent and hopeful. But we couldn't recognize a single one of our individual faces amongst the crowds. We saw photographs in the papers of politicians making their speeches with dramatic gestures. We read many things, but nothing remotely resembled the riot.

And for the first time I began to think of history as a dream rewritten by those who know how to change the particulars of memory. I began to think of history as fantasy, as shadow reality. Then I thought of it as the reality we never lived. Who lives our lives for us?

The papers said the rally was so successful that, to ensure the peace continued, and to prevent jealous reprisals from the other party, the interim government was imposing a dusk to dawn curfew. Soldiers paraded the city on the backs of armoured trucks. Waves of them poured down our street, with guns under their arms, eyeing us as if we were the most visible threat to the forthcoming elections. The soldiers swept through our street, disappeared, and then kept returning. They paraded our boundaries.

None of the papers wondered about our rage, or about the devastated houses, the burnt petrol station, the incinerated cars, the torn streets, and the ten dead bodies which still lay under the insurgent sun, hectored by flies.

And because the riot had never happened, because our rage had been a collective hallucination, no one asked questions about the reasons for the riot. No one asked questions about anything. The unasked questions accumulated in the new air of the curfew. Without any answer, they grew bigger. The questions took the form of the unexplained dead. Birds of prey, whose wings grew heavier, fed on that perfect food of night.

The birds of curfew beat sinister rhythms into our sleep. And the unasked questions, joining with the fetor of Madame Koto's disintegrating myth, produced a combined stink in the air of the nation's birth which made us seem stupid and sleepwalking, slow and slightly deaf.

We began to wonder if our rage so much as affected a single shadow in that hard world they rewrite as history.

TEN

Living in a paradox

We began to distrust things. When the blind old man wept about the untimely death of Madame Koto we merely took him for a dream that we could not agree upon. We watched his demonic mourning with solitary eyes. The solitary eyes of those who cannot trust others with their perceptions. We watched him in groups, but saw him each in our unique isolation. If he was a fact, we did not discuss it. If he was a dream, we did not share him.

But when the blind old man's public mourning reached its climax on the sixth day, scaring the dogs and cats with his hyena-like noises, kicking like an upturned beetle on the ground, in his striped hat and yellow sunglasses, we started to wonder if we hadn't misjudged him. And we became a little terrified at the strength of his bereavement.

As his mourning reached its climax, Madame Koto's body began to shrivel. Her flesh shrank beneath her gold-braided robes. Her eyes were at their most swollen. We had no idea that the final chapter of her mythic life was being brought to an end. Then we heard that her swollen eyes had burst and yellow liquids drooled down her shrivelled face, staining her pillow-case with her agonized weeping for the dreams beyond death.

On that seventh day of her death, when we couldn't sleep for the steel rings of curfew round our lives, Madame Koto's corpse appeared in our street.

We saw her at the front seat of her Volkswagen, with party banners draped round the little car. She wore dark glasses, and seemed as imperious as we had ever known her to be. She was driven up and down our area. She was so impervious to our gaze, so indifferent to the world, and so solid in her being, that we could be forgiven for thinking that we were the dead, and that she was of the living. This also made us suspect that we had never been real, and what we took as the facts of our days were merely the intense dreams of our ghosts. We began to suspect that we had been living in a paradox. Living and suffering in a shadow universe, the terrain of the dead. Living in an underworld of mythic time where all the failures and dreams of our lives were concrete things.

We had been living in death. Waiting to be born. Mistaking the dreams in our deaths for realities. I began to understand our eruptions, and why we had such a poor effect on the solid world of history. I understood that a pre-condition for a good birth is patience. But those who rewrote our lives deprived us of the choice of patience. They had foreshortened our possibilities with their corruption and their lies. Everything got spoiled because of the essential questions no one asked. And I saw how we could live other people's entire histories in such a short

349

space of time, be blessed with plenty, and yet find ourselves beggars in the wide world.

And all this before a tree bore its first fruit.

ELEVEN

Turning death into power

On the seventh day we began to realize the implications of that great myth fallen. But it took Dad, who couldn't hear anything, to make us realize what was happening. The funeral had finally come upon us. It had been searching for us for seven days through all the realms of reality.

The curfew narrowed our lives. But only Madame Koto, who had become an old woman of a corpse in rumour, with her crushed smile and her yellow teeth, found freedom in the night. The curfew was her liberation. Under its cloak the rituals were organized which would transfer her powers into their control. Under the cloak of curfew dread sacrifices were performed, designed to turn her death into power, her myth into domination, her disintegration into unity, the dust of her flesh into the gold of a living force.

In the dreams of death, riding in her Volkswagen up and down our street, her smile turning fiendish, she became the negative will which paralysed us.

TWELVE

The mysterious funeral (1)

On that seventh day the blind old man sent word round that we were all invited to Madame Koto's funeral. We were suspicious of the invitation and no one sent word back that they would attend.

The funeral music of drums and trumpets and dirge accompaniments filled the air. We heard that several funerals were taking place for Madame Koto simultaneously in different parts of the country. There were funerals in deep creeks, in remote villages, on hilltops, and in the original home of the great black rock. The biggest funeral took place in her secret palace. No one knew where her body was, and in all the different sites of her diverse funerals, coffins supposed to be containing her body were buried.

That same day, a great Mass was held for Madame Koto in the Cathedral of Saint Mary in the city centre. She was buried to halting renditions of Mozart's great unfinished Mass in C minor. The service drew a huge congregation composed of nuns from the cloisters, bewigged judges, bespectacled soldiers, bishops with glittering crosiers, garri traders, rich businessmen, famous musicians, local governors, sundry church elders, marketwomen, trade unionists, the Governor-General with his two trusted deputies, and the future Head of State with his tentative cabinet. There were also the beggars who had come into the church to shelter from the drizzle which was slightly flavoured with a rainbow. And all manner of people who had never heard of her, bicyclists and hawkers, poets and thieves and street urchins, had been drawn into the cathedral by the sheer magnitude of the occasion.

All kinds of people were magnetized by the instant legend of the event and by the cathedral, with its whimsical dome, its stained-glass windows and syncretic images of saints, its vaulted ceiling. And all were awestruck by the mighty resonances of the cantatas and fugues which poured out of the cylindrical organ pipes and created circles of curious crowds outside the cathedral doors. The surrounding streets were taken up by bystanders and city-folk, all amazed by the cars parked around, the armed guards, the soldiers with guns, and by the mystery of the personage who was being honoured in so unprecedented a manner. It was as if a great ancient mother were being sent on her way to the land of everlasting legends.

The service was such a great success, with speeches from all sorts of luminaries, that the church enjoyed a multitude of conversions.

THIRTEEN

The mysterious funeral (2)

And while the service was taking place, the other funeral began at Madame Koto's bar. There was much feasting and much music-making, but none of Madame Koto's followers attended. They had all fled into a world of shadows, condemned to be haunted by all the things Madame Koto's eyes had seen while she lay in state.

But the funeral was attended by a great many musicians, who warred amongst themselves for the sustenance of her myth. All sorts of people turned up. Midgets with ears stained purple. A white man who had helped her flee from the Gold Coast. Peculiar-looking women with golden bangles who brought sacrificial goats, odd-looking yams, wild birds, and baskets of palm kernels. There were men in white robes, soldiers with guns, policemen with batons, and people who had travelled long distances, who made themselves comfortable on mats in her room. None of the revenants returned. Those who attended the funeral were people we had never seen. We marvelled at the many dimensions of her life.

As the day wore on and the feasting progressed, we saw the emissaries of kings, all in royal attire, bearing sacrificial gifts. We saw diplomats from obscure and great nations. There was a delegation from the future Head of State. There were delegations from all the major and minor political parties. There were journalists and photographers, finance ministers, makers of cages, trainers of parrots, keepers of secret keys. It was as if we had only ever known one small aspect of the many lives of Madame Koto, who seemed to grow more august with her death.

Among the many strangers who attended the funeral preparations, there was one in particular who exerted the strongest pull on my spirit-child imagination. He was the most quiet, and the most mysterious. He seemed vaguely familiar though I had never seen him before. He had a smallish head and serene eyes and only three fingers remained on his right hand. He was dressed like a hunter, and he didn't speak to anyone. A silent power emanated from his wiry frame. And I, the spirit-child, who knows the wondrous destiny of human beings beyond the earth, I could not penetrate the protective serenity of his aura. I could not enter his thoughts. His realm was beyond me. When he stared at me with deep-set eyes the most mysterious flicker of a smile lit up his face as if he knew who I was and had already perceived my destiny in advance. I did not see him much during the tumultuous events of the funeral. I did not see him for the strangers that had moved into our area and who poured out of their houses to pay their last respects to Madame Koto. They were the only ones amongst us who answered the blind old man's call.

While the bar resounded with funereal music and

bustlings and arguments about the different regions – terrestrial and superterrestrial – of Madame Koto's domain, many of us hung at the barfront watching the proceedings.

But we did not see the secret preparations around Madame Koto's body, or one of her many bodies. We did not witness the final shaving of her beard for the funeral rites. We did not witness the plaiting of her hair into fantastic braids. And we did not know anything of the commotion that surrounded the construction of her coffin.

FOURTEEN

The power of the dead

Madame Koto, in spite of having shrivelled in rumour into an old woman, went on growing till her last day. We did not see the fury of the blind old man, who had to keep sending orders to the specially hired carpenters. They rebuilt her coffin three times to accommodate her breasts which had grown preternaturally large. Then they had to extend the coffin in length because, rather late, they had discovered that her legs were growing as well.

In the end, the blind old man, fearful of this inexplicable growth, ordered a coffin made of the hardest steel. And then he sent off dimensions so extraordinary that the workmen, to this day, believe that they constructed a coffin for the burial of a giant bull.

FIFTEEN

'They have taken her heart!'

There was great tumult when the coffin arrived. Eight stout men, the veins in their necks bursting from exertion, carried the coffin on their heads. And when they dropped it, the foundations of the house trembled. It was a coffin so mighty that it could easily have served as a small room for a family of four. The musicians, noting this crucial detail for the embellishment of Madame Koto's myth, were significantly silent. The women released awesome ululations. The blind old man, waving the flywhisk in his hand in a gesture of admonishment, banished their cries.

Silence followed. He ordered the room to be vacated. Then he drew an impenetrable veil of spells around the inner circle as they began the final rituals which would remove the powers from Madame Koto's body.

I heard Madame Koto's voice cry out during the last rites. No one else heard her cry. No one registered any dread. I heard the cry again. It was hyena-like, piercing, like the cry of sacrificial victims who have their hearts torn out from their bodies, under their own gaze, and under the power of ancient sorceries.

'They have taken her heart!' I shouted, and someone slapped me so hard on the face that I found myself reeling in the thoughts of the funeral attendants.

SIXTEEN

Death is cultural

I wandered through the dimly-lit corridors of the white man's mind. He was thinking: 'People's experience of death is cultural'; and then he inwardly smiled. Along the corridors of his mind, beyond its transparent walls, there were places lined with statues and ritual images, chapters of unfinished books, and details for memoirs about the untamed heart of Africa that would never be written. There were also lighted places filled with iridescent warmth and I found myself liking the gentle edges of his consciousness.

Another knock stunned me into another mind. Dark and heated and full of potent sounds. Grim rivers. Tidewash of memories. Pictures of Madame Koto as a young girl. She was beautiful and had that peculiar green light in her clear eyes which had been an early indication of her unusual birth and destiny. She floated in an air of sandalwood incense. The bones of rare animals on a chain round her neck. I saw her naked. Saw the wild red flower of her vagina. Her heaving breasts. Saw her open mouth and her eyes rolling around. And heard her orgasmic cry deep in the river-wash of that dark mind. I saw two fingers in an enamel bowl. Saw Madame Koto and the man fleeing through the bushes. Living in the forest. I dimly witnessed her initiation into the ancient cults. Then the darkness of that mind closed on me.

I opened my eyes and found myself surrounded by women. Faces hard as bitterwood. Eyes deep with emotion and therefore emotionless. Faces like benevolent masks of fertility rites. Mum was amongst them, and she was cradling me silently. When I got down from her arms, I found everything weaving. My head was unsteady. Silently we watched as the strangers gathered at the barfront in that air of disintegrating myths.

SEVENTEEN

Old trees are impossible to replace

The musicians played, and the blind old man supervised the building of the three temporary huts for the funeral event. They dug holes for the sticks and soon constructed huts with raffia and bamboo. The roofs were made of fresh palm fronds.

Women were wailing. Musicians produced plangent notes from ivory trumpets, seven-string harp lutes, and raft zithers. They beat out fearful syncopations from gigantic talking drums. Every now and then they broke into soulful threnodies.

The highest paid mourners in the land had been assembled. They took over the blind old man's weeping. They wept and wailed and threw themselves dramatically on the ground at crucial moments. When they had wailed for a while, hurled themselves about for a bit, and rolled on the ground, they got up, dusted down their clothes and went to help themselves to large quantities of fried guinea fowl, stewed rice, baked plantain and beer. They ate and drank voraciously.

Madame Koto's followers had fled but her earliest women, many of them prostitutes, returned. They had all gone on to become prominent figures in society. Some had married judges, politicians and army generals. Many of them were entirely successful in their own right.

All the originals, who had been at the most discernible beginnings of her myth had come back, like returning daughters. They had left their husbands and children for the duration of the funeral. They had left their thriving concerns, famous restaurants and high-class salons where traders from Beirut, jewellers from Antwerp, Indian tycoons and beautiful women congregated, had scandalous parties and did excellent business. These original women of Madame Koto's bar had left their estates, their farms, their cloth-dyeing concerns, their shops and kiosks, to come and participate in the obsequies for the great woman who had opened their roads for them. They had all prospered. And they all had the shadow of secret lives and fetishes beneath their impeccable make-up.

All the original women were there. The innocent virgins who had fled from tyrannical fathers, from dreadful backwaters where people were thrown into brackish creeks to see if they were witches. Young women who had fled the rapes committed on them by uncles, or fathers' friends. The girls who had escaped the stifling provinciality, the immemorial superstitions, the crushing negativity of isolated villages. Others who had fled from convents and were quickly trained in the art of seduction. All those who had fled from crude religions, from a life of drudgery to a life of city dreams. The faithful ones of the earliest times. They had all returned. And they prepared the feast, cleaned Madame Koto's rooms, organized the orderly dismantling of her realm, and

363

determined for her an honourable funeral, because they knew that great old trees are impossible to replace.

EIGHTEEN

The beautification

The women dedicated themselves to the beautification of Madame Koto. Her body was wrapped in a red cloth from the neck down. Painstakingly they made up her face. They deepened the blackness of her eyebrows, applied rouge to her damp cheeks, powdered her forehead, painted her lips with rose-red lipstick, wove her hair into long braids, and wove the braids into the shape of a pyramid. They made her look so beautiful that it was as if they were preparing her for the great wedding she had planned for after her party's victory at the elections.

NINETEEN

The procession

After the coffin had been treated with potions and libations, the funeral procession began, to the accompaniment of music and songs. The coffin was placed on top of the Volkswagen, but was so heavy that the car could barely move. The more the driver tried, the deeper the car sank into the rain-softened earth. In the end ten strong men, most of them strangers, bore the bier on their heads and led the solemn procession down our street.

On both sides of the bier, paid mourners wailed in alarming voices. Musicians played their threnodic accompaniments. The women wept. The blind old man, led by a young girl of startling beauty, kept contorting himself in grief.

The procession, with its eerie magnetism, drew a great number of people who had never been in a procession before. Mum at first didn't want to go along. Dad stayed at home, sitting on his legendary chair, deaf to all the noises, absorbed in the voices and sweet lamentations he heard from other spheres. Mum finally joined the tail end of the crowd of mourners, the curious, the ragged, seekers after spectacle.

The procession went to one of Madame Koto's

secret palaces. We all gathered at the backyard, while the musicians performed their myth-making music. We gathered under the darkening sky as night fell. Lamps and bamboo torches were lit all over the area.

A dense veil hung on bamboo poles. Behind it the ground had been prepared. Paid mourners outdid themselves in piety. But what was being done behind the veil, where the coffin lay like a little house, was obscured from us all. The women bustled. Cows and rams, goats and sheep, were tethered to trees and poles. Peacocks made vain noises. Chickens squawked. Children ran about naked. Hurricane lamps were lit in niches. Huge party banners fluttered in the night-wind.

I couldn't go behind the veil. Stout men with red wrappers, machetes in their hands, ritual scarifications on their chests, stood sentry to make sure the uninitiated didn't witness the last rites.

TWENTY

Behind the veil

But I saw it all. I, the spirit-child, who knows something of the bright heavens, of shallow and mythic glories, I saw it all. I, who can travel in the corridors of minds, play in the interspaces, dance to the seductive whispering of spirits, slip through the eye of a sacrificial needle, and who finds great cities in the narrow space of palm kernels, I saw the ministrants as they loaded Madame Koto's possessions, her tortoises, her rich garments, her jewellery and her gold, her rare beads, her flywhisk and her chief's fan, her trinkets and brocaded lace, and buried them with her in the coffin.

Her remaining peacocks were slaughtered, her tortoises crushed, her parrots beheaded, her monkeys killed, and their blood was poured into Madame Koto's sacrificial earth. Their bodies were her companions to the other world, keeping her company in the great illuminated darkness of the grave. Musical instruments were placed in the coffin as well. Xylophones and trumpets. A talking drum and an iron bell. The blind old man's accordion was also placed in the coffin, so that she could be entertained in the antechambers of eternity.

They didn't forget to bury with her a beautiful

new lamp, a gramophone, a telephone (so that she could be reached in the other world), her favourite cooking utensils, a new broom, yams and fruits, alligator pepper seeds, a smooth-browed calabash, cassava plants, cola-nuts to give to the ancestors, dolls and toys for the spirit-children she would meet on the other side, presents for her predecessors, gifts to the elder spirits, pens for the spirit-scribes, bangles and clippings of children's hair for the great mothers of the spirit realms, kaolin and loincloths for the silent fathers, portions of mingled earth from all over the country for the gods and goddesses of new-born nations, a red pair of sunglasses for the bright new sunlight of the first mountain beyond, seeds of rare plants for the numinous beings who must be bribed before her spirit could cross the shady interrealms, bones for the dogs of the earth, spells and fetishes and potions and magic words written backwards on papyrus leaves to charm or battle with the wayward spirits of the unknown boundaries, books to read, newspapers to tell the ancestors some of the things that had been happening here and to show what little improvement had been made since they departed, photographs and maps, state documents and love letters, all the paraphernalia of her cultic powers, and a gourd of scented palm-wine, to remind her of one of her lives on earth.

Also placed in the coffin were a bronze stool, the gift of a king; gold bracelets, gifts of the market-women; bales of cloth, with illustrations of her life-story, gifts of all the original women of the earliest days. As night grew darker, and as the ululating noises of the cultists sounded from the trees, the earth, the remote distances, the near and far houses, as the ululation grew more complex, more chilling, the ministrants placed the jackal-headed masquerade with all its cinderous features into the coffin with her, along with shimmering fragments of the black rock of her myth.

But before the coffin was covered and sealed and locked with seven padlocks, and after the contents of the coffin had been neatly arranged so that it looked like a dreaded treasure chest that was being buried for future generations and solidly locked so that only the rightful inheritors could gain access to the buried riches and nightmares – before all this was done the original women and the close associates and the inner circle were summoned. They danced behind the veil, and paid their last respects. The musicians beat their drums, their copper bells rattled our ears. The paid mourners cried themselves hoarse.

The women and the cultists, whose eyes were red and inflamed from too much weeping, their faces bony from the heat and the anxieties, shuffled behind the veil and beheld Madame Koto, sitting on a golden stool, draped in red, wearing red sunglasses. Her face was ghoulish with all the rouge, the red lipstick and leaking embalming fluid. She sat with a ghostly and magisterial tranquillity, as if ready to listen to their last entreaties, their declarations of everlasting loyalty and love, their regrets and confessions, their hopes and dreams; and having listened to the deepest things in their spirits, to absolve them of all worry and fear.

TWENTY-ONE

An omen

The moon came out and conquered the darkness with its sepulchral radiance. The dancing stopped. Under the instructions of the blind old man, the corpse was wrapped in brocaded lace and in a specially-treated red-dyed mat. It was conveyed by chosen women to the edge of the grave. The women, weeping, placed their numerous gifts beside the corpse. Another ritual ensued. I saw two corpses, and didn't know which one was real.

The blind old man ordered that the coffin be brought to the graveside; and ordered that Madame Koto's body be gently placed on the prepared mattress in the coffin, lying face upwards, with her red spectacles on, as if she were eternally contemplating the ineluctable mystery of heavenly constellations, surrounded by earthly comforts and companions. The coffin was then shut. But as they began their attempts to lower it into the earth, something snapped and everyone fled, screaming.

It was discovered that two of the seven padlocks had sprung open. The ministrants tried to hurry the last obsequies, for this peculiar occurrence was interpreted as a ghastly omen.

But the blind old man read the omen differently:

that she was not yet ready to go, that there were more rituals demanded, and that she still had more things to accomplish. He commanded that Madame Koto be removed from the coffin, and seated on a regal chair, that she might perform her last great functions as one of the mothers of the earth.

TWENTY-TWO

Half a ton of concrete

Then began the round of entreaties. Addressing the regally seated Madame Koto, the women and the cultists prayed to her to pass messages on to their ancestors, and to intercede for them in the world of spirits. Childless women prayed to be made pregnant. Men whose businesses weren't doing well asked for success. Kneeling in fervent pleas, the supplicants implored their ancestors to grant them prosperity and health, longevity and happiness. They asked that evil never enter their lives. They prayed that their feet would never go astray on life's road. They asked for protection from seen and unforeseen eventualities. And they begged that their lives be rich with blessings. They addressed all their claims and their problems, their hopes and their fears, to Madame Koto, whom they saw as their best advocate in the powerful realm of the dead.

Madame Koto listened to their supplications with the solemn air of her impassive greatness. She absorbed all their concerns into her death. The greatness of her myth gave certainty to the supplicants that she would deliver all their messages and intercede on their behalf to the mighty divinity. They poured on to her all their longings, all their cravings, all their disputes, all their complications, all their illnesses, and all the curses that had secretly dogged them ever since the day they had innocently entered the fate-laden stage of the world.

Their demands to ancestors and remote gods went on for so long that many of the rituals had to be delayed. The wailings and inconsolable weeping and the endless entreaties dragged on so much that the blind old man, impatient and exasperated, commanded that the burial commence. The rituals were speeded up. The women increased their wailing; in a harsh voice, the blind old man ordered them to be removed. The women had to be dragged away from the edge of the deep grave.

Madame Koto was then carried to her gigantic coffin and laid finally in her position of rest. A giant ammonite was placed in her hand. The coffin was shut, the seven padlocks applied and tested, and then the lowering began amidst prayers, rites, and dances. Powerful herbalists, in deep shadow, operated on the vibrations of the air. Mysterious forms of witches and wizards flew restlessly everywhere, infecting the atmosphere with a mood of terror, hallucinations and awe.

The men lowered the great coffin into the earth and it went a long way down, as into a deep well, before we heard the ropes snap. Then the slightly delayed crash of metal on the hard floor of the grave. Again people fled. They feared that the omen was becoming reality, and imagined that Madame Koto, inextinguishable even in death, was fighting to get out of her coffin.

They buried her deep in the earth and filled the

grave with half a ton of concrete and planted potent spells around the seven corners of her grave. They had learnt from the case of the dead carpenter that certain people can be more terrifying dead than alive, that they can escape from the grave into the air, that they can enter into myth and enjoy a second and more unfettered life. A life of terrifying vitality, hurling their dreams of death upon us who dwell in the shadow realm of reality.

TWENTY-THREE

Gun salutes

After her grave had been sealed a huge soapstone statue was placed over it. The statue towered over the other images and cenotaphs in the courtyard, and rivalled the height of the orange tree. Madame Koto stood in a bold gesture, one arm raised, the pose of a warrior.

We were there all night. The night was lengthened by an unknown goddess. It was a long vigil. We suffered heat stupors. Red ants crawled about everywhere, released from their homes in the earth. Mosquitoes were intense in the still air. Fireflies and midges and mean little flying insects tormented us. We suffocated under the peculiar heat of the moon.

Some of the women fainted from exhaustion, dehydration and weeping. We were marginally revived with music. We bought food from the clustered food-sellers around, not daring to eat from the feast. We ate fried mudfish, yams, skewered lamb, Jollof rice, and drank soft drinks. Tapers blazed all around in the softening darkness.

Then, as we were beginning to revive in the still air, we were overwhelmed with the thunderous booms of the seven-gun salute to the great dead woman. The salute was answered in seven distant places. The whole area woke up. Dogs barked. Children cried. The salute lasted only one minute but it woke us up for the rest of the night and far into the early hours of the morning.

TWENTY-FOUR

We did not weep

The faces of our neighbours were hard throughout the ceremonies. They remained hard during the most moving moments. The women's faces were stony. The men still looked partly deaf and dumb. Even when Madame Koto's original followers wept, even when people who didn't know much about Madame Koto fell into wailing for the sheer infectious solemnity of the rituals, our neighbours' faces remained stony and their expressions remained dislocated.

None of us shed a tear. Our eyes were dry as the hearts of impervious stones. Nothing contorted our faces.

The paid mourners went into fresh paroxysms of grief. The lone white man stood apart from it all, fanning himself. It came as a shock to us all suddenly to see him crying. He was led into the house, consoled by weeping women.

But most puzzling of all was the erratic behaviour of the man with three fingers who was dressed like a hunter. He maintained an almost haughty dignity through the proceedings. But as soon as preparations were being made to transfer us all to the bar, where the proper feasting would take place, he broke down and contorted himself on the sand and threw himself about and wept uncontrollably. I suspected, at that moment, that he might have been her husband. I remembered him from a photograph in Madame Koto's room. I remembered the two fingers preserved in alcohol. The women rushed to him as he wept. They covered him with a red cloth and led him into the house. He wailed like a frightened child all the way. We never saw him again.

None of this shifted the solid stone of our resentment. We did not weep and our faces were so hard that we began to look inhuman, mask-like, under the bitter heat of that night. We were so hard-faced that none of the grieving touched us and my eyes hurt from seeing the stony faces of our neighbours who had been so traumatized by Madame Koto's relentless domination, by her almost mythic tyranny, by the way she had disturbed our sleep with her infernal powers, the way she had sucked energy from us, and poisoned our days and filled our nights with inscrutable terror.

From the severity of our neighbours' eyes, from the bitterness of their gaze, it seemed as if they had come to the funeral to ascertain for themselves that Madame Koto was indeed finally dead.

They stayed to witness the sealing of her grave. They stared at her statue with mortally offended eyes.

TWENTY-FIVE

Celebrations for a legend

After the burial and the gun salutes, the procession returned to our street to witness the feast meant to celebrate the continuity of life, and the persistence of her myth.

We did not join in the funeral feast. We watched as seven cows and twelve goats, intended to celebrate her party's victory in advance, celebrated her death.

We stayed in the shadows and watched the mourners dancing and weeping. We watched the bacchanalia which followed. Visitors and participants got sated and drunk and lay sprawled in the intoxication of a ritual celebration of death. We watched the hundreds of cartons of beer, the endless bottles of whisky and the innumerable gourds of palm-wine consumed by the celebrants as they mourned and told stories of Madame Koto's incredible feats, of her extravagant generosity.

The blind old man sent huge portions of fried goat, stewed rice and beancakes round to us, but none of us ate the meat of her myth. None of us partook of the rice and palm-wine of her legend.

As we watched, lingering in the shadows, witnesses to the end of an era, we noticed that apart from the ghoulish wailing of the blind old man, only the women truly mourned her.

TWENTY-SIX

Lingering in the shadows

We became ugly in the shadows because of the hardness of our faces. Our eyes were dull. We had the listlessness of people whose sleep has been continually sabotaged.

In the shadows we watched the young girls. Many of them were bare-topped. We stared at their hard and shining breasts. We watched the girls who were cultic priestesses in training as they bore white basins with the legend 'Koto' on them. The basins were weighed down with food prepared in unknown animistic convents. The girls had kaolin on their faces, their eyes remote. Their young bodies were golden with a deep sensuality, and when they began to dance the men were entranced. The men were electrified, their desires made more intense because they were forbidden intimate contact with the girls. As the musicians conjured ethereal strains from their instruments the girls danced with such vigour and insanity that I feared further transformations. But as they got lost in the ecstasy, they passed from mere dancing into a somnambulistic trance.

Then, utterly possessed, three of the girls ran towards us in the shadows. They pointed their fingers at us, their thighs shaking, breasts quivering.

They hissed like snakes. They ululated. They pointed at us accusingly. It occurred to us that we were being blamed for Madame Koto's death.

One of the girls stepped forward from the rest. She was of extraordinary beauty, and had kind eyes. Her fine pointed breasts were oiled and looked like polished mahogany. She knelt in front of us, as we stood resentful in the shadows. Then she began a puzzling entreaty, begging us without stating the particulars of her plea. She knelt there with a sad expression on her face, rubbing her hands together in profound pleading. She had tears in her eyes. She kept begging us, without ever making it clear what for. Then she quivered. A spirit took her over. She screamed and begged, and then the men, flashing their eyes at us, came and rushed her away. As she was borne away, she was still pleading.

We who had lingered in the shadows, our faces harder than dead wood, retreated from the funeral celebrations. We dispersed to our different rooms. Our faces hurt in fixed severity. We remained slightly deaf and dumb, bewildered by the inexplicable acceleration of time.

TWENTY-SEVEN

When I cried out the pain eased

We found Dad standing on his head, upside down, against the wooden window.

'Who is crying for forgiveness?' he asked as we came in.

We said nothing. We sat in silence on the bed.

'Someone is crying for forgiveness,' Dad said again.

We didn't understand him. All around we could hear Madame Koto's women ululating, could hear them howling into the dawn, as if they were trying to break down the mysterious doors of the earth, the doors that separated the living from the dead.

The room was dark. There were no candles lit. Dad remained standing on his head, his eyes shining oddly from the ground as if he were a sinister cat, or a mischievous spirit spying on our lives in the soft darkness.

A rebellious wind rattled our rooftop. After a while there was silence. We waited for the sound of Madame Koto's wailing women to return, ghostly in that strange night. The darkness in the room was that of the earth. I saw the spirits of trees in our living space, their leaves an ethereal green. The spirit-trees flourished in their invisibility. I was seeing them for the first time in a long while. All things continue their dreams, both living and dead. All living things continue even when dead. Their shadow selves, their spirit entities, keep on growing as if nothing had changed. The world is full of superimpositions.

'I can hear a baby crying,' Dad said.

We couldn't hear anything. The silence was deeper than the night. We were in the seabed of silence. Silvery fishes swam across the hardness of our faces. The silence was so deep it obliterated time. Only Dad's breathing anchored us to the world of darkness.

As we sat in the silence, the stigmata in my palm suddenly came alive in pain. The stigmata burned as if I had just sustained a wound in the middle of my palm. Under the sudden lash of that pain I cried out, cracking the silence asunder. When I cried out, the pain eased. When I stopped, the pain returned.

'I can hear someone crying,' Dad said, from the floor.

Mum fetched a candle and lit it and asked what was wrong. I showed her the stigmata. It had now grown so vivid it seemed as if jagged glass had been twisted into my palm. Or as if someone had stuck a red-hot taper in my palm and left it there. Mum fainted at the horrid sight, dropping the candle. Dad scrambled from his upside-down position, relit the candle, and revived Mum. Both of them stood perplexed. They said nothing. They stared at me with suspicious eyes, as if I were transformed.

The wind blew out the candle. Dad stayed kneeling in front of me. Mum was crouched beside me. The silence deepened.

'It doesn't hurt any more,' I said.

They stayed silent. Then we began to hear new tones of weeping. The weeping drifted in from the adjacent rooms, the rooms of our neighbours. All the women in our area, all in their different rooms, began weeping at once. It was quite ghostly. Like a circling chorus, circling the air, swirling and rising in sorrow. Mum's face was hardened in the darkness. She looked to me like the masks they use to frighten off bad spirits.

TWENTY-EIGHT

As if they had all just lost their mothers

'They are all crying,' Dad said, with wonder in his voice.

Then, like kerosene exploding into flame, Mum broke down too. She crumpled on the bed, contorting and kicking. She wept hysterically, and couldn't be stopped.

'Why is she weeping?' Dad asked in utter amazement.

I was astonished at his question. I was astonished because Dad could hear.

'You can hear, Dad!' I said.

'I know. But why is your mother weeping, eh?'

I couldn't see Dad's face in the dark. Had he been on a long journey and just returned? Had he been wandering in a world of echoes and voices that he took to be reality?

'I think it's because of Madame Koto.'

'What has she gone and done now?'

'She's dead. They buried her today.'

Dad didn't say anything. He went on another long journey, wandering amongst memories.

In silence, we listened to the lamentation. Even the

ones who hated Madame Koto the most wailed all night. They wailed inconsolably, as if they had all just lost their mothers.

TWENTY-NINE

A little night music

As I sat there, a beautiful glow appeared all around me. Out of the enveloping glow came the merest hint of sublime music. I listened to the purity of the music and said, very gently:

'Ade, it's you isn't it?'

The spirit of my dead friend appeared next to me. His brilliant white hat was the only sign and star in that sad darkness.

'Why do you bring such lovely music when there is such misery here on earth?' I asked, in a whisper.

'Be grateful for the music,' he replied.

I thought about what he said. I could hear a cooling wind blowing over the land. He stayed silent. His silence made me more aware of the music.

'Why do we lose the highest points in our life?' I asked.

'To go either higher, or lower.'

'Why do we lose the best dreams of our lives?'

'Because we forget.'

'How can we stop forgetting?'

'By renewing ourselves.'

'How?'

'By becoming a child again every seven years.'

'Do we always have to lose our best dreams?'

'Yes.'

'Why?'

'To find them again, anew.'

'How?'

'By listening.'

'To what?'

'To the agony or the laughter of angels.'

'Where?'

'Within yourselves.'

The music was fainter now. The fainter it was, the more beautiful it became. It was almost unbearable. My friend's presence was fading. The glow was diminishing. He was leaving me behind again, in this dark place, among the hard things of the world.

Then he smiled, and was gone. But he left me the music. Its tenderness lingered in the silence.

THIRTY

Softened faces

Mum fell ill. Most of the women in our area came down with mysterious fevers. Dad entered a state of shock that lasted a week. Madame Koto kept appearing to me. She kept begging my forgiveness, which I tried to give, but did not know how.

A new era crept into our lives. When I woke up on the morning after Madame Koto's burial, I felt as if I had been overcome by a curious illness which had no discernible symptoms. The pain of the stigma had lessened. I alone was aware of the illness. To my parents I was perfectly well and normal. When they sent me on errands I was happy to obey. The illness took the form of a curious spaciousness in my spirit. I felt lighter, as if a part of me had floated away.

Everyone remarked on how well I looked. I felt tranquil. But I knew that soon the other world would begin invading me. I became vigilant. I thought often about the seven-headed spirit who was coming to get me. I kept expecting the voices of my spirit companions, who were still angry with me for betraying my pact to return to them in the spirit world. I awaited further appearances of Ade. I had unexpected longings for the disembodied singing and the wonderful melodies that I alone heard, which haunted my childhood. But nothing happened. The lightness, the spaciousness, remained.

I felt prone to simultaneous visions. I felt like one perpetually on the verge of a fit or a seizure. Still nothing happened. I suffered the lingering expectancy, the sense of something ominous about to happen, but endlessly deferred.

There was one lovely thread woven into the fabric of that period. After the weeping, and after the fevers, a gentle change came over things. It gladdened my heart to see how the faces of the women had lightened, how their eyes shone. It touched me also to see that the men had lost their vaguely stupid expressions. An inexplicable pestilence had been lifted from our collective air.

I noticed also that after Mum had wept all night her face softened, and her beauty returned.

There were no masks among us in the respite that followed Madame Koto's burial.

THIRTY-ONE

Time quickens

The respite was brief, and time quickened. We woke up one morning to find curfew hours extended. We woke up on another morning to find massive obituary notices for Madame Koto in all the newspapers. The obituaries took up three full pages of every single newspaper in the land. We saw big photographs of her sitting on a wicker chair. The obituaries appeared for an entire week. They all bore condolences and deep regrets at her passing. It was strange how she had become more public and more famous dead than alive.

We had hardly recovered from that shock when, on another morning, on awakening, we found that the much delayed elections were upon us.

The elections would seal the fate of the unborn nation.

THIRTY-TWO

The karmic dust of angels is everywhere.
The secret side of things is open to us.
The time of innocence is gone.
The age of dreaming has come.

Old ways are dying.
We who live through turbulent mysteries
Do not know that a whole way is passing.
We do not know the things to come.

We go on living as if history is a dream.
The miracle is that we go on
Living and loving as best we can,
In this enigma of reality.

1989–1998
London

www.vintage-books.co.uk